Edgar Wallace was born illegitimate
adopted by George Freeman, a porter
eleven, Wallace sold newspapers at Ludgate Circus and on leaving
school took a job with a printer. He enlisted in the Royal West Kent
Regiment, later transferring to the Medical Staff Corps and was sent
to South Africa. In 1898 he published a collection of poems called
The Mission that Failed, left the army and became a correspondent
for Reuters.

Wallace became the South African war correspondent for *The
Daily Mail*. His articles were later published as *Unofficial Dispatches* and
his outspokenness infuriated Kitchener, who banned him as a war
correspondent until the First World War. He edited the *Rand Daily
Mail*, but gambled disastrously on the South African Stock Market,
returning to England to report on crimes and hanging trials. He
became editor of *The Evening News*, then in 1905 founded the Tallis
Press, publishing *Smith*, a collection of soldier stories, and *Four Just
Men*. At various times he worked on *The Standard*, *The Star*, *The Week-
End Racing Supplement* and *The Story Journal*.

In 1917 he became a Special Constable at Lincoln's Inn and also
a special interrogator for the War Office. His first marriage to Ivy
Caldecott, daughter of a missionary, had ended in divorce and he
married his much younger secretary, Violet King.

The Daily Mail sent Wallace to investigate atrocities in the Belgian
Congo, a trip that provided material for his *Sanders of the River* books.
In 1923 he became Chairman of the Press Club and in 1931 stood as
a Liberal candidate at Blackpool. On being offered a scriptwriting
contract at RKO, Wallace went to Hollywood. He died in 1932, on
his way to work on the screenplay for *King Kong*.

The Admirable
Carfew

This edition published in 2001 by House of Stratus, an imprint of Stratus Holdings plc, 24c Old Burlington Street, London, W1X 1RL, UK.

www.houseofstratus.com

Typeset, printed and bound by House of Stratus.

A catalogue record for this book is available from the British Library.

ISBN 1-84232-657-0

We would like to thank the Edgar Wallace Society for all the support they have given House of Stratus. Enquiries on how to join the Edgar Wallace Society should be addressed to: The Edgar Wallace Society, c/o Penny Wyrd, 84 Rigefield Road, Oxford, OX4 3DA. Email: info@edgarwallace.org Web: http://www.edgarwallace.org/

Contents

CARFEW II

It was an idea; even Jenkins, the assistant editor, admitted that much, albeit reluctantly. Carfew was an erratic genius, and the job would suit him very well, because he had a horror of anything that had the appearance of discipline, or order, or conventional method.

In the office of *The Megaphone* they have a shuddering recollection of a night in June when the Panmouth Limited Express, moving at the rate of seventy miles an hour, came suddenly upon an excursion train standing in a wayside station beyond Freshcombe.

The news came through on the tape at 5.30, and Carfew was in the office engaged in an unnecessary argument with the chief sub-editor on the literary value of certain news which he had supplied, and which "the exigencies of space" – I quote the chief sub, who was Scotch and given to harmless pedantry – had excluded from the morning's edition.

Carfew had been dragged to the chief's room, he protesting, and had been dispatched with indecent haste to the scene of the disaster.

"You can write us a story that will thrill Europe," said the chief, half imploring, half challenging. "Get it on the wire by nine, and for heaven's sake, give your mind to the matter!"

Carfew, thinking more of his grievance against an unwholesome tribe of sub-editors, who, as he told himself, suppressed his copy from spite, had only the vaguest idea as to where he was being sent, and why.

1

The flaming placard of an evening paper caught his eye – "Railway disaster" – as he flew through the Strand in a taxi-cab, and then a frantically signalling man on the side-walk arrested his attention.

"Hi – stop!" shouted Carfew to the driver, for the signaller was Arthur Syce, that eminent critic.

Now, it was rumoured that there was some grave doubt as to the authenticity of the Riebera Espanolito, recently acquired by the National Gallery, and Carfew was hot for information on the subject. Indeed, it was he who had planted the seeds of suspicion concerning this alleged example of the Spaniard's work.

The great news agencies sent in their disjointed messages of the railway smash – they came by tape-machines, by panting messengers, by telegrams from the local correspondents of *The Megaphone* at Freshcombe – but there was no news from Carfew. Ten o'clock, eleven o'clock, eleven-thirty – no news from Carfew. Skilful men at the little desks in the sub-editors' room, working at fever speed, pieced together the story of the accident and sent it whizzing up pneumatic tubes to the printer's departments.

"If Carfew's story comes in, use it," said the despairing chief; but Carfew's story never came.

Instead came Carfew, with the long hand of the clock one minute before twelve, – Carfew, very red, very jubilant, almost incoherent in his triumph.

"Hold half a column for me!" he roared gleefully. "I've got it!"

The editor had been leaning over the chief-sub's desk when Carfew entered. He looked up with an angry frown.

"Got it? Half a column? What the devil have you got?"

"The Spaniard is a fake!" shouted Carfew.

He had forgotten all about the railway accident.

If he had not been a genius, a beautiful writer, a perfect and unparalleled master of descriptive, he would have been fired that night; but there was only one Carfew – or, at least, there was only one known Carfew at that time – and he stayed on, under a cloud, it is true, but he stayed on.

Newspaper memory is shortlived. Last week's news is older than the chronicles of the Chaldeans, and in a week Carfew's misdeed was only food for banter and good-humoured chaff, and he himself was sufficiently magnanimous to laugh with the rest.

When the dead season came, with Parliament up and all the world out of town, somebody suggested a scheme after Carfew's own heart. He was away, loafing at Blankenberghe at the time, but a wire recalled him:

"Be at office Tuesday night, and follow instructions contained in letter."

To this he replied with a cheery "Right O!" Which the Blankenberghe telegraphist, unused to the idioms of the English, mutilated to "Righ loh." But that by the way.

"Do you think he will understand this?" asked the editor of his assistant, and read:

"You will leave London by the earliest possible train for anywhere. Go where you like, write what you like, but send along your stuff as soon as you write it. We shall call the series 'The Diary of an Irresponsible Wanderer.' Enclosed find two hundred pounds to cover all expenses. If you want more, wire. Good luck!"

The assistant nodded his head. "He'll understand that all right," he said grimly.

The chief stuffed four crinkling banknotes into the envelope and licked down the flap.

Then came a knock at the door, and a boy entered with a scrap of paper. The editor glanced at it carelessly.

"Writes a vile hand," he said, and read: " 'Business – re engagement.' Will you see him, Jenkins?"

His second shook his head. "I can't see anybody till seven," he said.

The editor fingered the paper. "Tell him – oh, send him up!" – impatiently.

In the waiting-room below was a young man. He sat on the edge of the plain deal table and whistled a music-hall tune cheerfully, though he had no particular reason for feeling cheerful having spent the two previous nights on the Thames Embankment. But he was blessed with a rare fund of optimism. Optimism had brought him to London from the little newspaper of which he was part-proprietor, chief reporter, editor, and advertisement canvasser. His part-proprietorship was only a small part; he disposed of it for his railway fare and a suit of clothing. His optimism, plus a Rowton House, had sustained him in a two months' search for work and a weary circulation of newspaper offices which did not seem to be in any urgent need of an editor and part-proprietor. More than this, optimism had justified his going without breakfast on this particular morning that he might acquire a clean collar for the last and most tremendous of his ventures – the storming of *The Megaphone* editorial. He had tossed up whether it should be *The Times* or *The Megaphone* and *The Megaphone* had won. He had a sense of humour, this young man with the strong, clean-shaven face and the serene eyes. He was whistling when the small boy beckoned him.

"Editor'll see you," said the youth.

"That's something, anyway, Mike."

"My name's not Mike," said the youth reprovingly.

"Then you be jolly careful," said the aspirant for editorial honours as he stepped into the lift, "or it will be."

The chief glanced at his visitor, noted the shining glory of the new collar and the antiquity of the shirt beneath, also some fraying about the cuff, and a hungry look that all the optimism in the world could not disguise in the face of a healthy young man who had not broken his fast.

"Sit down, won't you?" he said. "Well?"

"Well," said the young man, drawing a long breath, "I want a job."

This was not exactly what he had intended saying, though in substance it did not differ materially. The chief shook his head with a smile and reached for a fat memorandum-book.

"Here," he said, running the edge of the pages through his fingers, "is a list of three hundred men who want jobs; you will be number three hundred and one."

"Work backwards and get a good man," said the applicant easily. "There are not many men like me going." He saw the chief smile kindly. "I'm like one of those famous authors' first manuscripts you read about, going the rounds of the publishing offices and nobody realising what a treasure he's rejecting till it's snapped up by a keen business man. Snap me up."

The chief's smile broadened. "You've certainly got a point of view," he said. "What can you do?"

The young man reached for the cigarette that the other offered. "Edit," he said, knocking the end of the cigarette on the desk "partly propriate, report, take a note of a parish council, or write a leader."

"We aren't wanting an editor just now," said the chief carefully, "not even a sub-editor, but – " He had taken a sudden liking for the brazen youth. "Look here, Mr —, I forget your name – come along and see me at eleven tonight. I shall have more time to talk then."

The other rose, his heart beating rapidly, for he detected hope in this promise of an interview.

"I shall be able to give you a little work," said the chief, and walked to the safe at the far end of the office, unlocked it, and took from the till a pound. "This is on account of work you might do for us. You can give me a receipt for it. I've an idea that you'll find it useful."

"I'm jolly certain I shall," breathed the young man as he scrawled the IOU.

He went down the stairs two at a time. He was a leader writer at the second landing, managing editor by the time he reached the ground floor, and had a substantial interest in the paper before the swing doors of the big building had ceased to oscillate behind him. He was immensely optimistic.

He engaged a room in the Blackfriars Road, paying a week's rent in advance, and breakfasted, lunched and dined in one grand, comprehensive meal.

The greater part of the evening he spent walking up and down the Embankment, watching the lights, that had a cheerier aspect than ever they had possessed before. Some of his dreams were coming true. He had never doubted for a moment but that they would; it had been only a question of time.

Eleven o'clock was striking when he stepped into the lobby of Megaphone House. There was a new boy on duty, and, in default of a card, the visitor wrote his name on a slip of paper.

"Who is it you wish to see, sir?" asked the boy.

"The editor."

The boy looked at the slip. "The editor has been gone half an hour," he said, and the young man's heart sank momentarily.

"Perhaps he left a message?" he suggested.

"I'll see, sir."

Anyway, he thought, as he paced the narrow vestibule, tomorrow is also a day. Perhaps the chief had forgotten him in the stress of his work, or had been called away. Cabinet Ministers, it was reported, sent for the editor of *The Megaphone* when they were undecided as to what they should do for the country's good.

There was a clatter of feet on the marble stairs, and a man came hurrying down, holding his slip of paper in his hand.

"I'm sorry, sir," he began breathlessly, "but the editor has asked me to say that he has been summoned home unexpectedly. I should have come to meet you, but I have only recently been appointed night secretary, and I have not had the pleasure of meeting you" – he smiled apologetically – "so I should not have recognised you." He handed an envelope to the young man. "The editor said I was to place this in your hands, and that you'll find all instructions within."

"Thank you!" said the youth, breathing a sigh of relief. It was pleasant to know he had not been overlooked.

He had left the building, when the secretary came running after him.

"I didn't make a mistake in your name, did I?" he asked a little anxiously.

"Carfew," said the youth – "Felix Carfew is my name."

"Thank you, sir, that is right," responded the secretary, and turned back.

Mr Felix Carfew – not to be confused with the great Gregory Carfew, special correspondent to *The Megaphone* – made his way to a little restaurant opposite the Houses of Parliament with his precious package at the very bottom of the innermost pocket of his aged jacket. (Gregory Carfew had light-heartedly missed the boat connection at Ostend, and at the moment was playing baccarat in the guarded rooms of the *Circle Priveé*.)

"Now," said Felix, having ordered coffee, "let me see what my job of work is to be."

He opened the envelope and, making involuntary little noises of astonishment, took out four pieces of white paper, whereon the admirable Mr Nairne promised to pay fifty pounds to bearer; then he opened the letter and read it. He read it three times slowly before he grasped its meaning.

" 'Go anywhere!... Write about anything!....' " he repeated, and drew a long breath.

" 'Earliest possible train!'...You may be certain of that, O heavenly editor!" he said, and paid his bill without touching the coffee he had ordered.

Earliest train – earliest train! Now, where did the next train leave for – the next train that would carry him out of London, away from the possibilities of recall, supposing that this too-generous light of the newest and best journalism repented his hasty munificence?

He whistled a taxi-cab, and made up his mind before the car stopped at the kerb. "Victoria," he said. At any rate, Victoria was near, and if there was no train, he could go on to Euston and catch the northern mail. It was half-past eleven as he drove into the station-yard, and he had an uncomfortable feeling that it was very unlikely that there would be a train for the Continent at that hour. (He had unconsciously decided on Paris as his objective.)

"I want a train for the Continent," he told a porter.

"What sort of train, sir?"

"Any sort you've got?" said Felix generously.

"I mean, are you one of the gentlemen who are going by the special?"

"Yes," said Felix, not knowing exactly what the special was, or who were the gentlemen going thereby.

"Well, you'll have to hurry," said the man, galvanised of a sudden out of his normal restfulness. "Come this way, sir."

Since the porter ran, Felix thought it no shame to follow his example, and they came to an ill-lit bay platform just as a whistle shrilled and a very short train began to move.

"Special, Bill!" shouted the porter, and the guard beckoned him furiously.

There was an empty carriage next to the guard's van, and into this Felix leapt. He turned to throw a shilling in the direction of the porter, and then sank back on to the soft cushions of the carriage and wiped his perspiring forehead.

It was a corridor carriage, and he had recovered some of his lost breath when he heard the snap of the guard's key, and the official came through the bulkhead door into the corridor without.

The man nodded civilly. "Nearly lost it, sir," he said. "Have you got a ticket, or are all the tickets on one voucher?"

"Eh?" said Felix, and then began to realise dimly that there was some sort of explanation due to the guard.

"The fact is, guard," he explained, "I am going to the Continent."

Into the guard's face came an expression of distrust. "Are you one of the party or not, sir?" he asked briefly.

"I am, and I'm not," said the cautious Felix. He felt in his pocket and took out the envelope with the notes. These he extracted and smoothed deliberately on his knee. He felt that this was a moment of crisis. He had evidently boarded somebody's special train, and it was up to him to demonstrate his respectability. A cynic might have been vastly amused at the tender solicitude which suddenly crept into the guard's tone.

"I am afraid, sir," he said gently, "you have got aboard the wrong train. This is a special ordered by his Excellency the Ambassador of Mid-Europe."

"Tut, tut!" said Felix, apparently annoyed. "What am I to do?"

The guard pondered, tapping his teeth softly with his key.

"You keep quiet, sir," he said, after a while; "I'll fix it up for you. There are no passengers on this bogie, and nobody need have any idea that you're aboard."

With these words of cheer, a touch of the cap and a smile, the guard went forward to attend to the official passengers, and Felix stretched his legs to the opposite seat and reviewed the situation. The first part of his instructions was carried out. He had left London by the earliest possible train. At any rate, he could get as far as Dover. Would his Excellency the Ambassador of Mid-Europe have chartered a special boat to enable him to cross the Channel? Anyway, one could cross by the first boat in the morning. And then for Paris! What should he write about? A visit to the Morgue, full of grisly details in restrained but vivid language? That had been done. Or a night in the Montmartre as seen by the eyes of one who had absorbed six absinthes? He had a notion that had been done too.

Perhaps he might hap upon some big, exclusive "story" – his luck was in. The Opera House, crowded with the beauty and wit of Paris, might collapse, and he be the only journalist present. That was unlikely in a city where one man in every three owned a newspaper, and the other two wrote for it.

A brilliant thought struck him. An interview with the Ambassador of Mid-Europe!

Everybody was interested in Mid-Europe and its erratic Empress. She had recently delivered an impassioned and bellicose speech, obviously directed towards Great Britain, and diplomatic relationships, in consequence, had been somewhat strained.

Felix Carfew's eyes sparkled at the thought. If he could secure the interview, his fortune would be made, the faith of this trustful editor of his fully justified. How pleasantly surprised *The Megaphone* would be to receive, say, a thousand words from Paris, beginning:

"I have been accorded an interview with H E Count Greishen, who gave me his views on the recent utterances of the Empress."

The tremendous possibility of the thing gripped him, and he jumped to his feet. The train was roaring and swaying through the sleeping country. Rain had begun to fall, and the carriage window was streaked with flying drops.

As the idea took shape he did not hesitate. He was on the train; he could not be thrown off, because this was evidently a non-stop run.

He was out of the compartment and in the corridor before he remembered that the guard had gone to the fore part of the train, and would be coming back in all probability. Reluctantly he returned to his seat and waited. He had to wait a quarter of an hour before the official returned, and for another five minutes he chafed inwardly whilst the guard made polite conversation, which was mostly about people who caught the wrong train and found themselves stranded in little, out-of-the-way stations. At last the man in uniform turned to go; then it was that Felix remembered that he was under an obligation.

"Oh, by the way, guard," he said, "can you change a fifty pound note?"

The man favoured him with a melancholy smile.

"I couldn't change a fifty-penny note, sir," he said; "but" – brightening up – "I could get it changed for you."

Felix handed over the note. "What time are we due at Dover?" he asked.

"One o'clock, sir," said the man.

"Then hurry up with the change." Felix was growing impatient; he had little more than half an hour to carry out his plan. He wondered exactly how the guard would get change, and his curiosity on this subject was satisfied when, in a few minutes, the man returned with a handful of Bank of England notes.

"I suppose you wonder how I got that?" he said, as he counted out the money. "The steward of the Embassy is on board, and, leaving hurriedly, of course he had no time to change his small money."

He rambled on in this strain for a few minutes, but Felix was not listening toward the end.

"Leaving hurriedly!"

When ambassadors "leave hurriedly," taking with them their whole staff – leaving so hurriedly, indeed, that special trains must be ordered – it has a significance.

He tipped the guard a sovereign, and sat down with his head in his hands to think.

There was a timetable on the rack over his head, and this he took down. Turning the leaves, he discovered that the last ordinary train for the Continent left London at nine o'clock. What was the urgency of the case that compelled a special at eleven-thirty?

"Felix, my boy, you've found news!"

He had made up his mind before the train ran alongside the ocean quay. It was a mild, wet night, he had no overcoat, but this did not worry him. He stood back in the shadow of the train and watched the Ambassador's party descend. There were fourteen in all, and they made their way along the quay to where lay one of the smaller channel steamers.

"Chartered," said Felix to himself. He took the landward side of the train and stepped out quickly. Halfway along the deserted platform he came upon a solitary seaman-porter. With a recollection of a previous calling, he asked:

"Can you get me an oilskin?"

The man hesitated. "I've only got my own, sir," he said.

"I'll give you a sovereign for it," said Felix.

"It's yours," said the other promptly, and stripped it off. "I've got a sou'wester kicking about somewhere," said the porter, pocketing the coin. "You'll want it if you're crossing. Wait here, sir."

Felix waited for a moment, when the man came running back, the hat in his hand.

"Here you are, sir! Hurry up if you're going by the special!"

"I'm going by the special all right," replied the confident youth. "Would you like to earn a sovereign?" he asked suddenly.

In the darkness he could not see the man smile at the absurdity of the question.

"I should say so," he said.

"Come along to where there's some light."

Under a flickering arc lamp Felix wrote a brief message on the back of his blessed envelope.

"Get through to London on the telephone," he said. "You'll be able to do it, if you persevere – and send this message."

"I can do it from the post-office, or from one of the hotels if I tip the night-porter," said the man.

"Well, tip him; here's another half-sovereign."

The steamer at the quayside hooted warningly, and Felix thrust the money and the message into the porter's hand.

"You'll have to dig out the telephone number," he called back, as he hastened his steps to the ship.

None challenged him as he ran down the slippery gangway to the heaving deck of the steamer. The Ambassador's party had disappeared below, and a sailor directed him to the saloon.

"Thanks, I'll stay on deck," said Felix.

He waited until the pier light slipped astern, then made his way below. Along the main deck on either side ran an alleyway, and a door abaft the engines opened to a flight of stairs leading to the saloon of the steamer.

Very cautiously he stepped inside. From where he stood he had a capital view of the saloon. A long table had been laid for a meal, and round this the various members of the Embassy were grouped.

Felix recognised the old Count, with his fierce, white moustache and his shaggy eyebrows, sitting at the head of the table.

They were talking in a language Felix did not understand, but he used his eyes with some effect, and by and by he saw the Ambassador take from his pocket a leather case, open it, extract what was evidently a long telegram, and compare it with a sheet of paper which had been folded with the wire.

"Those are his instructions," said Felix; "they are in code, and that paper is the translation. I'm going to have those if I die in the attempt."

The danger would be, he told himself, that the boat would arrive at Calais before he had time to put his plan into execution; the party might sit at their meal until the harbour was reached. He prayed fervently for a choppy sea or a gale of wind that would send them flying from the saloon; but the sea was like oil, and the drizzle of rain was a sure indication that no wind could be expected.

He went up to the top deck to think out a scheme. Over to starboard a bright light flashed on the horizon at regular intervals.

"What light is that?" he asked a passing deckhand.

"Calais, sir."

"Calais! Oh, of course, we leave Calais on the right?"

He put the question carelessly.

"Yes, sir, for Ostend."

"Oh!" said Felix, who had secured the information he wished. For an hour he paced the deck enjoying the novelty of the position. Then there was a stir at the companion-way, and half a dozen men came up, heavily coated, and made their way to a covered shelter behind the funnel. The Ambassador was not one of these, and the adventurer moved forward to investigate. He went below again. There were a number of cabins opening out on to the main deck, and he had time to see the broad back of Count Greishen disappearing into one of these.

"You'll excuse me," said Felix, switching on the light, "but I want to get your views on the European situation." It was the sort of thing he would say if he had been interviewing the member for East Poshton, and the respectful tone was all that could be desired.

An elderly diplomatist, awakened at two o'clock in the morning by an imperturbable youth in oilskins and sou'wester, might be excused a feeling of irritation; but when the awakening is performed by the sudden switching on of an electric lamp, and the first greeting he receives is a request for his views on the political situation, his wrath, however great, may be pardoned.

He was speechless for a moment, the while Felix produced a conventional notebook and seated himself on a settee.

"In cases like this – " he began, when the Count found his voice.

"Who are you, sir, and what do you mean by coming here? I'll have you arrested, you – you – "

Felix raised a warning hand. "Do not let us forget that we are gentlemen," he said, with dignity. "Now, on the question of diplomatic relationships, don't you consider that your people are behaving like goops? Now, take the question of that silly speech of the Empress – "

"Sir," said the diplomat, with terrible calm – he was sitting up in his bunk, and the fact that he wore green-striped pyjamas detracted somewhat from his impressiveness – "you are going too far. I gather that you are a journalist?"

"Carfew, of *The Megaphone*," said the young man proudly.

"Mr Carfew – I shall remember your name," said the Ambassador. "You have forced your way by some means on to a boat which has been privately chartered. Now you force a way into my cabin, and I shall have you removed. In all my life I have never – "

"I dare say you're right," interrupted the youth graciously; "but that's beside the point. What we have to arrive at now is a *modus vivendi*. A similar situation occurred in Pillborough, where the mayor had a terrific row with the borough surveyor, and wouldn't sit in the same room. You needn't try to ring the bell, because I've cut the wire outside. Now, your Excellency, let us talk this matter over. You've had instructions to return immediately?"

"This," said the Ambassador, trembling with anger, "is an outrage against every civilised law!"

"Let me ask you a few questions." Felix poised his pencil. "You have been recalled – yes?"

"I refuse to answer."

"As a result of the recent speech of our Prime Minister – "

"Your Foreign – Confound you, sir, I won't answer your beastly questions!" roared his Excellency.

"Very good," said Felix writing rapidly.

" 'As a result of the speech of the Foreign Secretary, my Government recalled me. The instructions did not reach me until after nine – ' "

"How do you know that?" demanded the astonished diplomat.

"We have sources of information undreamt of," replied the young man gravely.

14

For the greater part of an hour they sat – the persecuted and the persecutor – until the slowing of the engines warned the reporter that the end of the journey was at hand.

Another man had been aroused in the middle of the night, to his intense annoyance. This was Gregory Carfew, to whom, at 3 a.m., came an urgent telegram:

"Your telegram received: have confirmed facts. We send you this to hotel in the hope you will call in for wires. Let us know if you were able to get aboard *Seabird*."

Now, Carfew was really a great correspondent, and, albeit, bewildered by the character of the message, he scented a story, and lost no time in dressing. The *Seabird* he had never heard of, but in the dark hours of the morning he found a marine superintendent who afforded him some important information.

"*Seabird*, m'sieur? Yes, it is one of the smaller of the packets. It is strange that you should ask, for we have just received a wireless message from her; she is seven kilometres outside. She has asked for police to be present to arrest a suspicious character who is hiding aboard."

" 'Curiouser and curiouser,' " quoth Carfew, settling himself down on the wooden quay to await the arrival of this mysterious steamer.

After a while, six Belgian policemen came and took up a position on the jetty. Then, in the grey light of dawn, the little paddle-boat came stealing into the harbour and made its stealthy way to the pier. The policemen were the first aboard, and Carfew followed.

Since the interest would seem to centre round the police and their presence, he followed them at a leisurely pace and came upon a group. An elderly man, speaking volubly in French, was talking, and instantly Carfew recognised him.

"By jove," he ejaculated, "it's old Greishen!" and elbowed his way through the little crowd.

"I do not think I should recognise him," the Ambassador was saying. "He kept his hat on all the time, and when the engines stopped he fled... But he is on board the ship somewhere."

"Pardon me, your Excellency" – Carfew pushed his way forward – "can I be of any assistance? My name is Carfew, and I am on the staff of *The Megaphone*."

"That's the man!" roared the Ambassador, and rude hands seized the astonished correspondent. "You have made a mistake, my friend," said the Count, his English failing him in his excitement. "You carry this off with a bloff, but I will put you where your mischievous pen will rest for a day or two. Listen, my friend!" He wagged a fat forefinger in the face of the paralysed Carfew. "If you had published what you had discovered last night, what you stole from me – yes, I have detected the loss of my despatch – if you had published, you might have made serious embarrassment for my country; but when you publish all the world will know. Two days, three days, you will go to prison, and then we can afford to release you. *Marchez*."

Carfew I was swearing terrible as he was hustled across the gangway, what time, snugly hidden in one of the boats that swung not two yards from where the arrest had been made, Carfew II was busily making notes for the story which was to establish his fame in the London newspaper world.

CARFEW, WITHINGTON AND CO, INVENTORS

Carfew could never quite make up his mind whether he would like to be a millionaire, or whether he would prefer to jog along with five or six thousand a year. He lived in Bedford Park, and occupied the period of time it took him to walk from his lodgings to Turnham Green Station in setting his affairs in order. Thus, he would never make a will. It is much better to be magnificent living than munificent dead. The newspapers would record both qualities, giving as much space to either, with the added advantage that the living philanthropist could read all about it in the morning newspapers.

His favourite distribution of wealth was as follows:

Foundation of scholarships (the Carfew Foundation for the Children of Journalists), fifty thousand pounds.

Endowment of a children's hospital, two hundred thousand pounds. (A baronetage would probably follow, though Carfew was democratic, not to say socialistic.)

The establishment of an ideal newspaper, and the maintenance of same without advertisement revenue, one hundred and fifty thousand pounds. (Carfew had had bitter experience with advertisers, who blankly refused to "come in" to the little sheet of which he had been part-proprietor, and he had rehearsed some exceedingly nasty things he would say to would-be advertisers. "No, sir, we cannot print your advertisement. I don't care if you offered me twenty pounds an inch – I would not insert an announcement concerning your infernal soap!")

Motorcars handsomely furnished, lit with electric light and replete with down cushions, say, ten thousand pounds.

Mansion in a lovely park, where he would live alone, one hundred thousand pounds. ("Who is that sad-faced young man?" strangers would ask the inhabitants of the village. "Him? Why, don't you know?" the rustics would reply, in hushed but respectful tones. "Yon's Squire Carfew, the millionaire. They du say that he be a turruble man to cross in anger.")

Such possessions demanded the application of the millionaire's schedule, and were infrequent. In the main, Carfew was content with five thousand a year and a life of travel.

One morning in April Carfew was busy endowing a hospital or an orphan home. He had reached the point where His Royal Highness had declared the building open.

Carfew was kneeling on a red velvet cushion, and the Prince's sword was raised for the accolade, and Carfew had stopped in his walk that he might enjoy the emotion of the moment, when he came into collision with an elderly gentleman, who, after carefully closing the gate of his suburban villa behind him, had bumped into the stationary figure standing wrapped in thought on the side-walk.

He was a very fierce old gentleman, somewhat spare of build, grey-haired and grey-moustached, and he had the ruddy-pink complexion of one who had served his country faithfully and had written to the papers about it.

"Your Royal Highness," began Carfew genially, "I regret – "

"Why on earth don't you look where you're going?" asked the elderly gentleman.

"I usually do," said Carfew; "but apparently the accident was caused by my not looking where I was coming from."

"You are an impertinent puppy!" fumed the other. "By jove, sir – "

He flourished his silver-knobbed walking-cane suggestively.

Carfew evaded the waving cane, then took a leisurely survey of the street.

"If you are endeavouring to attract the attention of a wandering motor-bus," he said, "it is my duty to tell you that you are off the line of route."

The bristling gentleman shrugged his shoulders elaborately. "Puppy!" he repeated, and walked on, giving vicious little tugs to his frock-coat and patting himself here and there. A gladiator strutting from the gory floor of the *Coloseum* might so have arranged his disordered dress.

Carfew followed at a respectful distance, his heart filled with mild resentment.

He did not object to the hasty appellation – he strongly resented the interruption to the interesting ceremony of which he was the central figure. Carfew at the moment was out of elbows with fortune. He had been fired from the staff of *The Megaphone* – that great organ of public opinion. He had fallen with what the provincial reporter loves to describe as a "dull, sickening thud."

This happened two months before Carfew collided with the military gentleman in Bedford Park. Three months' salary paid regularly lasts three months. Three months' salary paid in advance lasts exactly six weeks. I do not explain this economic phenomenon – I merely state it as a fact. And here was Carfew counting the change from a shilling at the Turnham Green booking office. And here was Carfew, who became severely practical in a train, debating in his mind whether he should tell his landlady exactly how he stood financially, or whether he could bluff it out another week.

When he had left *The Megaphone* he was not decided in his mind whether he would start a rival newspaper, or whether he would take employment with a rival journal. He had, with a pencil and paper, worked out a scheme whereby he could produce a paper which would show a profit of two thousand pounds a month, but convinced nobody but himself. He was no more fortunate when he decided to offer his services to other journals.

There was a conspiracy designed to keep him unemployed. Nobody wanted him. The editors in Fleet Street gave him audience readily enough, were immensely polite, but unsatisfactory. They felt that, in the present state of journalistic depression, they could not offer him the salary which his services deserved. Every single newspaper, daily or weekly, to which he applied, informed him that his visit coincided with a period of rigid economy.

It may have been that the modest estimate he made of his own value was not sufficiently modest. Be that as it may, Carfew, on this memorable spring morning, was "up against it, good and hard." He alighted at Temple Station, and turned on to the Embankment. It was a glorious spring day. The world was flood with April's yellow sunlight. The trees were bursting into green, and through the railings of the Temple he saw great splashes of vivid colouring where the tulips bloomed in beds of stiff and orderly formation.

Carfew squared his shoulders and stepped out briskly, for he was young and buoyant and had faith in Carfew. And the world was bright and beautiful and sunlight fretted the waters of full Old Thames with criss-cross patterns of gold, and there was a fat, black tug pulling a string of lazy barges against the stream.

Carfew decided to cross the broad thoroughfare to get a better view of the river. There was a man walking in front of him – an elderly gentleman, with a jaunty silk hat and a frock-coat cut tightly in at the waist. The back view was familiar. Half way across the broad thoroughfare, Carfew suddenly reached out his hand, grasped his elder by the shoulder, and unceremoniously dragged him back.

The fact that half an hour previously he had called the other a puppy did not seem to Colonel Withington sufficient justification for the assault.

"Sir!" he gasped awfully.

A motorcar whizzed past within a few inches of where they stood. The chauffeur flung a sinful observation in passing about people who did not look where they were going.

"I have saved your life," said Carfew modestly, "but do not, I beg of you, thank me. I am sufficiently repaid by the driver's offensive remark."

He released the Colonel, and they crossed the remainder of the road together.

"I am awfully obliged," growled the elderly gentleman. "I didn't hear what the man said."

He added his opinion of the man with true soldierly frankness.

"He told you to look where you were going," said Carfew sweetly.

"Humph!" said the Colonel. They reached the side-walk in safety. Carfew, with a courteous little bow – one he had invented specially for the occasion of his presentation to Royalty – turned to the parapet. The Colonel hesitated, walked on a little way, stopped and looked round at the unconscious youth, drinking in the beauties of the river, then, after a moment's hesitation, walked back to him.

"Excuse me," he said, and tapped his shoulder lightly with his cane.

Carfew turned.

"Can you spare the time to walk a little way with me?" said the Colonel gruffly. He was a trifle stiff, being an uncompromising, explosive colonel, not given to graciousness. In his lifetime he had sentenced many guilty soldiers to cells, had presided at courts-martial, and had spent many hours of his life shouting incomprehensibly at eight hundred men, and the eight hundred men had done exactly what he shouted without so much as saying: "Excuse us, sir, but haven't you made a slight error?"

Carfew fell in by the other's side.

"My name is Withington, Colonel retired," said the Colonel briefly. "I am greatly obliged to you. I am afraid I was rather rude to you – apologise."

"Certainly," said Carfew; "I apologise, though why I should apologise for your – "

"Huff!" said the Colonel. "You misunderstand – I apologise. What's yours?"

"Thank you," said Carfew; "but, if you don't mind, I'd rather have a cup of tea. Any kind of drink – "

"What's your name? What's your name?" demanded the military gentleman, testily. "I'm not inviting you to drink. You don't suppose, my good fellow, that I'd walk into a public house, eh? What on earth do you think I am – eh?"

Carfew did not tell him; instead, he offered vital information.

"I am Carfew," he said. That was all. He was Carfew. Everybody knew Carfew. It had appeared in the papers – it had been printed.

"Don't know you," said the Colonel, "but I'm awfully obliged to you. What d'ye do?"

Carfew was annoyed.

"I am Carfew," he said distinctly – "Carfew the journalist – *the* Carfew."

The Colonel looked at him suspiciously.

"Reporter, eh?" He wagged a warning finger. "Don't put anything in your beastly paper about me: 'Famous Inventor's Narrow Escape: Rescued from Death on the Thames Embankment!' None of that! I know you!"

Carfew was speechless. If there was one thing in the world he hated more than another, it was being called a reporter. He felt as the Colonel might have felt had he received a letter addressed "Lance-Corporal Withington."

And the arrogance of the old man! He thought himself famous! And he did not know him!

"You need not trouble," he said brutally; "you're worth about three lines, including your biography. You are what we call a 'fill.' "

They walked on in wrathful silence, crossing Queen Victoria Street by the subway.

"I don't dislike you," said the Colonel suddenly, as they emerged from the underground passage. "Are you free?"

"As the air," said Carfew, mastering his annoyance.

"Then come along – come along," said the Colonel.

They walked on in silence for a while, the soldier twirling his cane and humming a mutilated fragment of a song which was popular enough in the 'sixties, and the words of which, as far as Carfew could gather, were:

Ta looral um, looral um, oh,
Ta diddy, la diddy, hi hay,
Oh, dee dum ti tiddle,
Oh, loorum lum liddle,
Oh, tumpty, would anyone say!

"Three lines, eh?" said the Colonel suddenly – "three lines? Ah, you're a child – you do not know!"

He went on with his song, the second verse of which did not differ materially from the first.

Now and again he shot a swift glance at the lean-faced youth at his side. What he saw satisfied him, for of a sudden he remarked explosively:

"I'll make your fortune! Hang it, I'll make a millionaire of you!"

Carfew was impressed. A dream had been realised. Somewhere in the background of his life there had ever lurked a munificent old gentleman who would adopt him.

"I have no parents," he said encouragingly, "and no relations whom I know. I have always felt the need of such a father as you would make, Major – "

"Colonel!" snapped the other. "And don't talk to me about my being your father! I'm not old enough, sir, to be the father of a big gawk like you. I don't suppose there is twenty years between us." He glared challengingly at Carfew.

"How old are you?"

"Twenty-four," said Carfew.

"Hum!" said the Colonel. "I'm over forty – just a little over forty."

Carfew was sufficiently discreet to stop himself saying that he looked older.

"Here we are." They turned into a block of offices facing the Salvation Army Headquarters. In the vestibule the Colonel grasped his arm and pointed with his cane to the white-enamelled indicator.

"Colonel G Withington, Inventor," he read. "The Withington Compass Company, The Withington Dry Plate Syndicate, The

23

Withington Gun Recoil Company, The Withington Patents. Fourth floor."

Carfew read all this, and the Colonel was gratified to note that at every enterprise his young companion nodded his head approvingly. The liftman, who was also the hall-porter, saluted the inventor punctiliously.

"Man of my old regiment," introduced the Colonel, with a jerk of his head. "Eh, Miles? Got you this job. Out of work and starving – three children – foolishly improvident!"

"Yes, sir," said Miles, who had long since ceased to be embarrassed by the crude recital of his misfortunes. "Left the regiment sixteen years ago. You were Major – "

"That will do, Miles," said the Colonel loudly. The lift rose slowly to the fourth floor and they stepped out. Immediately facing was a door on which was painted the Colonel's name and the title of his companies.

The tenant unlocked the door with a flourish – he did everything with a flourish – and waved Carfew inside.

"No clerks," said the Colonel. "No spying, prying, lying – er – "

"Trying," suggested Carfew.

"No, sir – no clerks. Here's my little home – my little gas stove – I make my own tea – my desk, my drawing-table, my modest library. Take a chair."

He opened a cupboard, and took down a soiled velvet coat and a faded smoking-cap, such as you see in the earlier Du Maurier drawings.

"Work, work, work!" said the Colonel. He opened a drawer of his desk and took out a flat tin of tobacco and a large pipe, and, whilst he filled it, Carfew recovered from his disappointment.

For this was no millionaire's sanctum. It was a poverty-stricken little office. There was a file of newspapers, an antiquated filing cabinet, a bureau, which combined the useful functions of desk and bookcase, two chairs, the gas-stove, and a few almanacks.

"I like you," repeated the Colonel. "You are the type of man I have been looking for – pushful, resourceful, thick-skinned – a bluffer."

Carfew looked thoughtful.

"I'm an inventor," said the Colonel. "Does it pay? No, sir. When I am dead, some rotter will be rolling in luxury, sir, on the fruits of my genius. This time fifty years – millions; today – that."

He banged down on the desk a handful of money, hastily drawn from his pocket. Carfew noted with dismay that it was in the main made up of coppers.

But his dismay turned as quickly to laughter – good-natured laughter – and the Colonel's grim face relaxed.

"We're in the same boat, sir," said Carfew, and chuckled at the humour of it.

The Colonel's uplifted hand stopped him.

"But we are at the end of our penury," he said. "Read this!"

He pushed a letter towards the young man. It was headed "Swelliger and Friedman," and read:

"DEAR SIR, – We have to thank you for your favour of even date. We have gone into the question of your patents, and we are willing to acquire two – namely, the Withington Compass and the Withington Gun Recoil Patent. We offer you the sum of three hundred and fifty pounds for these, though, in doing so, we feel it is our duty to tell you that we regard neither as being of such commercial value as will recoup us for our speculation. – We are," etc.

Carfew read the letter again. Here was a firm of financiers offering three hundred and fifty pounds for something they expected to lose money over.

"We'll go into this," said Carfew with energy. He spent a busy morning examining curious and boring specifications. He found the Colonel a most extraordinary mixture of shrewd worldliness and childlike innocence. At eleven o'clock Carfew was a partner in the most promising business in London. At twelve he had been summarily reduced to the ranks, deprived of his living, the partnership dissolved, and degraded to the honorary position of ignorant jackass. (This was the direct result of his questioning the value of the patent compass; the Colonel was a little annoyed.)

At one o'clock they went out arm in arm to an ABC shop, Carfew being at the moment managing director with authority to act.

He had many vicissitudes that day; for the Colonel, who, as he proudly confessed, had neither chick, child, wife, nor any other master but the King, God bless him! – "Amen," said Carfew piously – was unused to being dominated. Carfew had a method of his own. He had energy; he had that supreme contempt for the world which every proper journalist possesses; he had business knowledge and a commercial diplomacy which only comes to the country reporter who has learnt that an advertisement must be balanced with a flattering editorial notice of the advertiser. He had, in fact, all the qualities that the Colonel lacked.

For three days Carfew worked at top speed, reading specifications, strenuously grappling with drawings which he but imperfectly understood – the Colonel had been an RE – sorting out the correspondence which had been neglected. He found that there were all sorts of little sums due to the inventor – little royalties, too small for the magnificent seeker of millions to notice. These he claimed peremptorily. In the meantime came an urgent letter from Swelliger and Friedman, begging the favour of an immediate reply to their letter.

But Carfew had gone into the question of the patent compass and the patent recoil. The compass he understood, the recoil carried him into a dark desert of dynamics, through which he vainly groped a way.

"Let 'em have it – let 'em have it," said the Colonel impatiently. "They are thieves! The compass is worth a million of anybody's money, but let 'em have it."

"What is the recoil worth?" asked Carfew.

"Millions," said the Colonel impartially, "but no commercial value, my dear boy. Limited output, limited income. I worked it out to amuse myself."

Carfew knew a man who was manager to a firm of scientific instrument makers, and to him he went. Briefly he explained the compass and exposed a model.

"Now, I am not trying to sell this to you," he said, "and I want you to forget you're in an office, and try to think you're in a church. What is the value of this invention?"

The man looked at it and laughed.

"I've seen it before," he said; "we examined the specification for a client. It is worth nothing."

"Absolutely?"

"Absolutely. There are compasses on the market that do all the funny things that this does, and more."

"Would you be surprised to learn that Swelliger and Friedman want to buy it?"

"I should not only be surprised," said the manager carefully, "but I should be incredulous."

That afternoon Carfew had a letter typed asking the financiers to fix an appointment for "our Mr Carfew" on the following day at two o'clock. On the morning of that day the adjutant – he accepted the rank and appointment from the Colonel's hands with gratitude – called at the War Office, and sent his name up to His Majesty's Principal Secretary of State for War.

I do not explain how it came about that the interview he sought was immediately granted. There are, you must remember, two Carfews. I would not dare to suggest that the card – inscribed "Mr Carfew, *Daily Megaphone*" – had anything to do with the invitation, "Will you come with me, sir?" of the liveried messenger.

The War Secretary was tall and thin, and a little severe. He looked over his pince-nez at Carfew, and appeared to be surprised.

"I thought you were Mr Carfew," he said. Carfew bowed, and the Secretary of State, who was a tactful man, as one should be who had to deal with a Service jealous of influence, indicated a chair.

"I know the other Mr Carfew," he said pleasantly. "Now, sir?"

Never a word-spinner, Carfew said all he had to say in five minutes.

"An invention," said the Minister, and shivered slightly. "It sounds valuable. I think I know Colonel Withington." He pressed a bell on his table, scribbled a note on a card, and when the messenger appeared, "Take this gentleman to Major-General Vallance," he said. He offered a mechanical hand to Carfew, favoured him with an almost automatic smile, and, "This officer will attend to you," he said.

Carfew was taken down a long corridor, and after a wait he was ushered in to Major-General Vallance, a little man, very bald and very unhappy.

"Invention?" He shook his head sadly. "Guns — recoils? Let me see?"

Carfew handed the typewritten sheets, and the officer read them carefully. Then he examined the drawings, and then he re-read the specifications. Then he looked at the drawings again, and checked certain sections with the description. With his head between his hands he read the specification again. When he had finished he said "Ha!" and looked at the ceiling.

He folded the papers carefully, replaced them in their envelope, and handed them back to Carfew.

"It is an invention," he said — "a good invention — we have proved it — but of doubtful value to us. It would mean pulling all our QF guns to pieces to introduce it, and that would never do."

"But," said Carfew, "wouldn't it be better than your present system?"

"If we had guns of another pattern," said the officer carefully, "and we anticipated their employment in circumstances — er — different, so to speak — well, we might consider the matter."

"I see," said Carfew glumly. He saw himself accepting the three hundred and fifty pounds offered by the speculative financiers.

"It would mean pulling our guns all to pieces," mused the General, "and, of course, very careful and detailed experiments before we paid thirty thousand pounds for an invention like that. You would be well advised to accept a lower offer."

Carfew sat bolt upright. "Thirty thousand pounds?" he repeated huskily.

The officer nodded. "That was the sum you mentioned in your letter, I think."

He did not observe Carfew's agitation as he pulled out a drawer of his desk and lifted out a little folder. This he laid on the desk before him and opened.

He turned over two or three letters before he came to the one he sought. "Yes," he said, reading, "thirty – oh – er – um!" He hastily folded the portfolio again. "I see. Yes, wrong letter. Confusing you with somebody else."

But the mischief was done. Carfew had seen the magic words "Swelliger and Friedman," and rose to the occasion.

"That's all right, General," he said, getting up from his chair; "the offer was made to you through our agents, Swelliger and Friedman. I thought I'd see you myself. We can always sell the patent, but naturally Colonel Withington wanted you to have the first refusal. Before I left the office this morning the Colonel said: 'Whatever we do, Carfew, we must persuade the British Government to take this. If it's worth sixty thousand pounds to Germany, it is worth thirty thousand pounds to Great Britain!' "

"Very proper," murmured the General – "very proper indeed. I wish we could – "

"Fortunately," Carfew went on with quiet dignity, "neither Colonel Withington nor I are in need of money – the question of payment does not come into the matter. We naturally have to protect our shareholders."

"Naturally," agreed the officer cordially.

"If the Government would pay us a couple of thousands pounds to secure the option – " suggested Carfew.

The General hesitated. "It would mean pulling our guns to pieces," mourned the General plaintively; "and – er – I think we have already got the option."

"Wow!" said Carfew, but he said it to himself.

He slipped the envelope into his breast-pocket, lingered a while, received no encouragement to stay, and took his leave.

He and the Colonel lunched frugally, and he told the senior partner all that was necessary for him to know.

"Did you mention the compass?" asked the Colonel anxiously.

This compass of his was very dear to him in every sense, for he had spent a small fortune in protecting it.

"No, I did not," confessed Carfew.

"Then you're an ass!" said the Colonel vigorously. He banged the marble-topped table at which they sat, to the scandal of the habitués of the ABC shop. "You have failed, sir, in your duty! You undertake a mission entirely on your own initiative; you bluff your way into the presence of the most incompetent minister of modern days, sir; you bluff your way into the office of that old fool, Vallance; you have opportunities, sir, and you fail to avail yourself of them! I should never have gone to the War Office – I have a supreme contempt for it – but had I gone there, sir, I should have played my strongest card – the Withington Luminous Compass. You're a fool!"

Carfew sniffed and suffered. "You had better consider yourself my clerk," growled the old man – "attend to correspondence, do nothing without orders! You are not fit to be a partner."

"Shall I pay the bill, or will you?" asked Carfew.

"You!" snapped the Colonel. "You know very well I paid for the postage stamps this morning, and there is that infernal milkman to be paid today."

(It may be mentioned that the partners made their own tea.)

Carfew was junior clerk for nearly half an hour, till a discreet word of praise for the Withington Vacuum Brake, on which the Colonel was engaged, restored him to his managing directorship.

At two o'clock, prompt to the minute, Carfew presented himself at Swelliger and Friedman's portentous offices in Lothbury.

He was shown into a waiting-room, and was detained ten minutes, at the end of which time he sent a message to the effect that he was a very busy man, and, if the partners could not keep their appointment, he must forego the pleasure of the interview.

"Could he call back again in half an hour?" asked the messenger.

"In half an hour," said Carfew, putting his hand into his watch-pocket and examining his palm, "I must be at the War Office."

In twenty seconds he was in Mr Friedman's room. It was a beautiful room, "more like," described Carfew subsequently, "a blooming boudoir than an office."

The carpets were thick, the tables and desk were highly polished; there was a magnificent chimneypiece, and an Old Master above it.

Mr Friedman, however, had not been delivered with the furniture. He was not in the scheme, and harmonised neither with the soft-hued carpet nor the Louis Quinze electrolier.

He was very short and very stout. He had side-whiskers and a moustache, and his pockets bulged with hands. He took one out reluctantly and offered a limp greeting.

"Sit down, won't you?" he said, with the aplomb of one who was rich enough to be affable to his superiors. "Now, what's all this about, hey? What's all this about?"

He sat heavily in a gorgeously-upholstered chair, and stuck his short legs forward stiffly.

"You're from Colonel Withington, ain't you? Now, what about this invention – these inventions, I mean to say – of his?"

"We'll sell," said Carfew.

"That's right – that's right," said Mr Friedman. "It's a speculation for us; but then, as the old sayin' goes: 'If you don't speculate, you don't accumulate, hey?'"

"We'll sell," said Carfew, "at a price."

"Three-fifty, I think," said Mr Friedman.

"Three-fifty, I don't think," said Carfew.

Mr Friedman said nothing. He gazed long and earnestly at the young man.

"What d'ye want?" he asked.

"For the compass – " began Carfew.

"Don't separate 'em, my dear lad – don't separate 'em," said Mr Friedman.

31

"For the compass," said Carfew, "I will take three hundred and fifty pounds, and for the recoil – "

"Yes?" Here the financier became alert.

"Twenty-five thousand pounds," said Carfew slowly.

Mr Friedman wriggled in his chair.

"Hear him," he said appealingly to an invisible deity – "hear him! Twenty-five – No deal!"

He got up and held out his limp hand.

"Goo'bye," he said.

"For all rights," said Carfew, ignoring the hand – "American, French, German, Austrian, Italian, Russian and British."

"Goo'bye," he said.

"For the British rights alone you'll get thirty thousand pounds," Carfew went on. "We want a quick deal, or we should sell direct."

"Glad to have met you. Goo'bye," said Mr Friedman.

"It will pay you handsomely," said Carfew thoughtfully. "You've been making experiments, and you know that the thing is genuine. The War Office expert has approved, and it's only a question of a thousand or two one way or the other with them."

Mr Friedman shook his head vigorously. "Experiments cost us nearly a thousand," he said, "an' you expect – Bah! Well, I'm busy. Goo'bye."

Carfew shook the extended hand and walked to the door. "Here," said Mr Friedman suddenly – "come back! Be a sensible young man. Sit down."

He pulled open a drawer and took out a box.

"Have a good cigar," he said. "You can't buy those in London under five shillings."

"I shan't try," said Carfew, and selected one. He puffed in silence for a few minutes.

"Now, be sensible," begged Mr Friedman, "and I'll be frank. You said you wanted twenty thousand. I'll tell you what I'll do. I'll give you five thousand, half cash down. Now then?"

"I said twenty-five," corrected Carfew, "and I'll take twenty-five, cash down."

Mr Friedman was undisguisedly upset. "Compromise," he said severely, "is the essence of business. Meet me fair, and I'll act fair. I've got all sorts of irons in the fire, and it does not matter to me whether I do a deal or whether I don't. I'll give you ten thousand, an' that's my last word. How's the cigar drawin'?"

"Fine," said Carfew.

"I pay five shillin's each for 'em wholesale. Here, put a few in your pocket. Now, man to man, is it a go?"

"Twenty-five thousand pounds," said the obdurate Carfew.

"Goo'bye!" responded Mr Friedman with such energy that the young man knew that this was the end of the interview. As he opened the door, a clerk came in with two telegrams.

Carfew had left the office, and was walking along Lothbury, when the same clerk came running after him.

"Will you go back to Mr Friedman?" he asked.

"No," said Carfew, but his heart quaked at his own temerity.

He stood irresolutely at the end of Lothbury, watching from the corner of his eye the building he had left. By and by he saw the top-hatted Friedman come hastily forth and walk in his direction.

Carfew leisurely signalled a taxi. "Here," said Friedman – "one word with you, Mr What's-your-name." The cab drew up. "My last word with you," said Friedman solemnly, "is fifteen thousand pounds cash."

Carfew shook his head. "I am sorry, Mr Friedman," he said. Then to the driver: "The War Office, and afterwards to the German Embassy."

It was a mighty guess, but he felt Mr Friedman's fat fingers grasping his arm.

"Your price is my price," said the financier. "You're an obstinate young man."

He shook his head in reproof and admiration. Carfew smiled.

"Will your clerk pay the cabman?" he asked. "I have no change."

"Certainly, my boy," said Friedman with boisterous good humour; and he himself, from his august pocket, with his own imperial hand, produced a shilling.

33

This saved Carfew some little embarrassment, for the liquid assets of Carfew, Withington & Co at that moment were eightpence, and the Colonel had sixpence of that to pay the weekly milk bill.

THE AGREEABLE COMPANY

A man who attracted money to him by the exercise of one set of qualities, and repelled it by the employment of another set, money in Carfew's hands was inflammable. It went with a flare and the roar of a kerosene refinery after the president's son – new from college, but strange to the business – had dropped his cigarette end in the basement.

Carfew came to the Grand Western Hotel with six thousand golden sovereigns standing to his credit in the L & S Bank.

He came in a taxicab, with a worn portmanteau and a chequebook, and he spent a glorious week of life tearing out the little pink slips till they were exhausted. After which he got another chequebook.

In the meantime he had got another portmanteau, a remarkable wardrobe, and the reputation of being an American bank robber.

"For," argued the gorgeous German hall-porter of the Grand Western, "he could not his money with such profusion spend if he had it honestly acquired."

Carfew was indifferent to the opinion of the hall-porter, being in that stage of superiority which allowed him to wear heliotrope socks without shame. People came to see him – people who wanted to render him invaluable services. Some wished to lead him to the private road which cuts off ten miles of the dreary path to fortune; some had ideas that only wanted money.

These latter Carfew laughed to oblivion, for he had ideas of his own – and money.

His money enabled him to indulge his taste in his own particular ideas, which ran in the direction of the Burlington Arcade, and took expression in artistic cravats and socks that spoke for themselves. It is a grand thing to be rich – to be able to write "Pay bearer five thousand pounds," without running the risk of being arrested.

His vices were inexpensive. He did not drink. He was no epicure, he loved fresh air and taxicabs. Theatres could not cost him more than three guineas a week, for of all the vices to which men are victims, he was least troubled by the greatest – he had no friends. He was dressing for dinner one night when the valet announced a visitor. "Show him up," said Carfew.

There came to him a tall, cadaverous man, with a profusion of hair and a certain untidiness of dress which usually marked the unsuccessful genius.

"Carfew?" he demanded.

The young man nodded. "Your hand," demanded the other briefly. "Your name I know – I have heard of you. My name is Septimus."

"Glad to meet you, Mr Septimus," said Carfew formally. "And what goods can we show you this evening?"

Carfew wanted amusement; he could spare this unpromising stranger at least half an hour.

"You don't mind my dressing?" he asked, as he lazily adjusted his tie before the glass.

"Not at all – not at all," said Mr Septimus, with a fine sweep of his hand. "A busy man – I am no hog." He seemed pleased with the negative illustration, and repeated in a whisper that he was no hog. "Mr Carfew," the visitor went on, "I have heard of you. You are the man who negotiated the sale of a certain patent, receiving as your share of the sale many thousands of pounds."

"That's true," said Carfew modestly; "I am best known, perhaps, as Carfew the Inventor."

"I do not know you as Carfew the Inventor," said the seedy man deliberately. "You have a title to fame more wonderful, more extraordinary, more far-reaching for humanity; you have attracted the attention of three men of gifts. Sir, will you honour me with your company this night?"

"My dear chap," said Carfew reproachfully, "tonight! Now be reasonable."

"Tonight," said the weird-looking visitor dramatically. "It is not unreasonable, believe me."

He was very earnest, so earnest that Carfew looked at him more closely. His clothes were old and stained, his cuffs were frayed and not over-clean, his neck was innocent of collar; a black silk cravat clumsily tied in a bow left a space of scraggy throat between neckband and neckwear. He had two days' growth of beard, and yet there was an undefinable air of refinement about him which puzzled the young man. His hands, long, thin, and white, were scrupulously tended.

"We're rather at cross purposes," said Carfew, kindly. "I would do anything to oblige you except" – he was on the point of saying "lending you money," but instinct arrested the speech – "except commit myself to a promise that I might not be able to fulfil. Now, exactly what is it you want?"

The man clicked his lips impatiently.

"I want nothing – absolutely nothing," he said, with a shade of annoyance in his voice. "I have no single desire in the world; there is no material with which, if money could fulfil, would remain unsatisfied. Look here."

He thrust his hand into the baggy pocket of his Inverness, and drew out an untidy bundle of papers. "You think I am a needy adventurer," he said, and it was apparent that his anger was rising; "you imagine that I have come here with some hare-brained scheme – "

"My dear sir!" said Carfew, somewhat embarrassed by the truth of the man's utterance.

"You think this – bah!"

He flung the bundle of papers into the air; they scattered on bed and floor. One fell at Carfew's feet.

"My dear chap," he expostulated, as he stooped to pick it up, "you're only – "

37

He stopped suddenly, for the paper he held was a Bank of England note for one hundred pounds. There was no doubt whatever as to its genuineness.

And the floor was covered with them.

There was a round dozen on the floor, two or three on the eiderdown which covered the bed, two on the dressing-table. Carfew, bewildered, hastened to collect them.

"Money," said the strange visitor bitterly – "money! Do we live for nothing but money? Is that the be-all and end-all of things? Is that the ultimate aim of humanity? Take it – keep it! Add it to your puny store. Tell your friends that Septimus of the Agreeable Company made you a present of it!"

He hitched his worn cloak round his shoulders and flung open the door. "*Au revoir!*" he said haughtily. "We are not likely to meet again."

He was halfway down the corridor before Carfew recovered from his surprise. "Hi, come back!"

Carfew darted down the corridor and caught the man by the arm. "Come back, come back, for heaven's sake!" he begged. "You mustn't go away and leave me with this money. I don't want the beastly stuff."

"Do you mean that?" There was suspicion in the stranger's frowning glance.

"Absolutely. Just give me a minute."

Reluctantly the man returned, and as reluctantly he took the notes from Carfew's hand and stuffed them into his pocket.

"Count them," said the anxious young man. "One might have gone astray."

"What matters?" responded Septimus carelessly. "I shall be little worse off. Let the man who finds it keep it."

Carfew gazed on him in awe, and for the first time a faint smile played round the thin lips of the seedy visitor.

"I think," he said quietly, "you are a little astonished at my indifference to money – perhaps you think it is an affectation. The truth is, money is of the least importance to me and to the Agreeable Company. For every sovereign you possess, I have probably three hundred. That would make me more than a millionaire, wouldn't it?"

He smiled again pityingly. "Money does not count, believe me," he said seriously. "There are three men in the Agreeable Company, and if you were to add their fortunes together, they would – But I will only say that I am the poorest of the trio." Again there was that odd little mannerism, for he repeated, speaking to himself in a voice which was scarcely more than a whisper: "The poorest of the trio – the poorest of the trio!"

Now, Carfew was by every instinct a journalist. His very faults might be traced to this quality, for he would jump at the shadow of a "story," and miss the bone of probability.

And here, indeed, was a story – the Agreeable Company of Millionaires!

"If you could tell me exactly the object of your visit," he said, "and just how I can serve you, I am quite willing to accompany you tonight."

"Are you?" Septimus leant forward eagerly, his eyes shining. "Are you really? Now, that is good of you! I want you to meet Decimus. You will adore Decimus. He is a man after your own heart – a brain ingenious, terrifically introspective, and with the idea."

Carfew, dazed by his tremendous character of the unknown Decimus, could only nod his head.

"The idea is the thing," the stranger went on. "I can see by your eyes that you think I am a little mad – perhaps more than a little. You think we are all a little mad!"

Carfew blushed guiltily.

"Ah, you do! But you shall see," exclaimed the stranger. He rose, hitched up his cloak again, and smiled. "It is now twenty-three minutes past seven by your new watch."

Carfew started and pulled out his new chronometer hastily; it was exactly twenty-three minutes past seven. "How on earth – " he began.

The stranger was amused. "Simple, very simple. You have a new watch – all young men who suddenly acquire wealth have new watches – and new watches keep perfect time. I know it is twenty-three minutes past because it is exactly eight minutes since the clock struck the quarter after. I know it is eight minutes because I have counted four hundred and eighty seconds. One half of my brain is counting all the time. But that is beside the point. It is now twenty-six minutes past seven. Will you meet me in front of the National Gallery at nine o'clock?"

Carfew did not hesitate. "I will," he said.

Septimus stood at the door. "If you have any nervousness, if you are in any way afraid of the consequences of your adventure, I shall not complain if you come armed."

And, with a profound bow, he departed.

Carfew went down to dinner in a condition of mind which it would be difficult to analyse. He had embarked on that variety of enterprise which is dear to a young man's heart – the enterprise which has the necessary envelopment of mystery, and the end of which could not be surmised. He finished his dinner in half the time it usually took, hurried back to his room and changed into a tweed suit. The night was damp and chilly. It offered him an excuse for wearing an overcoat and a soft felt hat, which the remarkable character of the interview justified. Prompt to the minute he took his stand by the steps leading up to the National Gallery. The clocks were striking nine, when a big motorcar, driven slowly from the direction of Pall Mall, drew up, and the stranger got out. By the light of a street standard, Carfew recognised him, though he might have been excused if he had not.

For now Septimus was a radiant being. Dressed in an evening suit of perfect cut, his long hair trimmed and brushed, his lean, intellectual face innocent of scrubbiness, he was the pattern of propriety. He came quickly toward Carfew and held out his hand.

"I am one minute late," he said; "these clocks are slow."

Carfew suddenly realised his own wilful shabbiness. "I am afraid I have changed my kit," he said, and felt unaccountably sheepish.

Septimus smiled. "Please don't bother," he said, and held open the door of the car. "Decimus is no hog either."

Carfew sank back into the luxurious cushions as the car glided noiselessly across Trafalgar Square, and tried to adjust his whirling thoughts.

"I suppose," said his companion, who seemed possessed of a fiendish power which allowed him to read men's minds, "that you are mentally quoting Mr Pickwick when he found himself in the middle of the night chasing the electric Jingle and the erring sister of Mr Wardle."

He had put off his eccentric style of address with his seedy costume, and Carfew noted that his voice was soft and cultured. All the extravagance of attitude and language had disappeared. He spoke easily, fluently, of men and things, the news of the day, touching lightly on politics, merely observing that the trend of recent legislation seemed to be in the direction of Socialism. He thought that such legislation was bad for property. It did not affect him, he said; all his money was fluid capital. This was an astonishing statement, for Carfew had never heard of a man whose wealth was so placed.

"I lend money," the other explained – "short loans, you know. It means a quick profit. I would not do this but for Octavius, who is the mortal enemy of laziness. He says that idle money does more mischief than idle men. What a brain that man has – what a brain!"

It was a return of the old enthusiasm, and Carfew waited, but Septimus said no more. The car had crossed Westminster Bridge, had passed through the tangle of traffic at the Elephant and Castle, sped quickly along the gloomy stretch of the New Kent Road into the bustle of the Old Kent Road.

Not another word said Septimus, and Carfew was content to engage himself with his own thoughts. They were climbing the steep hill that leads to Blackheath when Septimus again spoke.

"I have only one request to make to you," he said, "and that is that you do not make any mention of the Straits Settlements to Decimus."

"The – ?" asked Carfew, not a little bewildered.

"The Straits Settlements," said the other calmly. "It is the one subject upon which I fear the otherwise perfectly-poised brain of the good Decimus is not too delicately adjusted."

It seemed a subject easy to avoid, and Carfew said as much. The other nodded gravely.

The car flew up the steep hill, turned to the right, and began skirting the heath. Halfway round, it slowed and turned into some grounds through two gaunt gates, along a short, dark avenue of trees, and pulled up before the gloomy door of a big house. There was no light in any window; even the hall was in darkness.

The two men descended, and Septimus, mounting the steps, rang the bell − Carfew heard its far-away tinkle. They waited a little time before the door was opened. The only light in the hall was the candle held by the man who had admitted them.

As the door closed upon them Carfew became conscious of the magnificence of the servitor who held the light.

He was a footman of imposing proportions. Clean-shaven, with a quiet dignity of mien, he wore a livery such as the personal attendant of a reigning monarch might have adopted. His coat was of royal blue velvet, thickly laced with gold; his breeches were of white satin, his stockings of rose-pink silk. On his feet he wore the shiniest of patent shoes, adorned with jewelled buckles that flashed back the light of the candle as only diamonds can. His hair was powdered white, the whitest of snowy ruffles were at his wrists, the most snowy of cravats at his throat; across his breast he wore a string of medals such as the domestics of royal households wear. Carfew noted the blue and white of the British House, the yellow and scarlet of Spain, the diagonal stripe of the German, the green and yellow of Austria.

"Messieurs Decimus and Octavius await your Excellencies," said the man, and his voice had exactly the quality of humility which his office demanded.

Septimus nodded. He handed his coat to the man, and Carfew followed suit. Now, it must be said of Carfew that he was not easily overcome by outward show. He was by instinct and training a journalist, and no journalist permits himself to be impressed. Yet there was something awe-inspiring in the spectacle of that gorgeous lackey in the unfurnished hall.

The dim light of the candle accentuated the desolation of the place. A huge black stairway led to the upper floors. The hall itself was innocent of chair or table, yet the candlestick in the footman's white hand was of silver and most beautifully designed.

The footman led the way along the passage till they came to a door which evidently opened into a room at the rear of the house. He knocked, and a gruff, grumpy voice said: "In!"

The man opened the door and entered. "Mr Carfew and Monsieur Septimus!" he announced.

Carfew followed him. The room, unlike the hall, was furnished; but such furniture! It proclaimed its origin loudly. It was frantically, garishly new; it was painfully common. "Hire purchase " was written on every stick of it, from the saddlebag suite to the fumed oak sideboard.

In the centre was a table draped by a blood-red cloth, and at this table, one on either side, were two men, who rose as Carfew entered. The first was stout, a fact emphasised by his costume, for he wore tight-fitting evening dress, with black satin knickers and black silk stockings. He was clean-shaven, and his white hair was brushed smoothly back from a low forehead.

"Mr Carfew," he said courteously, and extended a fat hand that blazed with brilliant rings, "this is indeed an honour."

His voice was a musical growl, and as he spoke, he blinked continuously, as one whose vision is slightly defective.

"My comrade Octavius," he introduced, and the second man bowed without offering his hand.

He was a man of middle height, and wore conventional evening dress. His face was thin and peaked, and a pair of rimless glasses sat on the high bridge of his long nose.

His mouth was thin and tightly pressed, and his appearance was not improved by the fact that his head was clipped as closely as any convict's.

"Honour!" he repeated automatically, and, without removing his eyes from Carfew, put his hand behind him and groped for a chair.

"Sit down, sit down," said Septimus, the most human of the three, Carfew thought.

There was an awkward pause as the young man took his place at the table.

Again the only light was that afforded by candles. There were seven candles, and they were inserted in a golden candelabra that stood in the centre of the table.

Carfew observed that whilst the stout Decimus and his guide gave their whole attention to him in the subsequent conversation, the melancholy Octavius stared steadily, uneasily, almost apprehensively, at the burning tapers.

"Mr Carfew" – the stout man clasped his glittering hands together and leant forward over the table – he sat opposite to Carfew – "you may wonder why we have sought you out, and why we have invited you to our poor dwelling?"

Carfew nodded, and Decimus repeated the nod. So, too, did Septimus, and even the other man absently jerked his head.

Decimus smoothed a newspaper cutting that lay under his hand.

"I read," he said, "that great interest has been created in City circles by a deal which the brilliant young journalist, Felix Carfew – I am quoting the cutting – made on behalf of Colonel Withington, the inventor. The paragraph goes on to say:

" 'The advent of a financial genius is an event which should not be passed unnoticed. We understand that Mr Carfew cleared a profit of twenty thousand pounds on the transaction.' "

He folded up the paper and looked at Carfew, and the financial genius nodded again, without shame.

"These interesting facts," Decimus went on, speaking slowly and deliberately, "appeared in *The South-West Herald*, and I do not doubt that you wrote the paragraph yourself."

Carfew felt himself blushing, and was annoyed.

"I do not doubt," Decimus proceeded gravely, "that twenty thousand pounds was a pardonable exaggeration, and that you made no more than six thousand pounds out of the transaction."

Carfew wriggled uncomfortably, but was saved the embarrassment of an immediate reply by Octavius, who, with sudden acerbity, demanded: "Must we have seven candles?"

"I think so," said Decimus gently.

"Seven candles all burning at once?" asked the other, with a show of irritation.

"It is a big room, Octavius," soothed Septimus.

"These candles cost twopence each," the obstinate Octavius protested. "Fourteen pence! Can't I put one out?"

"I think we will keep the whole burning, if you will allow us," said Decimus firmly.

Octavius muttered something about "ruin," and continued his gloomy survey of the candelabra.

"If you will allow me to say so," said Carfew, "I can't see how the authorship of that paragraph or the truth of its contents – "

"Has anything to do with me, eh?" Decimus smiled broadly. He had a large face, and Nature had afforded him generous provision for making his amusement visible. "That may not be apparent to you, Mr Carfew." He was intensely earnest of a sudden. "Mr Carfew, if I handed you securities for a million and a half pounds – securities which I could realise, and you could realise in twenty-four hours – would you undertake to initiate on our behalf a daily newspaper?"

To say that Carfew was stricken dumb with the proposal is to adequately convey his emotions; that which would deprive him of speech was no ordinary proposal.

And it was the dream of Carfew's life to initiate a London newspaper. It is the dream of every well-balanced journalist's life.

There is no journal that was ever printed that the average newspaper man could not improve upon. And the million and a half pounds!

Why, one could do anything with that sum! One could produce a paper that would influence Olympians. The best writers of the day and hour would write for it; its columns could be filled with the genius, the wisdom, and the wit of the language. There should be a Blowitz in every capital; exorbitant charges would be made to advertisers.

"Would I undertake it?" he said huskily. "Yes, I think I would."

Octavius, staring the flames of the candles out of countenance, spoke without relaxing his attention.

"Would he undertake to steadily castigate – you know?"

He nodded mysteriously.

Septimus looked at Decimus imploringly.

"May we say it?" he asked.

Decimus frowned and pursed his lips.

"Yes," he said, with a touch of bitterness in his voice.

"Would you undertake to show up the Straits Settlements Affair?" asked Septimus in a whisper.

Darker and darker grew the cloud on the brow of stout Decimus.

"I can't bear it," he said harshly. "Do not use those words again, I beg of you – say 'SS.' I thought I was strong enough. Don't do it, Sep – don't do it, dear lad!"

He covered his face with his hands. "My dear Decimus," said the other, greatly concerned, "I'm so sorry. I am a brute!"

It was some time before Decimus recovered his self-possession. "The question we have to ask you," said Septimus, speaking quickly, "is this: If we hand you tomorrow the sum of one and a half million pounds, are you prepared to found and edit such a paper? Secondly, will you undertake that such a journal shall be in the hands of the public three months from today?"

"I am," said Carfew, with the alacrity of a small boy offered his first ride on a locomotive.

"This candle is quite unnecessary," interrupted the distressed Octavius. "Let me, I beg of you, extinguish it."

He raised a little snuffer imploringly. "Seven candles," he muttered, with an angry sniff. "It is a monstrous waste!" Then of a sudden he checked himself. "Security," he said shortly, and turned his head to his companion – "ask him about security."

"My dear Octavius!" Decimus was reproachful.

"It is an elementary safeguard, an elementary precaution," persisted the other doggedly. "He may be a man of substance – he may not be. A million and a half is a lot of money; people would say that we were mad, not knowing about the SS. I insist upon some form of security."

"I protest!" Decimus was very angry, but Carfew had now recovered his grip of the situation.

"I think Mr Octavius is perfectly justified," he said. "I have security up to six thousand pounds, but beyond that I can promise nothing."

"More than enough, and altogether unnecessary – altogether unnecessary," said Decimus shortly. "You agree, Septimus?"

Carfew's guide nodded. "I should certainly not have asked Mr Carfew here if I had any idea that such a thing would have been demanded," he said sharply.

Octavius, in disgrace, returned to a contemplation of the candles, but from his tightly-pressed lips Carfew gathered that the little man was obdurate.

"Let him come tomorrow with six thousand pounds," he said obstinately, "and I will hand him my share."

There was another uncomfortable silence.

"Tomorrow night I shall be here," said Carfew, with a smile, and rose.

"It is altogether unnecessary," said Septimus again, rather angrily. "I am humiliated, Octavius – humiliated, Decimus."

He accompanied Carfew from the room. Near the door stood the gorgeous footman, patiently standing, candlestick in hand.

"One moment." Septimus caught the young man by the sleeve and drew him out of hearing. "If you have any difficulty," he said, in a low voice, "cash this." He handed an oblong slip to the other. It bore an almost undecipherable signature, and was a blank cheque on the Bank of England. "Fill in the amount you want up to fifty thousand," he said, "but do not, I beg of you, give hint to Octavius that I have done this. He is – er – a little eccentric."

Carfew pushed back the cheque smilingly. "You know the amount I can guarantee," he said. "Thank you a thousand times for your generosity, but it is unnecessary."

"Take it," urged Septimus, and thrust it into Carfew's hand.

To humour him Carfew accepted the cheque. In a few minutes he was being driven back to London alone.

His brain was in a whirl; he could not think consecutively. Only he realised that a dream, a wild, extravagant dream, was to be realised. He would call the paper *The Monitor*. It should be the last word in up-to-date journalism. He would offer the foreign editorship to Macraltan, who had been so decent to him on *The Megaphone*. He would ask the great GSB to do the dramatic criticism.

It was nearly three o'clock in the morning before he fell asleep. He breakfasted in bed, and in the midst of the meal the waiter told him that a gentleman wished to see him.

"Show him up," said Carfew. He expected to see Septimus, and was disappointed to find that his visitor was a complete stranger. He was a tall, broad-shouldered man, with a brown, clean-shaven face and a twinkling eye.

Carfew looked at the card the waiter had brought. "T B Smith," it ran.

"Well, Mr Smith?" said Carfew.

The visitor seated himself by the side of the bed. "Well, Mr Carfew," he smiled, "they tell me that you are going to organise a big engineering work."

Carfew's puzzled frown was the reply.

"Or a paper, perhaps?" hazarded the other.

Carfew nodded. "I haven't the slightest idea how you came to know," he said, "or why you should have thought it was an engineering work."

The tall man laughed.

"You have been associated with newspapers and with inventions, you know," he exclaimed. "Anyway, what I want to ask you is, do you want a manager?"

The young man regarded him suspiciously.

"I am afraid matters are not sufficiently advanced," he said coldly, "to justify my making any arrangement with you."

"Aren't they?" Mr Smith was disappointed, and did not conceal the fact. "I'm sorry. I'm used to managing big affairs. I've had control of a company with a capital of fifty thousand."

Carfew smiled a superior smile at the ceiling. "My dear old chap," he said tolerantly, "you talk of fifty thousand as though it were all the money in the world. Now, I purpose spending that amount in a month."

He impressed Mr Smith, and was gratified.

The visitor rose. "I see, sir," he said respectfully, "I'm not much good to you. Yet you might want an assistant. You are very young."

Now, there was nothing that annoyed Carfew more than to be told in a certain tone of voice that he was very young, and that was exactly the tone the visitor adopted.

"I am old enough to know how to spend money," he said shortly.

"I suppose there is no chance?" Mr Smith said, fingering his broad-brimmed hat. "Perhaps, when the business is settled in a week's time – "

"It will be settled today," replied Carfew; "and, as far as you and I are concerned, you may regard it as settled now."

That ended the interview. Carfew was a little puzzled as to how the story of the new venture had leaked out. But he had little time to waste in idle speculation. He saw his banker that morning, drew out the greater part of his balance, and spent the afternoon sketching out the shape and substance of the new journal. He paid a lightning visit to Fleet Street, and decided that, wherever the temporary offices of the paper should be, the permanent *Monitor* building should be erected on the island site of the Strand.

He found time to read up the Straits Settlements, and was surprised to learn that the Government of the colony was a singularly inoffensive one. At nine o'clock the motor called at his hotel. This time it was Decimus who welcomed and accompanied him. The reason for the substitution Decimus explained. He felt that he owed Carfew an apology.

"Septimus has told me that he gave you a blank cheque," he explained. "I hope you have used it – I trust you have used it. It was so like Septimus – so delicate, so thoughtful."

"As a matter of fact, I haven't," admitted Carfew. "I never intended using it, though it was most kind of you both."

"Not used it? Sorry – very sorry!" Decimus shook his head sadly. "I am annoyed with Octavius. He is – how shall I put it in justice to him? – a leetle mean, eh?"

Carfew grinned. Octavius was a little mean skunk, yet his character was consistent with his wealth, if Carfew knew anything about millionaires. They arrived at the house, and were ushered into the gaunt hall by the identical footman. His uniform was now of orange, heavily braided with rich, black mohair.

"Ha, you notice Charles, eh?" said Decimus, smiling. "Different uniform every day; that's a fad of Octavy's, dear lad. More expensive than candles, eh?" He chuckled.

He received a warm welcome from Septimus and a chilly one from Octavius, now in a condition of abject misery, for two golden candelabras were set on the table, and each had seven candles burning recklessly.

Carfew plunged straight away into business. He produced his rough sketches, his memoranda, the scheme of publication. They discussed the matter dispassionately. Septimus suggested a correspondent at Constantinople. He would be expensive, but he was worth the money. Decimus would like paper of a certain quality, and Carfew said that it would cost a little more than he had estimated for. Then:

"Guarantees," said the sharp voice of Octavius.

"Take no notice," whispered Decimus. But Carfew put his hand into his inside pocket and produced a roll of notes. He pushed them along the table to Octavius.

"These are my guarantees," he said simply.

Octavius took the roll, smoothed it flat, and counted the notes with great deliberation.

"Six thousand," he said. He held one up to the light. "Good!" he grunted, "I will apply the test."

Carfew met the good-natured smile of Decimus.

"Humour him," whispered the stout man.

Very slowly Octavius rose from the table, and as slowly walked to the door, muttering to himself. He had no need to open the door. It was opened for him by a tall, strong man, who stepped into the room with a whimsical smile on his face.

"Good evening, gentlemen," said the stranger genially.

Carfew recognised him as the impertinent visitor of the morning.

No word said Septimus, Octavius or Decimus.

"Pleasant evening," said the smiling intruder. "You know me, Tony?"

Octavius gave a sickly smile. "I know you, Mr Smith," he said – "it's a cop!"

"A fair cop," said T B Smith, of Scotland Yard, vulgarly. "I want you three. My men have got your gorgeous pal. You've got some money, I think, belonging to this gentleman. Thank you…if you don't mind." With a dexterity born of practice he snapped a pair of handcuffs on the delicate wrists of Octavius. "You're the only dangerous man of the bunch, Tony," said Mr Smith in extenuation. "Now, then, if you are all ready, I will run you down to Blackheath Hill Station in your own car."

"The fact of it is, Mr Carfew," explained the detective, "I could have saved you the undesirable publicity of this case, only I did not want to spoil the coup. Those three friends of yours are confidence tricksters. They work for big money, and are always prepared to spend a thousand to get six. They played on your imagination with their mysteries, their millions."

"I am a perfect howling jackass!" said the crestfallen Carfew.

"You are very young," said the detective, and Carfew was unaccountably annoyed.

CARFEW IS ADVISED

He was young and he was rich. That is to say, he had more money than he had ever had before, and any man who has more money than he ever had before is rich; whether the sum be five pounds or fifty thousand pounds.

Carfew had a little office in the City. He had no business, but he had an office. He once made money – not much, from the point of view of Lord Kullug, but, oh, so much from Carfew's standpoint.

He increased that little fortune of his, and learnt something that was worth learning at the same time and in quite an unexpected manner.

Carfew, who was spending a holiday in the country, saved the life of Lord Kullug's daughter.

This is romantic, and I am very sorry, but it couldn't be helped. Lord Kullug's daughter was punting in the little river which runs through the home park, and Carfew, sitting on the bank with his back to a board which informed him that "Trespassers will be shot by order," or words to that effect, was idly watching her.

She was a slim, pretty girl, but not Carfew's kind. So he was telling himself when her punt came abreast of him, and she stopped poling to eye him severely.

"I say," she said, "what are you doing in our park?"

He rose and took off his hat. "I beg your pardon?" he said.

"What are you doing in our park? This is private land."

"I was sitting down," said Carfew.

"But you mustn't sit down in our park," said the girl petulantly. "My papa is Lord Kullug, and you will be prosecuted."

"It seems a very inadequate reason," said Carfew, very calmly.

"You are not an artist, are you?" she asked suddenly. "My papa does not allow artists in our park."

"I am not an artist," said Carfew impressively; "I am a gentleman."

He thought she looked dubiously at him, and was nettled.

"You ought to go away," she said; "we don't want strangers in our park."

Carfew sighed wearily. "Can't you think of something else to say?" he asked. "This 'our park-ing' of yours is getting on my nerves. I never turn people out of my park."

She was ready to be annoyed with him, but curiosity and interest got the better of her.

"Have you got a park?" she asked.

"Yes," said Carfew carelessly, "I have several – Regent's Park, Hyde Park, Battersea Park – "

The girl uttered an exclamation of annoyance, stooped to pick up her pole, overbalanced, and fell into the stream. She gave a little scream, but picked herself up and began to wade ashore.

"Isn't it any deeper than that?" asked Carfew from the bank.

"Go away, you wretched man," she snapped.

"Because," said Carfew, "if it isn't, I'm coming in to rescue you."

And, with no more ado, he stepped boldly into the water. It was by no means a simple task the rescue of Lord Kullug's daughter, for the bottom of the stream was full of little holes and pitfalls, and she was glad to have the assistance of this blatant young man. Twice he made a false step and went up to his neck in water, and when at length he reached the bank, he was pardonably indignant.

"You told me it wasn't deep," he said reproachfully. "I might have lost my life. Really, for a person who owns a park, you are very inconsiderate."

"If you hadn't bothered me, I shouldn't have fallen in," she said, and she was very angry.

"If I hadn't been here when you had fallen in," he replied gravely, "I shudder to think what might have happened to you."

All the way to the big house he talked to her, telling her of the danger she had escaped, describing similar accidents which had occurred to friends of his – they were all people of eminent position, and most of them were great public characters – until the girl began to believe that she had indeed escaped deadly peril, and that she had figured in the adventure of her life. He praised her coolness in the moment of danger, and compared it with the panic into which Lady Baglord fell when she was thrown into the sea off Cowes from Carfew's yacht.

"She gave me twenty times the trouble you gave me," said Carfew reminiscently, "and I assure you there was no more danger than if she had fallen into my private swimming bath at Blenheim House."

Carfew was a good talker, and in the half-mile walk he brought about a revolution in the girl's opinion of him and his conduct. In the end, she forgot that he was a trespasser, and that his outrageous conduct had provoked the accident. If she did not forget, she certainly did not tell her father.

Carfew was taken to a room, clothing of approximate fit was found for him, and he was invited to stay to dinner.

"I cannot tell you how greatly obliged to you I am," said Lord Kullug.

He was a tall, gaunt man, hard-featured, and with an eye which chilled. Carfew, having carried matters so far, wisely declined the invitation to dinner.

"Come and see me in the City one day, and lunch with me," said his lordship. "All that you tell me about my daughter's – er – courage, is very pleasing to me. She comes of – er – a good stock."

Carfew smiled sympathetically. "That I know," he said.

He knew the Kullugs to be what they were. Old George Kullug had been a storekeeper in Kimberley in the early days of the diamond fields. He had made money and had evaded the law. He left two millions to his middle-aged son, who had added considerably to his inheritance.

Carfew went back to London elated, for this adventure was one after his own heart. He was a rescue specialist. Once, on the Thames Embankment, he had rescued from death an elderly colonel of Engineers – at least he had told him to "look out" at the approach of a taxicab – and that colonel of Engineers had laid the foundation of Carfew's fortune.

He went back to Blenheim House – which is situated in Bloomsbury Square, and for the use of one room in which lordly establishment he paid twenty shillings a week – whistling a little tune. He was still whistling when he turned on the tap of his private swimming bath, to the intense annoyance of the medical student who occupied the chamber next to the bathroom.

Three days later Carfew presented himself at 843, Lombard Street, which is the London office of the Manhattan Deeps, Manhattan Deeps being a most prosperous Johannesburg gold mine, of which Lord Kullug was chairman and board of directors.

Carfew had looked up the concern in the "Stock Exchange Year Book," and noted the directors' fees were one thousand pounds per annum.

"He'll probably make me a director," he thought, "and give me the necessary stock to qualify."

There were other and kindred concerns – the Weits Consolidated Goldfields, Limited, the Licker Deeps, Limited, the Turfontein Associated Claims, Limited, the Johannesburg District Land Syndicate, Limited – all having offices under the same roof, and Carfew, working out possibilities with the aid of a pencil and the "Year Book" aforesaid, computed the maximum benefits which might accrue to him as being in the neighbourhood of five thousand pounds a year.

"Not bad," said Carfew complacently, and wrote to Lord Kullug telling him he would call.

Lord Kullug's secretary replied that he regretted his lordship would be out of town on Tuesday, and would Thursday suit Mr Canfam? Which annoyed the young man very much, because his name was not Canfam, though, as he signed it, it looked very much like it.

He sat down and wrote to the secretary in reply:

"DEAR SIR, – I am directed by Mr Felix Carfew to thank you for your letter of even date. In reply, Mr Carfew asks me to say that though he was leaving town for his country place at Harrogate, on Thursday, he will put off his journey till the following day, and will be pleased to call on Lord Kullug at the hour named."

He signed the letter "Adolphus Brown," and dispatched it with the comforting sense of having held up his end.

Punctually to the minute he arrived at the Lombard Street office. He would have come in a hired electric brougham, but, having surveyed the office on the evening previous, he decided that it was very unlikely that Lord Kullug's private office would be in the front of the building, and less likely that his lordship would witness his arrival, even if the office were so situated, for, as Carfew knew, millionaires did not spend their days looking out of windows.

He was ushered to a reception-room, and, after a reasonable period of waiting, a uniformed attendant led him along a carpeted corridor, tapped respectfully on a rosewood door, and showed the young man into a room which contained a map, a square of carpet, a big desk, an easy-chair, and Lord Kullug.

The millionaire removed his glasses and nodded to Carfew.

"Sit down, Mr – er – "

Carfew refused to help him.

"Mr Carfew, eh? Well, I'm sorry I could not see you before."

He looked at his watch. "A little too early for lunch. Now, just tell me something about yourself. I am under an obligation to you, and I should like to be of some service to you."

This was the kind of talk Carfew wanted to hear. And he told Lord Kullug something about himself. He related things and hinted at others.

He inferred that he – Carfew – was the type of man no great corporation could afford to be without. He suggested that the one idea that obsessed the important City houses was to secure his services on the board of directors. He spoke airily of contracts he had secured, concessions he had obtained.

"Let's go to lunch," said Lord Kullug.

They drove in his car to the Savoy.

Carfew pointed out, in a subtle way, the enormous advantage of youth. He hinted that he could influence the Press to an extraordinary degree, but never yet had had occasion to do so. He admitted that he held no directorships, because he had fought shy of anything but the best companies, besides which he did not care for industrial concerns.

"Here we are," said his lordship.

A table had been reserved for them, and when the choice of the wine had been made, Carfew continued:

"I'm rather at a loose end," he confessed. "A young man with money, energy and initiative who achieves some distinction in a quiet way, is inclined to let himself go to rust, if opportunity does not offer itself. As I was saying to the German Ambassador some time ago – we were travelling together – "

(The conversation in question took place when Carfew – a very young and confident reporter – forced his way into his Excellency's state cabin and bullied him into giving an interview.)

Of course, Carfew explained, he did not wish to take advantage of so small a service as saving his lordship's daughter. After all, there was very little danger to himself, he added modestly, though at one time he had thought it was all over.

Carfew talked and talked, and the more readily he talked, the more readily did his host accept the position of audience.

He interrupted Carfew once to ask him what capital he had. Carfew said he had exactly fifty per cent more than he possessed.

At the end of the lunch Lord Kullug found an opportunity.

"You're an interesting young man," he said, "and you should go far. I can help you."

Carfew murmured his appreciation.

"I have considerable experience of the world," his lordship went on, "especially of the financial world, and I can put you in the way of a fortune."

"That," said Carfew, with dignity, "is the road I am looking for."

"I could, of course," Lord Kullug continued, "give you a directorship, but I haven't one to spare."

Carfew's hopes fell from 100° Fahr. to the place where you mustn't shake the mercury for fear it breaks.

"I give you instead" – he paused, and Carfew's hopes took the elevator to the fourth floor – "a little good advice."

The elevator rope broke, and Carfew found himself in the basement, alive, but dazed.

This precious advice was not forthcoming until Carfew and the millionaire were outside the building, and the door of the luxurious automobile had been opened for the peer to enter.

"You can make a fortune," said his lordship, "if you let the other fellow do the talking. Good afternoon."

Ten minutes later Carfew was walking slowly in the direction of Bloomsbury, repeating the formula at every few steps.

He went to his room, removed his shoes, divested himself of his splendid raiment, and lay on the bed, thinking very hard. He went down to dinner in the same subdued mood.

At the end of the meal he leant across the table and said to the young medical student who sat *vis-à-vis*: "Do you want to make a fortune?"

The student growled wicked words at him.

"But do you?" persisted Carfew.

"Of course I do," said the other.

"Well," said Carfew, drawing a long breath, "let the other fellow do the talking. Good evening."

He went to bed that night to some extent mollified. He was not easily snubbed. People who boasted that they had snubbed Carfew were either untruthful or mistaken. But he had been snubbed, and it had been done with a thoroughness which left him no conceit.

He came down to breakfast next morning still digesting his lesson. There was a letter on his table, and the flap bore a crest.

"A rabbit rampant eating a carrot couchant," said Carfew disrespectfully. "I wonder if it is from – "

It was, and written in Lord Kullug's own hand. Would Carfew call at eleven?

Carfew called, and Lord Kullug rose to meet him. "I sent for you, Carfew," he said, with a grim little smile, "because I am afraid I did not make it clear to you that I know exactly what part you played in the rescue of my daughter."

Carfew said nothing. He shrugged his shoulders in self-deprecation.

"And I rather admired your audacity," his lordship went on. "Moreover, in the advice I have given you, I think you were more than repaid for the ducking you got. But there is one thing I did not ask you, and which I feel sure that you will not mind telling me. Exactly why did you seek an introduction to me?"

Carfew smiled, and the millionaire's lips twitched responsively. Carfew did not tell him that, in trespassing in the home park, he had no more idea that it was the property of Lord Kullug than he had that Lord Kullug was anything but a name.

"Look here, Carfew" – his lordship swung himself round in his chair and faced the young man – "we are both business men. Let us put our cards on the table. I think you will find it worth your while."

"Perhaps that would be wise," said Carfew, after a little pause.

"D'ye know," continued the elder man, "it never occurred to me till I was on my way home last night. I was chuckling over the snubbing I had given you, and, if you will pardon me, your discomfiture. I thought – you'll forgive the plain speaking – that you were a bumptious youth, pushing, arrogant and a little – er – boastful."

Carfew smiled again and shook his head, a little reproachful, a little amused.

"Yes – yes, but let me finish," continued the millionaire. "I was thinking this when the thought occurred to me – have Sieglemanns sent him?" As he said this, he leant forward and scrutinised the young man closely.

Carfew dropped his eyes for a moment.

"H'm!" he said.

"Sieglemanns did send you!" exclaimed his lordship. "They sent you to find out about the Turkish loan." He burst into a fit of laughter and leant back in his chair. "And I saw through it," he said at last. Then, banteringly: "Well, Mr Carfew, what did you discover? Are we going to float it? What shall we issue it at? And what do we get out of it?"

He gazed at Carfew with amusement and with the air of benevolence which is peculiar to the don who propounds a problem to which he only can offer a solution.

Carfew was silent. Then he rose. "I am afraid it will not interest you, Lord Kullug," he said, "to learn what I have discovered."

A look of alarm came into the other man's eyes.

"What have you discovered?" he asked sharply.

Carfew shrugged his shoulders. "Nothing," he said, and smiled meaningly.

He took his departure, leaving his lordship in some perturbation of mind. In the street Carfew bought an evening paper, but failed to discover any reference to the new Turkish loan. He went to the nearest Tube bookstall and purchased all the current financial journals, and studied them on his way back to Bloomsbury. Only one had reference to the matter.

"The uncertainty regarding the issue of the new Turkish loan," it said, "is affecting the tone of the Paris Bourse. A rumour is gaining currency that the French houses will not be invited to issue, and that it will be placed in the hands of one of the big London houses. Paris is without definite information on the subject, and, until there is an official declaration, French investors naturally display reluctance in reinvesting."

"Oh!" said Carfew. He had only the vaguest idea as to what it was all about, or exactly in what manner so ridiculously a minor point as the country in which a Turkish loan would be issued could affect the peace and happiness of Lord Kullug.

He found a wire waiting for him at Blenheim House:

"Call and see me at five o'clock, 104, Berkeley Square. – KULLUG."

He presented himself at the house five minutes late. He could have been there a quarter of an hour before the appointed time, but he thought better to arrive after the hour. Lord Kullug, pacing the polished floor of his library, was a little impatient.

"You ought to keep your appointments to the minute, young man," he said. "Sit down. Will you have a cup of tea?"

Carfew shook his head. "I have just come from the Ritz," he said simply.

"Seen Sieglemann?" demanded the other sharply.

Carfew smiled. "No," he said truthfully. "I have seen nobody but my doctor."

He had bumped into the medical student in the hall of Blenheim House, and, remembering the unpleasant things young Aesculapius had said, Carfew's description was a very kindly one.

"Now," said his lordship, "I want to know definitely what you have discovered."

"Nothing," said Carfew firmly.

"Did my foolish daughter say anything to you?"

Carfew shook his head. His lips were tight pressed as though to guard against an unwitting admission.

"I know no more than" – he paused, weighing his words – "than the Bourse suspects."

It was very bold of Carfew, and he was in a momentary panic lest he had said too much.

"Indeed?" said the millionaire grimly. "You know that, do you? I was right – I was right!" he muttered, and shook his head threateningly.

"When did you find out?"

Carfew hesitated. "I know nothing more," he said slowly, "than I knew after lunch yesterday."

"After lunch yesterday?" repeated the other. "After you lunched with me, you mean?"

"Exactly," said Carfew.

They eyed each other as the matador and the bull eye one another before the final coup.

"But I said very little," protested his lordship, speaking half to himself; "you did all the talking."

Carfew did not speak then.

"When do you make your report to Sieglemanns?" demanded Kullug.

"I may not make it," responded Carfew.

The millionaire sat nibbling the end of an ivory paper-knife. "I can pay, and pay well, for information," he said at last. "If you know anything worth knowing, you can sell your report to me."

Carfew again hesitated, but the millionaire opened his desk, and, taking out a chequebook, wrote with some deliberation therein. He tore out the slip and handed it to the other. "I have made it payable to bearer," he said.

Carfew took the form, placed it in his pocket, without haste took up his hat.

"The report?" asked his lordship.

Carfew smiled. "I have forgotten – everything," he said.

Lord Kullug nodded. "That is right – you will go far, my friend. And remember," he said, as they shook hands before parting, "the little piece of advice I gave you at the Savoy was meant in earnest. Let the other fellow do the talking."

"I shall never forget that," said Carfew with some emotion.

A DEAL IN RIFFS

It was in his house in Bloomsbury Square that Carfew met Willetts.

When I suggest that he had a house, I mean that he invariably spoke of "my house" and "my little place." As a matter of fact, the house was not his any more than it was the property of the fourteen other young gentlemen who boarded there.

Carfew came to know Willetts by accident. A new servant – there was a constant procession of new servants in Blenheim House, Bloomsbury Square – mixed the shoes – Willetts' varnished and pointed Oxfords with Carfew's square-toed brogues.

"A ridiculous mistake," said Carfew, annoyed.

"Very," said Mr Willetts.

They stood in their slippered feet on the landing, each holding a pair of shoes. Willetts was beetle-browed and studious, and wore gold-rimmed glasses, though he was a very young man.

"These shoes," said Carfew carelessly, "though not much to look at," he added hastily, as he caught the other's supercilious smile, "cost me thirty-five shillings. They are my favourite shoes."

"Indeed," said Mr Willetts politely. "For another ten shillings you could have got a pair exactly like mine."

They stood glaring at one another for fully a minute, and then the humour of the situation dawned simultaneously upon both, and they laughed.

This was the beginning of a friendship which entailed friendly calls from one room to the other, contemplative pipes smoked in silence, and the discovery of a mutual contempt for all the rest of the world harboured in Blenheim House.

Willetts was a stockbroker – spoke light-heartedly of millions – shook his head over Moorish loans, and said emphatically that not another farthing of Parker and Parker's – his firm – should go to Tangier till the French firmly established their rule from the coast to Fez.

"Cutting out all humbug, old man," said Carfew one evening, "what are you – senior partner or transfer clerk?"

Willetts swallowed something in his throat and admitted that though he was a clerk – not a transfer clerk – he had prospects, and was, moreover, trusted as no other employee of the firm was trusted.

It is an axiom of finance that no man is ruined by taking small profits. It is equally axiomatic that the man who sits tight and waits for shares to jump, usually does all the jumping himself.

Carfew, a rich man by the suburban standard, was taught a new game by Willetts.

There are certain American railway stock which you can buy, and, as sure as sure, they will rise a little. Then you sell out and rake in twenty pounds, thirty pounds, fifty pounds, or the like, according to the amount of your investments. Similarly, there are certain American steel stock that you can sell, and just as inevitably they will sag, and all you have to do is to ring your broker on the phone and tell him to cover.

When Carfew learnt the trick, he made money automatically. He would read, without understanding, the financial papers, and learn that his rails were up and his steels were down, then he would call "071 Central," and say in a most business-like voice: "Sell those rails of mine, Parker," or "Cover those steels," and at the end of the week along would come a pink form full of strange figures and a cheque, let us say, for forty-three pounds eight shillings.

One day in the autumn something happened in the United States of America. There was a law case between a big steel corporation and a big railway corporation, and the steel corporation won.

Carfew read the account of the trial in *The Times*. It was all about rebates and overcharges, and Carfew approved entirely the very strong remarks of the judge of the Supreme Court who tried the case, about the rapacity, unscrupulousness and general iniquity of the railway company.

"The decision of the Supreme Court," said *The Times* correspondent, "will have a far-reaching effect upon American railways."

"And quite right too," said the virtuous Mr Carfew. "It is really abominable that such things should be."

The next morning, Carfew, as was his wont, rang up his broker. Something had kept Willetts at the office so late the night before that he had not seen him.

"That you, Parker?" he asked languidly. "Sell those rails of mine and cover – "

"I should like to," said a grim voice at the other end of the wire. "Haven't you read the market report?"

Carfew frowned. "I never read market reports," he said. "What I wanted to say to you was this: Sell those rails of mine and cover the steels."

"Very good," said a voice acidly, and the telephone clicked.

The next day Carfew received a letter. It contained a pink form conventionally inscribed, and a letter requesting one thousand one hundred and fifty pounds "difference."

Carfew was astounded – he was outraged. He called up his broker and asked him what on earth he meant, and in a few plainly-expressed sentences the broker elucidated the situation.

It appeared that, as a result of the litigation which Carfew had so heartily approved, steel had gone up and rails had gone down, which was exactly the opposite way to that which the young financier had anticipated. Carfew paid the cheque with some misgivings as to his own sanity.

Willetts, a wise old man of twenty-six, heard Carfew's lamentations patiently.

"My dear chap," he said, "you haven't much to grumble at."

"I'm not grumbling at what I have," said Carfew with acerbity; "it's what I haven't got that worries me."

Willetts chewed a toothpick thoughtfully.

"You have had a good run," he said at last; "you can't expect all the luck to be on your side. Besides, when you read about that trial, you ought to have covered yourself."

Carfew surveyed him coldly. "I do not wish to make profit out of the misfortunes of others," he said with dignity; "and, besides, I did not think of it."

They were sitting at a frugal dinner in Soho. He leant across the table and emphasised his remarks with the salt caster.

"Willetts," he said solemnly, "I've got to get that money back. I will not be robbed because a fool of a judge, in his dotage, probably, passes offensive remarks about a poor wretched railway that – that wouldn't kill a worm, so to speak. Now, Willetts, you know everything there is to be known; you've got to pull me out of this mess."

Mr Willetts grew more thoughtful. "Perhaps, if you saw my principals – " he suggested.

"That seems an idea," said Carfew.

He wrote a little note requesting an interview, and was asked to call Messrs Parker & Parker's was a cold-blooded firm, and carried on its prosaic business in Moorgate Street.

Ordering Parker to sell steels and to buy rails was a different matter to interviewing Mr Augustus Parker with a request that he would show a clear and easy way for the early acquisition of wealth. Fortunately, Carfew was under no misapprehension as to his own sterling qualities.

Mr Parker was a man of fifty, suave and absent. He gave you the impression, all the time you were talking to him, that he was wondering whether he gave the newsvendor a half-crown in mistake for a penny on the previous night.

He was smooth of face, and had a little black moustache, and a fascinating trick of wrinkling up his nose when he disagreed with your point of view.

"Very unfortunate," he said gently, "very unfortunate, of course." He looked out of the window and frowned. Was it a half-crown he gave the man? He had had two or three, two shillings and several coppers –

"I am not crying about the money I have lost," said Carfew. "I hope I am too good a sportsman to worry about that sort of thing, only I want it back."

"Ah, yes!" murmured Mr Parker, mildly surprised and almost interested.

"What I want you to do," Carfew went on, growing confidential, "is to put me into something. I want to get a stock that is as low as it possibly can be, and must go higher."

"So do I," said Mr Parker sympathetically.

"You know much more about these things than I," Carfew admitted graciously; "you're in the heart of it. Now, what am I to do?"

Mr Parker was still looking out of the window, threshing out the question of the lost half-crown. He permitted his thoughts to stray back to Carfew, and half turned his head in the direction of his visitor.

"As I understand it, Mr Carfew," he said, "you want a miracle."

"Not a very large one," protested Carfew.

Parker smiled slightly. "We do not keep them in stock – of any size," he said. He turned his head to the window, then came back quickly, swinging round in his chair till he faced the speculator.

"Have you heard of Riffs?" he asked.

Carfew made a point of having heard of everything, but the business in hand was too serious for idle boastfulness. "I haven't," he confessed.

Again Mr Parker was silent, then he continued: "Riffs railways are at five shillings and sixpence," he said. "The road isn't built yet, but the company has the concession. It taps a vast agricultural district – the best in Morocco. As soon as that line is laid, those shares will be worth – anything."

"That's my stock," said Carfew with enthusiasm. "I'll buy – "

"Wait a minute." Mr Parker raised a manicured hand. "There is a possibility that the line will never be made, and then the shares are worth – nothing. I will explain."

He took a gold pencil from his waistcoat pocket; and drew a little map on his blotting-pad.

"Here is Tangier, here is Fez, here is the Riff. That portion of the Riff country through which the rail must run is hill country, and at the present it is held by a gentleman named El Mograb, who is by birth a Moor and by profession a brigand. The French are most anxious not to have trouble in that part of Morocco – it is too near Europe – so there is no question of forcing the rail through. They have tried moral suasion, and it was expensive. They sent a messenger with rich presents. It cost the Government two hundred and fifty thousand pesetas to ransom him – that's about ten thousand pounds."

He looked out of the window, and seemed rapidly slipping back to the problem of the lost half-crown.

"Well?" demanded Carfew.

"Well," said Mr Parker, with a weary smile, "El Mograb is the big bear of Riffs." He looked at Carfew curiously. "They tell me you are a very persuasive man," he said slowly. "You go out and persuade the Riffi people to let the railway through, and you'll make money."

"I see," said Carfew. "You'd pay my expenses?"

"If you succeeded," murmured Mr Parker, "I might induce the board to vote you something very handsome."

"A box of cigars or something?" suggested Carfew rudely.

"Very handsome," repeated Mr Parker, and shook his head at the vision these words conjured up.

"I'm a child in these matters," said Carfew with determination; "but I understand that, before I went on such an errand, your board would pay my expenses."

"A little," said Mr Parker hastily. "We are very poor. I hold a great deal of stock, and any heavy expenses would be detrimental to my interests."

"I am sorry you told me that," said Carfew; "it may keep me awake tonight. Now, exactly where should I come in?"

Mr Parker, by a supreme effort of will, withdrew his eyes from the contemplation of the street.

"If you buy shares at shillings and sell them at pounds, you come in all right," he said.

Carfew nodded. "I seem to have heard of options and things," he said. "Correct me if I am wrong, for I know very little about these things. For instance, you write me a little letter saying: 'My poor dear man, – In view of the fact that you are going to almost certain death, I give you or your executors the right to purchase ten thousand shares – "

"A thousand would be more reasonable," said Mr. Parker.

"Eight thousand shares in Riffi railways at five shillings."

"They are standing at five shillings and sixpence," corrected Mr Parker.

"Say five shillings and threepence," Carfew conceded, "at any time during the next six months. How is that?"

"Preposterous!" said Mr Parker, frankly. "Suppose Riffs go up – eh? My dear, good fellow – " He shook his head. "It is very unlikely that you'll do any good – the whole idea is fantastic. Now, I'll tell you what I'll do – on behalf of the company. I'll give you the call on one thousand at five shillings and sixpence for three months, and I'll adventure fifty pounds in the way of expenses."

"It's a bet," said Carfew.

Carfew had the faults of his genius. He took things for granted. He had confidence in his own judgment and did not seek advice. He might have saved himself trouble if he had sought out somebody who was acquainted with Morocco, and secured a few hints; but Carfew was superior to the advice of little men. He had a plan of campaign in his mind. It took him less than five minutes to form; once formed, it was immutable.

Three days later he left for Morocco by the shortest and most expensive route, and he carried with him three packing-cases which contained gramophones, a cheap cinematograph apparatus, beads of every variety and size and colour, gaudy clothes, cheap little mirrors, Birmingham ware from pocket-knives to watches, and gaudy picture books.

Certainly he took the advice of a porter at Victoria, and registered his baggage to Irun, and, save for a long and exciting debate with Customs officials at the Spanish frontier, he had no trouble. He went full speed through Spain by the new Gibraltar express, spent a few hours in Madrid, and came by way of Algeciras to Gibraltar in a reasonably short space of time.

He arrived at night, and left the next morning, with his packing-cases, by a little steamer, the *Gib al Musa*, for Tangier – which he learnt, for the first time in his life, had no "s" at the end of it.

Tangier, all white and glistening, with one green tower to mark the mosque, welcomed him with a babble of sound. He was fought for – he and his baggage – by ragged porters, and, after a breathless period of shrill recriminations, in which boatmen, porters, Spanish passengers and Customs House officials took part, he was landed.

He was taken in charge by a voluble, tattered guide rejoicing in the name of Rabbit, who swore with facility in Arabic, Spanish and English, and in time Carfew found himself, limp but triumphant, on the broad terrace of the Hotel Cecil, drinking tea.

He called upon the British Consul, carrying a letter of introduction, and was solemnly warned that, under no circumstances whatever, must he go anywhere near the Riffi country.

"You will have to get permission from the French authorities," said the immaculate Vice, "and you will have to provide yourself with an escort. It makes things a little easier for you that you're connected with the Riff Railway," he added, "because they have a sort of working arrangement with the Government. You see, if you're caught by El Mograb, nobody takes any responsibility for you."

"Trust me" – with confidence. "I am not without experience of native tribes."

"You speak Arabic, of course?"

"Like an Arab," said Carfew.

He made no attempt to secure permission from anybody. Rabbit assisting, he hired mules and loaded them one night, and, passing through the Great Sok at daybreak, struck out for the Riffian hills. It held him in assured faith in himself to see that none of the men of his caravan had any apprehension as to the outcome of his journey. They showed no sign of fear; they were light-hearted and cheerful, and their gaiety was infectious. Carfew found himself leading his column and humming a song, the burden of which was that all he wanted was love. "All that I want is you," sang Carfew unmusically, and addressing the twitching ears of his mule.

They passed the uncompleted railroad. Tall grass grew between the iron sleepers, and the rails were rusty. The debris of construction lay about – little wooden tool huts, abandoned barrows, here and there a rusty pick or the sheeted bulk of a crane.

"Rabbit," said Carfew, "you see this railway?"

"She no good," said Rabbit, and spat contemptuously.

"She's no good now," said Carfew, with a proud smile, "but, before many moons, the desert should bloom as a rose. This deserted plain will hum like a hive of bees."

"I bring you plenty honey bimeby," said the practical Rabbit. "You give me two dollar – I buy you good honey, yes."

They camped that night in the solitude of the plain. The next morning they resumed their journey. They passed little villages, where the charcoal-burners lived; once they saw in the distance a cloud of horsemen going in their direction. They kept level with them for a few hours; then the strangers disappeared.

Carfew camped at the foot of a hill. He was awakened before sunrise to find the camp occupied by a disreputable host of men who had bandoliers about their shoulders and carried business-like Mauser rifles in their hands.

Rabbit, a little nervous, enlightened him.

"This El Mograb man" he said. "Very bad feller, Mr Goodman." (This was Rabbit's stereotyped name for his patrons.) "Assassin – *comprenez?*"

"You look after those packages of mine, and keep close to me," said Carfew.

The leader of the party swaggered up and said something to Rabbit in Arabic.

"He says you go wit' him to El Mograb," said Rabbit.

"Bid him lead on," said Carfew magnificently. They traversed a rough road across the foothills, and Carfew found his captor by no means a bad fellow. He accepted with a smile the cigarette the young man offered.

"Tell him," said Carfew, "that I have come from the Great White King."

Rabbit translated, and the man replied shortly.

"He says, 'Which one?' " said Rabbit.

Carfew was taken aback. In all the adventure stories he had ever read, the invocation of the "Great White King" had invariably acted like magic. The illustrious Captain Cook, no less than Christopher Columbus and Carfew's other predecessors had uttered such words, and natives had thrown themselves at their feet with howls of reverence.

"Tell him I bring presents for his wife, who is the joy of his harem," said Carfew.

Rabbit was unmistakably shocked. "Mr Goodman, you no go for to say that, or he knock your head off, sire!"

Carfew was puzzled. "Tell El Mograb – " he began.

"This feller not El Mograb, Mr Goodman," said Rabbit contemptuously. "You *allez El Mograb toute suite*."

Carfew relapsed into a dignified silence. At noon, when the sun was hottest, they came to a camp pitched in a green place in the fold of the hills. He was taken to a tent, and, to his relief, his stores were put in with him. He was given food and water, and, through Rabbit, a salutary admonition.

"They say, you go run away, they shoot you."

"I shall not run away," said Carfew.

He was awakened from a doze in the evening, and informed that El Mograb would receive him.

Led by the man who had captured him, he approached the biggest of the tents. Here, under the shade of a striped tent fly, drawn out till it formed a canvas verandah, El Mograb awaited him – a tall, grave man in a spotless white jhellab. Carfew observed that he was white. Save for the brown eyes and the little curl of beard on his chin, he might have been an anaemic Frenchman.

"Tell him I come in peace," said Carfew, "and that the Great White – I mean the British Government – has sent me to have a little talk."

"Haj," translated Rabbit, "this man is a fool who wishes to speak with your Highness. I think he is rich."

"Tell him," said the unconscious Carfew, "that I bring him splendid presents."

"Mr Goodman," said Rabbit, after this had been translated, "he go send for your presents."

They were brought after a while, unpacked and spread before El Mograb, and the great brigand surveyed them without enthusiasm.

"Tell him – " began Carfew.

"I can save you the bother of the translation," said El Mograb quietly, and he spoke in perfect English. "You are Mr Carfew, of the railway, are you not?"

"*Oui*," said Carfew, who felt that the occasion demanded a display of his own linguistic capacity.

"And exactly what are these things?" he asked.

"Presents," said Carfew, a little feebly.

The Moor stooped and looked at a gramophone.

"This is one of the old pattern," he said; "those with the sound boxes are ever so much more pleasant. Did you bring any new records?"

"He squatted down in the Oriental fashion and turned over the discs. "There were a pretty waltz when I was in Paris a few years back – 'Rêve d'Or' – do you know it? – rather reminiscent of Offenbach at his lightest. I do not like Scotch comic songs," he said; "they are so like the songs of the barbarian hillmen south of Fez. Here is one I like." He extracted it and removed the paper envelope with deft fingers. "It is – what you call it? – an English *grande* overture."

He fitted the disc on the machine, turned the handle, and let the revolving top slip. He sat nodding his head to the tune, then he suddenly pressed the little brake.

"Too sharp," he said; "you haven't brought the right kind of needle."

He stood up. " Let us go within," he said, and clapped his hands.

The curtain that hid the interior of the tent rolled back and revealed a large, cool room, thickly carpeted, and furnished with divans luxuriously cushioned.

"Will you rest?" said El Mograb. "And have you acquired a taste for our coffee, or shall I order you a glass of mint tea?"

Carfew said "*Oui*" again.

"Will you tell me exactly what you came here for?" asked El Mograb.

Carfew had one great asset – he knew when to tell the truth, and he told it.

El Mograb listened attentively, and, when Carfew had finished, he nodded.

"You put the matter in a new light to me," he said. "Next week I will summon the hill people and we will talk over this matter."

That was all he said on the subject. He told Carfew much about himself – of his father, who had been the old Sultan's vizier; of his own education in England – a suggestion made by an English minister – of his return to Fez, of antiques and wholesale executions. Then Abdul Aziz came to the throne – Abdul the Foolish. El Mograb had joined in an abortive revolt.

"Now I am amongst my own people," he said, "and I have fought the Shereefian army many times. But I like Paris best," he said a little wistfully.

Carfew, in return, related his own life history – of a wicked uncle who had stolen his patrimony, of how this uncle had been murdered by a faithful servant of Carfew's, of how Carfew fled, and was pursued by two battalions of infantry, and of his final pardon.

"You are a jolly good story-teller," said El Mograb, "but you forget that I was at Harrow for three years."

No more was said of the railway. At daybreak Carfew and his men were conducted to the plains below, escorted by El Mograb's ragamuffins. Before he left, El Mograb came to say farewell.

"Will you send a telegram for me from Tangier?" he asked, and handed Carfew a slip of paper. "It is to an old college friend," said El Mograb.

Out of sight of the camp Carfew read the paper. It was addressed "Pollymog, London," and was in some sort of code. Two days later he was in Tangier. He arrived in London the following week, and Parker met him at the station.

"I got your wire," said the broker, "but I don't quite understand what you have done."

"I've seen El Mograb," said Carfew proudly. "I've persuaded him to allow the line to pass; I have argued with him, I have convinced him."

Parker eyed him absently. "I don't know that you have done much convincing," he said. "The beggar had a pitched battle with the Shereefian army yesterday and routed it."

Carfew was astonished. "But the shares have gone up already," he said; "I saw them listed in Paris, and they've risen to eight shillings."

Mr Parker scratched his head. "I know that," he said irritably. "Unless you've been buying, I can't understand it. Somebody has been buying them by the thousands."

They drove to Parker's office, that gentleman deep in thought. "If Mograb had come to terms with the Government, I could understand that people would jump in and bull the stock; but he is fighting, and as obstinate as ever."

Carfew stopped dead. "Do you know who 'Pollymog, London,' is?" he asked.

" 'Pollymog, London'?" repeated Mr Parker. "Yes, it is the telegraphic address of De Villiers. He's a broker who does a lot of buying for foreign investors."

Carfew remembered that El Mograb liked Paris best, and when, a week later, that famous brigand made peace with his Government and it was announced that he intended leaving his native land and settling in France, Carfew understood.

By this time Riffs stood at twenty-five shillings on a rising market, to Carfew's great joy – and El Mograb's.

CARFEW ENTERTAINS

Very few people know the truth about Sur Alto Don Jerome of Castile. Carfew knew, but, excellent man, he would never tell you, because, as he would inform you gravely, there are some secrets which even the gold of Ind could not purchase; besides which, he intended embodying the story in a book. As for the man from Mexico City, he will not tell the story for ten years to come. I owe my knowledge of the happening to Mr Collin of Cincinnatti.

Don Jerome arrived in England with his parents on March 4th. He spent a day or two at Windsor, a day or so in London, visiting his august relations; he went to Bognor for a week, for the bathing, and then left for his father's kingdom, via Ostend. I believe he went to Westende-Bains and stayed incognito at the Littoral, subsequent to his English visit; but that is a matter which does not concern either me or the Chevalier Carfew, a Commander of the Order of Santa Theresa. Still less does it concern Mr Collin, who now numbers amongst his clients a European monarch, an excellent substitute for the man from Mexico, who, I fear, will not gamble in stock for many, many years.

At the time under review, Carfew was snatching the fragments which were left to him after the failure of a certain bank. He had ventured some two thousand golden sovereigns into that promising concern, because it paid seven and a half per cent on deposit accounts, and seven and a half per cent is infinitely preferable to the two and a half per cent which Consolidated Funds offer.

His broker, his bank manager, and such of his friends as had any title to knowledge on matters financial advised him to give the bank a wide berth; but Carfew, secure in his faith – in Carfew – made a deposit and called his advisers "conservatives" and other harsh names.

The bank paid eight shillings and twopence in the pound, and people said that this was another instance of Carfew's extraordinary luck, because no sane person in the money world anticipated a dividend of more than the odd twopence.

"And I hope," said his broker, his bank manager, his friend who dabbled in markets, and such of his acquaintances as were on sufficiently familiar terms, "that this will be a lesson to you." Carfew made sniffing noises with his nose, which were intended to convey contempt, defiance, and an absolute indifference to the opinion of his fellow-creatures.

This was Carfew's state three days before the Court Circular announced the arrival of Sur Alto Don Jerome on these benignant shores.

Carfew was not only annoyed, but the cause of annoyance to others; for from extreme recklessness he proceeded to the extreme of caution.

Parker was pardonably annoyed when he discovered that Carfew had been pursuing inquiries as to his – Parker's – stability. Carfew's bank, being an inanimate corporation, was neither annoyed nor hurt when he sent peremptorily for its balance sheet, and answered the young man's inquiries – which were as to whether the bank had written down securities since the fall of Consols – with promptitude and civility.

"May I ask," said the heated Mr Parker, of Parker & Parker, Brokers, "what the devil you mean by employing a rum-soaked private detective to waylay and pump my clerks?"

Carfew looked him straight in the eye, as he would have looked the managing director of the bank that failed straight in the eye, had he had any suspicions: unfortunately he had had none – in time.

"Have you any reason to fear investigation?" he asked coldly.

Parker, who was worth half a million, went red in the face – Carfew suspected a guilty conscience, but that was far from the cause – and rang a bell.

A clerk entered. "Make out Mr Carfew's account," said Parker chokingly; "bring all the scrip we hold of his, and the chequebook."

Carfew waited till the door closed on the subordinate. "Do not," he said, with dignity, "allow your pique to lose you a trusted and, I may add, a valuable client."

"Valuable!" said Mr Parker, controlling himself. "Why, you foolish young man, you — foolish young man, your business isn't worth that" — snap! — "to me, not that" — snap! — "not that, sir!"

Snap! snap! snap! went Parker's fingers.

"Calm yourself," said Carfew. "I'm calm — why can't you be calm? I'm not going to take my business away from you, if that's what is worrying you."

"You are, sir — you are!" roared Parker. "That is just what you are going to do!"

"I am not," said Carfew firmly; "clear your mind of that fear. I merely set on foot a few inquiries, and from those inquiries the firm of Parker & Parker has issued, I may say, triumphantly."

The clerk was back now, with a bundle of share certificates, a chequebook and a long account.

"That will do," said Parker gruffly, and the scribe withdrew.

"Consider," said Carfew, as the other ran his fiery eyes over the account, "consider what the City will say when it comes to learn that I have withdrawn my account — it will soon get round."

Parker put down his pen and stared helplessly at the imperturbable young man; then his features relaxed into a smile, and the smile became a chuckle, and from that to a fit of uncontrollable laughter was a short step.

"You — you — " He could find no words to express himself.

"You have annoyed me very much," he said at last, and he was serious.

"You have often annoyed me," said Carfew serenely; "the best thing you can do is to put your annoyance to *contra*. And now we have settled that matter, I want to ask you something."

Parker's clerk came in with a card. "You'd better ask me tomorrow," said Parker, reading the inscription and frowning a little.

Carfew rose with a sigh, mechanically lifting one of Parker's priceless Egyptian cigarettes as he passed the open box on the desk. Outside the door he saw the new visitor and remarked him casually.

"American, and of a good type," said Carfew, who prided himself, not without reason, upon his ability to size up human beings.

Carfew wended his way to Bloomsbury, more settled in his mind than he had been for weeks. He knew the worst now, and the worst, since it was eight shillings and twopence in the pound, had not been so crippling as he feared it would be.

At the corner of Southampton Row he bought a newspaper, as was his wont, and, over a cup of tea in his room he skimmed the world's happenings with a professional eye.

It was here that he read that His Royal Highness Don Jerome had arrived in London, and he wondered exactly who Don Jerome was when he was at home, no less than what he was doing so far from home.

Being at heart a journalist, he took a proprietary interest in members of royal families; but since he could not immediately place Don Jerome, whether he wore a beard or contented himself with moustachios, he allowed that most Christian prince to retire from his mind, for not to be known by Carfew was half-way to oblivion.

He dressed for dinner – an unusual circumstance – and drove to a music-hall, which, without Carfew's express permission, it would be unfair to name. Fate was playing no pranks with him that he should find himself seated next to the man he had seen going into Parker's office, for Parker had sent the ticket to Carfew before their quarrel, and had probably disposed of the second seat to his other client.

None the less he had a grievance that Parker dared bestow his favours by halves, for, argued Carfew, there was no reason in the world why Parker should not have given him both seats.

He looked at his neighbour. He was a good-looking man of thirty, square-jawed, clean-shaven, and he was the possessor of a pair of piercing blue eyes, which looked steadily ahead from under the shaggiest eyebrows Carfew had ever seen on the face of so young a man.

He was correctly dressed, and looked what Carfew thought he was – a prosperous American merchant.

"Excuse me," said Carfew, "I think you know a friend of mine?"

The calm eyes surveyed him.

"Parker," suggested Carfew; "he is one of my brokers."

"Oh, yes," said the other, unbending.

"A very good chap," said Carfew; "I hope in time to give him the whole of my business."

The stranger regarded him with a new interest.

"A real nice man," he agreed, "though somewhat conservative."

Carfew nodded.

"I was trying to persuade him to do a little business with me. Why, I thought it was just simple business, but he just thought it wasn't so simple, so we let it go at that."

Carfew bent his head. "Now in my country," said the stranger, and he spoke with little or no punctuation, "which is Amurica, if I wanted to bear stock, I guess there'd be plenty around to advise me not to do ut, but when I'd made up my mind I'd just do ut – why, the broker would go right along and carry out instructions."

"And Parker wouldn't?"

"No, sir; your Mr Parker was willing to do ut, but he didn't want to indulge me in other matters, so we left it right where it was."

Now Carfew was immensely curious. There was no surer method of interesting him than by denying him information, unless it was by taking him a little way along the road and leaving him to grope the rest of the journey. He waited for his new acquaintance to continue, but he maintained a stolid silence. Presently he turned abruptly:

"My name is Collin – George K Collin. Likely you've heard Mr Parker mention it? No? I'm here in England on a mighty curious errand. Got into touch with some people in Mexico. That is in Amurica, but not in the United States of Amurica; it's a republic down south, but one of these days – However, that's neither here nor there. Well, this friend of mine, not exactly a friend, you understand, but just a man I've corresponded with in Cincinnati, that is a town in Amurica, and a most interesting town; I should be glad to show you round any time you're passing through; here's my card – well, as I say, I had some correspondence with this man – in fact, I've done some pretty big deals with him – and he heard I was in London, so he just wrote and asked me whether I'd oblige him in a pretty delicate business."

He paused for breath, turned his eyes to the stage and went on:

"This vaudeville is somewhat monotonous. Why, they wouldn't stand for this show in New York or Chicago. Chicago is a most wonderful city; it's about a thousand miles from New York, on Lake Michigan, and is one of the most prosperous cities in the world. Well, I was saying, this friend of mine from Mexico – Mexico City, which is the capital of Mexico proper – has got mixed up in a sort of family suit – a vurry unpleasant business, his wife being in it – and he asked me would I be good enough to take a child with me to some part of Europe, to get him away from his mother. Why, I thought it was the kind of work I wasn't exactly fitted for, so I said so; but he was urgent, and I do a lot of business with him, and he said it was impossible for him to take the child, because he had to stay here in London to fight the suit ; but if I'd go right across to Flushing by tomorrow night's boat, he'd be eternally obliged. You understand I'm trusting you as a friend of Parker's?"

"You may regard me as Parker," said Carfew, and felt he was flattering Parker. "But where does the bearing of stock come in?"

"Why," said Mr Collin, "this friend of mine from Mexico City told me I'd make quite a lot of money by bearing Spanish Threes – that's a sort of gold bond which one does not usually bear – and he gave me the information as some reward for my kindness."

"And you are taking the child?"

Mr Collin nodded and made the slightest of grimaces.

"Why, I'll admit that I don't like this transaction, and Parker doesn't like it, either. He's my London agent, but I do a big business for this man in Mexico City. I turn over something like two hundred thousand dollars a year, and he might think I'm disobliging. It was very unfortunate – very unfortunate that he knew I was in London."

It was not till the close of the entertainment that Mr Collin returned to the subject. They chatted on other matters. It was mainly Mr Collin who did the chatting, for he had a great deal of geographical information to impart, and was passionately fearful of the Englishman making such solecisms as the confusion of Portland Maine with Portland Oregon, *par exemple.*

Strolling from the theatre, Carfew suggested supper, and the two crossed to Leicester Square, and in an upstairs room at one of the famous hostelries which abound in the district, Carfew entertained his guest.

"And what did you want Parker to do in the matter?" asked the young man, when conversation switched on to the other's mission.

"Why," said Mr Collin hesitatingly, "I thought he might come along and see me off. See here, Mr Carfew, this is not my business, and I'm not accustomed to what may be termed the finesse of kidnapping, and I feel I should like a little moral support."

Carfew decided quickly. "I will come if you wish."

Mr Collin reached across the table and gripped the other's hand. "I was going to ask you, but I was just scared of getting another rebuff."

They parted that night, having fixed a rendezvous for the morrow.

Carfew loved profitable adventure, and if no profit promised, he was prepared to waive sordid gain for plain adventure.

It was raining the following night when the pair met at King's Cross and made their way to one of the solitary and gloomy squares which lie between the Euston Road and Bloomsbury.

Collin hired a prowling cab and gave the driver instructions. He was to drive slowly round Phillip Square till he was hailed by a gentleman who would be accompanied by a small boy. The moment that gentleman hailed the cab, he was to stop.

"You had better remain in the cab," said Mr Collin; "probably my friend from Mexico City would not be pleased if he saw somebody was with me. You can drive along to the station with me; my baggage is already there."

They had not circumnavigated the square twice when the cabman pulled up sharply. Standing on the side walk were two men and a small boy. It was difficult to see their faces, but, from the energetic gestures of one, Carfew gathered that he was the man from Mexico.

Collin sprang out, and through the open door, Carfew was an interested spectator.

The Mexican was talking eagerly, almost fiercely, to the child. It seemed to the unseen observer that he was all but threatening him. The boy was listening attentively, answering "Si, señor," "No, señor," in a musical voice. He wore a mackintosh which reached to his heels, and his face was hidden under the broad and dripping brim of a straw hat.

Then the man from Mexico broke into English. "I am obliged," he said with scarcely any accent, "for your kindness, frien' Collin – I have remembrance. This boy he will give you no trouble. At Flushing my brother will receive, and there will finish."

"Why, Mr Callaras," said Collin's voice, "I am glad to be of service to you, though I am willing to admit that it is not the particular variety of business – "

"I am thankful," said the other hurriedly; "there is not time to talk now." He seemed to be urging the boy and Collin into the cab. The boy came in first and sat facing Carfew. If he saw the other, he made no sign. Collin followed. He leant out of the window, partly to conceal Carfew from his exigent but valuable client, and to take farewell of the men. The cab was on the move before he withdrew.

"Why," said Mr Collin in perplexity, "this is a development I did not anticipate, for our young friend apparently does not understand English. The Mexicans, as you know, speak Spanish, Mexico being one of the first portions of the New World which came under Spanish influence. Until recently Cuba was – "

He traced the influence of Spain upon the Southern American continent from Euston Road to Cheapside. By such light as came into the dark interior of the cab, Carfew saw the boy. He was a handsome child, immensely grave and a trifle pale, as he sat in his streaming mackintosh, his wet little hands clasped on his lap. Carfew judged him to be nine, and was not far wrong.

"Where are we going?" asked Carfew suddenly.

"To Liverpool Street," said Mr Collin.

"But," said Carfew, "the Flushing boat-train goes at nine o'clock, and it is past nine already."

This was an indubitable fact. Though the public clocks of London do not, as a rule, agree, they were singularly unanimous upon that one point.

They sat in silence, a silence only broken by such lip noises as Mr Collin employed to emphasise his annoyance.

"We'll go back to my flat," said Carfew. He had risen to the dignity of a set of Bloomsbury chambers only a few weeks previous to this. "I can give you a shakedown and make up a bed for the boy. I suppose all your baggage is at the station?"

Mr Collin nodded.

"You can go off by first train in the morning."

"I shall have to wire my friend from Mexico City," said Mr Collin glumly. "Why, he'll be mad; but it was his own fault."

They stopped at an all-night office in Fleet Street, and sent their wire, and drove on to Carfew's flat.

There was a bright fire burning in his study. for which he was glad, for the child was shivering.

Carfew helped him off with his wet mackintosh. He was dressed in an ill-fitting sailor-suit, his brown legs were bare, and he accepted the chair which Carfew pushed to the fire with a smile of infinite sweetness.

The two men sat watching him.

"I suppose he'd like something hot," said Carfew ruefully; "but what the little beggar would like I can't imagine. Do you know any Mexican dishes?"

Mr Collin shook his head.

"I've heard of olla podrida," he said cautiously; "it seems a comprehensive sort of dish."

Carfew was dubious. He went to the tiny kitchen and found some milk. With great daring he put some into a saucepan and placed it over a gas fire. He bore the result to the boy, who drank it with a grateful smile.

Collin had taken a letter from his pocket, and was turning it over. "This is the letter I've got to give to the man who was to meet me," he said; "there's no address in it, or I'd wire him. I wonder – "

"Perhaps you'd find out if you opened it," suggested Carfew.

They looked at one another.

"It's mighty serious opening private letters," said Collin, and shook his head.

"The circumstances warrant it," said Carfew.

"We'll wait to see if there's any answer to our wire," said the other.

They waited talking before the fire till nearly midnight. Carfew did not put the child to bed, lest his father called for him, but in a big chair, propped up by pillows, his feet encased in Carfew's socks tucked into a pair of Carfew's slippers, the boy dozed.

Twelve o'clock struck, and Collin produced the letter.

"We can't keep the poor little lad out of bed," he said, and opened the envelope.

"It is in Spanish," he said.

"Perhaps I will read it, gentlemen."

They turned. The boy was awake.

"Oh, you speak English?" asked Collin in surprise.

"A little," said the boy, and took the letter in his hand. He looked up with a smile. "It is not perfect, my English, but you will understand." And he read:

"You will take the boy – (that is me," smiled the child) – "to a quiet Belgian *plage* – (what you call seaside) – Telegraph to me at my address; tell me where you are. I shall ask ransom, two million pesetas. I had great difficulty in getting boy from palace, but his absence will not be discovered before midnight. I am sending him by an Americano who thinks boy is my son. He is not very clever, this Americano, but he is honest, so I do not think he will be suspected."

"That is all," said the boy.

Carfew was on his feet staring at the lad.

"May I ask if your Royal Highness has any commands?" he said.

The child laughed gleefully. "You will please me if you take me to the palace," he said. "I am glad of your hospitality, but I haven't much English to say what I wish."

Carfew was pulling his boots on with feverish haste, and Mr Collin, sitting squarely opposite Sur Alto Don Jerome of Castile, was absorbing him.

"Say, Prince," he said solemnly, "you've put my friend and me in a hole." He shook his head. "Why didn't you tell us you were a prince?"

The boy kicked his slippered feet to the blaze. "They told me – the men who carried me from the palace – that if I did not give my word as a caballero that I would not tell you, they would kill me," he said simply. "But when I heard you speak, and knew you were Americano, I was sure you would find out, because" – he lifted his thin face smilingly to the seamed and tanned face of the American – "my father says that Americanos are always discoveries making, is it not?"

Carfew, returning from telephoning to the palace, found the boy asleep in Collin's arms.

"Say," whispered the man from Cincinnati, "I'm carrying Spanish gilt-edged stock all right – all right."

THE ECCENTRIC MR GOBLEHEIM

It is the truth that Carfew was no plodder. He said "Ha, ha!" in sardonic tones to people who talked of systematic labour and believed in dreams and portents. And people in the City knew this. Indeed, Carfew had something of a reputation for luck, which may have been unfair, for judgment played a part in many of his transactions.

He could reason out a plan of campaign, providing the effort took no longer than three minutes; but the calm detachment which enables men to make money from stock markets he did not possess, or, if he had the quality, he never exercised it.

Carfew believed that if the palm of his right hand tickled unaccountably, he was going to make money. He also knew that it was disastrous to put on one's left boot first. He never troubled about walking under ladders, because, as he said, he was not superstitious; but he surreptitiously crossed himself at the sight of a skewbald horse, because, as everybody knows, that is an elementary precaution which it would be criminal to evade.

One day, when Carfew was sitting at the window of his room overlooking Bloomsbury Square, thinking of nothing in particular, he was summoned to the telephone.

"Is that Mr Carfew?" said a deferential voice.

"Yes," said Carfew. "Who are you?"

"I," said the voice, with increasing deference, "am Lewis, of Lewis and Gobleheim, Mr Carfew."

"Oh, yes," said Carfew heartily, "of course!"

He had never heard of Lewis and Gobleheim, but that fact made little difference to Carfew, who was a natural opportunist.

"We would like to ask you, Mr Carfew," said the silky voice, "to see us at your convenience – 162, Austin Friars, Mr Carfew."

"Certainly," said the young man. "I think everybody knows your address – eh?" He laughed genially. "It is like addressing a man to the Bank of England, or to Madame Tussaud's, or – or the Tower of London. Certainly I will come along to Lewis and Grabhanger."

"Gobleheim," corrected the voice – "Gobleheim, Mr Carfew."

"I said 'Gobleheim,'" said the unscrupulous youth; "these telephones are terrible. At what hour would suit you?"

There was a long pause. Carfew judged that, with his hand over the transmitter, the other was consulting somebody. Then:

"If you could come today?" said the voice.

"At half-past two?" suggested Carfew.

Again the consultation. "That will suit us admirably, Mr Carfew. Shall we book that appointment?"

Carfew agreed, remarked upon the hideous character of the weather, mentioned casually that he was lunching with "a man from Rothschild's," hinted at an important board meeting which he would cheerfully miss in order to meet Messrs Lewis and Gobleheim, and hung up the receiver with that pleasurable sense of anticipation which a man possesses who sees unearned increment in the offing.

Lewis and Gobleheim sounded good. The mere fact that the firm bore such a name was evidence of its *bona fides*. A shaky concern would have called itself Graham and Fortescue, or, taking a leaf from Froissart, Ramsay and Mornay; but this was just plain Lewis and Gobleheim, and its very baldness of nomenclature advertised its stability.

Carfew looked up the firm in the telephone directory. It came as a mild shock to discover that the name did not appear.

"A conservative business," thought Carfew, "which, owing to the stress of modern conditions, is reluctantly compelled to adopt telephonic connections, but shrinks from advertising the fact."

When Carfew excused, he did so thoroughly and comprehensively. At two-thirty to the minute he presented himself at 162, Austin Friars, which is in the least pretentious block of offices in that crooked thoroughfare. In the cramped vestibule was an indicator, showing the names of the firms carrying on business. The most recently painted – and stencilled at that – was the name of Lewis and Gobleheim, and their habitation, said the indicator laconically, was "5th F." Up five flights of stairs Carfew toiled, and came at last to a door, on a glass panel of which a piece of paper was stuck, inscribed:

LEWIS AND GOBLEHEIM.

Carfew knocked, and a pleasant voice bade him enter. The room was innocent of furniture, save for a table and two chairs. An opened packet of stationery was deposited in the corner, a silk hat hung on a nail, and the owner of the hat came forward with springy step and genial smile to welcome the visitor.

Carfew took him in, from his glossy head to his brilliant feet. He was a nice young man, distinctly Hebraic and immaculate.

His frock-coat was cut by a master, his vest slip showed exactly the right margin, his spats were snowy, his cravat respectably black. His jewellery consisted of a solitary pearl in his necktie and the thinnest of gold chains. He was young and clean and pleasant.

"Let me offer you a chair, Mr Carfew," he said smilingly. "I must apologise for this wretched office, Mr Carfew, but the fact is, Mr Carfew, these are but temporary premises."

Mr Carfew inclined his head graciously, and the young man seated himself at the desk, flinging away his coat-tails with the dexterity which only comes to a man who lives in frock-coats, and surveyed Carfew benevolently.

"We will get to business, Mr Carfew," he said.

He unrolled a stiff sheet of cartridge paper from its brown wrapping, and Carfew saw that it was a map with rectangular sections coloured a brilliant green.

There was in Carfew's composition a sixth or seventh sense, which became instantly agitated when his good money was endangered – he felt it working.

"This," said Mr Lewis, carelessly indicating the plan, "is the Li Chow Mine, a concession which we have been able to secure from the Chinese Government, and which, in the course of the next three years, will be in full working order."

Carfew nodded. He was a little annoyed, but more amused that, with his reputation, any person should dare

"However," said Carfew to himself, "let us listen with good-natured tolerance."

"I must confess," said Mr Lewis with a smile, "that I should not have asked you to come and see me" – ("Infernal cheek!" said Carfew under his breath) – "had it not been for the superstition of my partner, Mr Carl Gobleheim, of whom you have doubtless heard."

"My partner," added Mr Lewis, with a sad smile, "is superstitious. That is extraordinary for a man of so practical a character. He believes in mascots, in luck, in omens." He laughed good-naturedly. "In fact, I am ashamed to disclose one-half of my partner's weakness, Mr Carfew."

"Extraordinary," said Carfew, who felt called upon to make some remark.

"Is it not?" said Mr Lewis.

He sat at the table, twisting his neat black moustache, somewhat disconcerted, so Carfew thought, by the chill reception of his confidences.

"And exactly how am I – " began the visitor; when Mr Lewis hesitated.

"I will tell you," said the other, speaking slowly and impressively. "My partner is putting this mine on the market at the end of this week. Now, it is his practice to find a man who is notoriously lucky. Do you follow me?"

Carfew did follow him. In fact, Carfew went ahead of him and anticipated all that was coming.

"Whenever we put a new thing on the market, Mr Gobleheim searches round for a lucky man. We keep a file of all the people who win lottery prizes, absurd as you may think the idea, and we usually choose one of those and sell him a few shares. Mr Gobleheim doesn't care if the mascot only retains possession of those shares for an hour – a minute – so long as he has actually possessed them, or they have been made out in his name."

"I see," said Carfew. Inwardly he was amused; his secret mind danced with laughter, and to the quantity of his merriment may be added a drachm or so of indignation. That any man in London, knowing Carfew's reputation as this man did, should imagine –

"My partner has heard of you, Mr Carfew," Lewis went on, with his ready smile – "indeed, one hears of you in all sorts of places."

"I see," said Carfew again.

He was a quick thinker, but he needed a lead.

"What do you suggest I should do?" he asked.

Mr Lewis shrugged his shoulders. "You might buy a few thousand," he said carelessly; "they will be issued at a premium. I am perfectly willing to take them back from you the day you buy – indeed, ten minutes afterwards – giving you a few shillings premium on each share."

So that was it. Carfew made up his mind. He did not disdain small profits even from the hands of a swindler. He had had some experience with confidence men before, and that experience should stand him in good stead.

He was something of an organiser, too, and his wits were working at top speed as he sat, his head bowed in thought, facing the bland and innocent Mr Lewis.

"When do you suggest that I should buy my shares?" he asked.

"Tomorrow," said the philanthropist.

Carfew nodded. "And you say that, if I purchased them, you would immediately repurchase at a premium?"

Mr Lewis signified his pleasure.

"At – er – what premium?"

The other pursed his lips and considered.

"I should say that the one pound Li Chow shares will be worth thirty shillings in a month, possibly – possibly, I say, for I should not like to promise too much – three pounds. Under these circumstances I feel I should be justified in offering two shillings per share."

Carfew, with a pencil and the back of a convenient envelope, made a calculation.

"So, if I bought five thousand shares I should make an immediate profit of five hundred pounds?"

"That is so," said Mr Lewis. "You would pay us five thousand pounds, I would transfer the shares to you, and all that I should have to do would be to hand back five thousand five hundred pounds, and receive your transfer."

Carfew drew a long breath. "You may expect me here at this hour tomorrow," he said, and held out his hand.

He was leaving the room when his benefactor called him back.

"Oh, I forgot to say, Mr Carfew," he said, "it is an eccentricity of my partner's that such shares should be paid for in cash – notes or gold, but preferably notes."

Carfew looked at him, and admiration and pity struggled for ascendancy in his eyes.

"I was wondering why you hadn't mentioned that," he said gently, for he felt a little sorry for the poor fellow who was essaying the heart-breaking task of freezing the great Carfew. "Anyway, I should have brought cash."

Mr Lewis bowed, and Carfew walked slowly down the narrow stairs into the street.

He looked up at the window of the room he had quitted and shook his head.

"My misguided friend!" he said mournfully. "Alas, my poor brother!"

Carfew could be very business-like.

First of all he called up his broker on the phone.

"Parker," he demanded, "are there any good Chinese mines on the market?"

"The Anglo-Chinese Properties are floating some," said Parker, "but you'll never get into those. There is practically no public subscription, they are taken up by an inner ring on flotation."

"Suppose," said Carfew, "some private individual in a little top-floor-back office offered you five thousand shares in a new Chinese gold mine, what would you do?"

"Send for the police," said Parker's voice. "I tell you that the Anglo-Chinese Properties have got all the mines worth floating."

Carfew hung up the receiver with a beatific smile. He hailed a taxi and drove to Scotland Yard. He knew some of the chiefs of the CID. McWort saw him readily, and Carfew unfolded his story briefly, suppressing the name of the firm, for he had no wish to set the machinery of investigation in motion; it made too much noise and might easily scare his birds.

"In fact," he explained, "I want this thing done quietly. Until I know I'm swindled I don't want to squeal."

The detective hesitated. "I don't see exactly what I can do," he said irritably. "I can put one man at the front of the office and station another within call."

"That is all I want," said Carfew. "I shall ask my bank manager to send an expert with me to handle the money. I rather fancy our friend will be disagreeably surprised when he rings the changes."

Carfew sat down before the great detective's desk and outlined the *modus operandi*.

"I know exactly what is going to happen," he said. "He will take my money, then whilst I am signing a transfer – flick! – in the twinkling of an eye, my bundle of notes will disappear and another will be on the table in its place. Then – "

"I am not," said the detective impressively, "without knowledge on the subject. Scotland Yard," he proceeded, "is an institution which was founded with the object of providing remedies for such social evils."

"Spare me your oratory, Demosthenes," said Carfew coldly.

Superintendent McWort was laughing as he accompanied Carfew along the corridor.

"I should be intensely amused," he said, "if this friend of yours actually got the better of you tomorrow."

"I shall grieve if you are denied a little morbid merriment," said Carfew politely.

"And," the officer went on, "I think it is extremely likely that you are going to be very sick over this business. Con Schriener is reported to be in London, and Con is the smartest man who ever traded a gold brick. Don't tell me that you have weighed the pros and cons," said the detective hastily. And Carfew, who at that moment was on the point of employing those very words, was visibly annoyed.

I doubt if ever in his adventurous career Carfew had elaborated his plans with such thoroughness.

The short space of time which was left to him he spent in stopping up every possible exit through which his good money might escape into a cold world. His motives did not bear examination. He hoped to make money quickly, failing which, his virtuous soul was enlarged with the knowledge that he would bring to justice "one of those parasites who prey upon foolish humanity."

(I am quoting from the skeleton report he had prepared for publication in *The Megaphone*, for at the worst he could sell the story to the press.)

On the morning of February 7, Carfew met the representatives of the forces he had set in movement. A detective called upon him before breakfast to receive his instructions; his banker, represented by a supernaturally solemn youth in spectacles, called after that meal. At ten o'clock Mr Grewer was announced.

"Show him up, please," said Carfew gravely.

Mr Grewer was short and stout and wheezy. He was red in the face and none too well shaven.

He brought with him the indefinite odour of cloves, superimposed on rum and milk, and he carried in his hand a thick stick and a hard felt hat, slightly worn at the brim.

"Sit down, Grewer," said Carfew, and leant back in his chair. Mr Grewer, with a groan, seated himself and said it was a fine day, considering.

"You have made a reconnaissance?" said Carfew.

Mr Grewer was frankly at sea.

"Made a which?" he asked huskily.

"You have had a look round?"

Mr Grewer smiled. "Oh, yes, I've had a look round, all right. You trust me." He leant forward confidentially. "I've 'andled more cases of divorce than any man in the profession. Look 'ere" – he raised a fat forefinger – "people say 'Ackits,' some say 'Molems,' but what do they do? They leave delikit bits to low subordinates? I take the matter through meself. No scandal, no upset in court, nothin' but pure, scientific – "

"I have told you that the regular police are engaged in the business," interrupted Carfew, "and they will not relish my employing a private detective, so I want you to keep out of the matter so far as you can. Now, what have you found?"

Mr Grewer produced a notebook. "One sixty two Austin Friars," he read. "Front entrance only. No back entrance. Small yard, where housekeeper keeps two guinea-pigs for housekeeper's child. That's against the lore," said Mr Grewer, looking up. "You could prosecute him under the Keeping of Livestock in Back Garden Act."

"Go on, Sherlock," said Carfew wearily. "I have no quarrel with the housekeeper."

"High wall," continued Mr Grewer; "no ladder available. Other side, high wall, small courtyard leading to other office premises."

"There's no escape there," mused Carfew.

"You can take it from me," said the confident Mr Grewer, closing his book, "that if the lady's there, we shall find her."

"There is no lady," said Carfew, testily.

He had learnt all that was to be known from this source. He paid the man his fee and dismissed him, to Mr Grewer's astonishment.

"You'll want a witness," he urged.

"Hop it!" said Carfew, who was versed in the vulgar *argot* of the day.

Shortly after two o'clock that afternoon an observer might have seen the preliminary acts of the comedy. First came Mr Lewis, walking briskly, an overcoat thrown over his arm. Then a lounger, who had been keeping observation, strolled across to the front of the office, and was joined by a second man. At two-thirty came Carfew, accompanied by a pale bank clerk. Lastly, and somewhat unsteadily, came Mr Grewer, unattached but curious.

In Carfew's pocket was a six-chambered revolver, in the bank clerk's hand a wallet, and in that wallet fifty notes, each of one hundred pounds value.

Mr Lewis seemed a little nervous. He welcomed Carfew, raised his eyebrows at the clerk, but relaxed his attitude of resentment when Carfew explained.

"Now," said Lewis, "we can get this business over quickly. You have the money?"

The clerk produced the notes and laid them on the table. Mr Lewis counted them with the dexterity of one who in his life had handled paper money in quantities.

"Correct," said Lewis.

Carfew glued his eyes to the notes; he had committed the numbers to memory.

"Here are the Li Chow shares, and here is the transfer," said the other.

Carfew read the document with one eye, and watched his money with the other. It was in order.

His own fountain pen was ready, and well it was so, because at that moment Lewis discovered that his ink-well wanted refilling.

"An excellent dodge," commented Carfew internally, and aloud: "I can save you the trouble." He signed his name with a flourish, and Lewis pushed back the notes. Carfew did not count them. Short of a miracle, nothing could have been abstracted or substituted.

He handed them to the clerk, who, as prearranged, counted them skilfully.

"Now you want your profit," said Mr Lewis pleasantly. From his hip-pocket he produced a flat pocket-book. He opened it and counted five notes of a hundred pounds. Carfew handed them to the clerk, who "snapped" each note scientifically and nodded.

"That is all, I think," said Mr Lewis.

Carfew noted a look of triumph in his eye, and went cold.

"That is all," he said unsteadily.

He descended the stairs, and at every step something inside him said: "You've been robbed! You've been robbed!"

With a nod to the detective, who was waiting outside, he stepped out into Broad Street, and, hailing a taxi, drove to the bank.

"There is nothing wrong with these," said his manager, after a careful scrutiny. "Either your confidence man smelt a rat, or else he is leading you on to further transactions. Certainly you are a hundred pounds in pocket at the moment."

A few seconds later the head clerk dashed into the manager's office fingering a revolver; but it was not the manager's death-cry he heard. Carfew was merely expressing his satisfaction in his noisiest fashion.

Carfew's broker was a man named Parker, and he had no prejudices save a not unnatural prejudice against losing money.

"Come into money, have you?" he said. "Have a cigar, and give me some of it."

He was in a genial mood, for that day he had transacted business which would considerably add to the amount of his death duties.

"I like you best when you're comic," said Carfew. "Yes, I've come into money, and I am in an expensive mood."

The broker eyed him thoughtfully. "I know the feeling." he said – "in fact, I feel the same today."

"I want to invest a few thousands in something horribly safe," Carfew went on. "I have been tempting Providence recently, and the reaction has set in. If you can put me on to something with a little more gilt on the edge than Consols, and which will pay, say ten per cent – "

The broker's face became serious. "Carfew," he said, " I think I can do you a turn – really. You might make big profits. You were talking to me about Chinese mines the other day over the phone. Now, the Anglo-Chinese Properties Company are putting a real first-class proposition on the market."

"Yes," said Carfew, interested.

"It will be issued at a pound premium; but you needn't worry about that – the shares will go to five pounds. The difficulty will be in getting any."

"Don't put difficulties in the way," pleaded Carfew.

"There are very few shares on the market. I have got a nice parcel because I know old Gobleheim."

"I beg your pardon?"

Carfew sat bolt upright.

"Gobleheim," said Parker. "He's a big gun in the Anglo-Chinese Properties. An eccentric old devil with a tremendous faith in luck. Why, do you know that if he thought you were what he calls 'wellstarred,' he would let you have those shares at par?"

"Would he?" asked Carfew faintly.

"It annoys his junior, Lewis – you've heard of Lucien Lewis? – like the dickens; and whenever the old man starts giving away good money, Lewis is generally round trying to buy it back quick and cheap. He offered me two pounds ten shillings a share for those Li Chow Mines I got yesterday."

"Li – Li Chow, did you say?" asked Carfew, like a man in a dream.

Parker nodded. "Those are the shares I advise you to buy. I think I could get some for three pounds."

Carfew rose unsteadily. "Suppose – suppose," he said shakily, "I had five thousand of these Li Chow shares at par, what profit could I have got?"

Parker laughed.

"Ten thousand easily; but you won't be able to get – "

"I'll come and talk business tomorrow," said Carfew, and went out into the street, a prey to various emotions.

PATRIOTS

You must remember about Carfew that he was an opportunist. Lots of people go wrong in appraising his character, because they fail to grasp the fact that he dealt with the forces of life as Napoleon dealt with the forces of his enemies – he readjusted his plans to meet the exigencies of the moment.

To follow another simile. When Carfew put down his nets into the ocean of finance, he usually did so with the expressed intention of hauling due east or due west, as the case may be. Those who called him unstable, fickle, inconsistent, or other harsh names, because he shifted his course to a point due north or south, are answered by the fact that he went after the fish.

Conservative men, who keep to their prearranged trawl, and wait for the fish to change their course, usually end their business careers at No. 16, Carey Street – I think that is the number of the building which houses the Official Receiver.

Carfew became a playwright after a none too brilliant season of theatrical management, wherein he discovered that, however badly the box office is doing, the treasury pays out with sickening and monotonous regularity.

Nobody wanted to produce Carfew's play in London. All the managers Carfew knew agreed that it was the finest comedy that ever happened. It was a "laugh," a "scream," or a "winner," and just the thing for "So-and-So." "So-and-So" agreed that it was a "laugh," a "scream," or a "winner," but unfortunately he had arranged for a French farce to be especially expurgated for his next production. Why not try Mr H?

Mr H said he'd read the play, and he'd laughed so much over it in the silent watches of the night – he lives in a house facing the entrance of the Zoological Gardens, that the keepers had turned out under the impression that a hyena had broken loose. But he couldn't produce it – it was over the heads of the common people.

Eventually the play was accepted by an American manager who agreed to produce it at the Fifth-Avenue Opera House, if Carfew would make a few alterations. So Carfew cut out the fourth act, rewrote the first, remodelled the second, and altered the third and changed the title – by which time he had written an entirely new play.

He had a final interview with the great impresario before he sailed to superintend the rehearsals.

"Pity we can't get Maisie Ellis for the leading role," said the presenter. He spoke round a big cigar, which gave his voice a complaining note. His attitude towards the events of life was that everything was a pity.

"Who's she?" asked Carfew.

"Pity you can't stop till you see her; she's opening in a month's time."

He shook his head gloomily, and remarked that it was a great pity.

Now, it may be said of Felix Carfew that when that eminent English author went out from London, with the object of introducing to the President and citizens of the United States humour as it really is, he never expected to return to England as soon as he did. He had mapped out a programme which had included flying visits to the principal cities of the United States, with periodical returns to New York to collect his royalties.

He came back under his arranged time because the citizens – the President being unavoidably detained in Washington – listened in stony silence to "Dog-Eared," that scintillating comedy, and applauded only – and with unmistakable heartiness – when the curtain finally fell.

101

On the morning he arrived, Carfew was interviewed by the reporters, and said that he liked New York and loved America with a deep, a true, and a passionate love; that he was seriously thinking of buying a house in Fifth Avenue, and that he thought American women were peachlike. He referred, being a humorist, to the sleepiness of Pennsylvania, the culture of Boston, the sinfulness of Portland, Or. – all of which facts he had gathered from a systematic perusal of the Sunday supplements and the book of a Gibson Girl musical comedy.

Just hold down Felix Carfew whilst I run along and fetch Gertrude Maisie Ellis. Look at her! She is a pretty girl, but, oh, so angry! Those soft cheeks of hers, that even two years of nightly make-up – to say nothing of two matinées weekly – have not spoilt, two big grey eyes shadowed by long, dark lashes, a great mop of goldy-brown hair, immensely unruly, lips generous and delicate of line, chin firm and rounded to perfection, the trimmest figure in cloth that ever delighted the eye of man, and all this under a hat which – well, it was just a hat. The shape was – it was trimmed and ornamented with soft billowy feathers – it was a hat.

She stood upon the deck of the *Kaiserin Catherin*. (She had intended sailing by the Cunarder, but would she sail under the red ensign of an effete and decaded nationality? Would she? Blazes!)

She went by the German line, rather than the English on purpose. She hoped the English people noticed the fact that she was returning home under the execrable white and black.

Oh, how she hated England! How she hated the English! How she loathed London!

It had not always been thus.

When she landed, she told a solitary and woebegone reporter that she just loved England; that it was like coming home; that the sight of the green lanes and the flowering hedges, the cute little primroses all in bloom, the poppies glowing in the dear cornfields, brought tears to her eyes.

The reporter, who knew enough of botany, horticulture, and natural science to realise that Gertrude Maisie Ellis had arrived three months too late for primroses, and three months too soon for poppies, substituted "violets coyly hiding beneath sturdy oaks," and wired a column up to London, which was cut down to a "stick" and tucked away between an inquest and a write-up par about the Gold Dust Twins.

She opened at the Marigold Theatre, Kingsway, with "Help-along Jane." "A play" – I quote from the agent's unbiased report – "which has placed Gertrude Maisie Ellis in the front rank of the world's great artistes, and has earned for her throughout the hemispheres the title of the American Bernhardt, not to say the Californian Duse."

"Help-along Jane" was a humorous play. It sold so on the programme. It was full of slang – good East-side slang as a Pittsburg author conceived it. Some of the lines were excruciatingly funny, but a stolid, thick-headed London audience did not laugh. No, it did not laugh, except in the wrong places. The London critics were gentle. They said the dresses were fine, the scenery was fine, the acting was fine. Some said "thin," but they really meant "fine."

Now, if Gertrude Maisie Ellis had been a normal leading lady, a conventional actress, or even just an ordinary sensible girl, she would have blamed the author. Every well-balanced leading lady blames the author if anything goes wrong, and calls a rehearsal, where the leading comedian says: "Suppose I came on with my trousers wrong side front, do you think I'd get the laugh?" And the leading man says: "Cut out the comedy, and I'll come down stage and seize you, Miss Ellis, and say, 'Let the stars be blotted from the velvet vault of heaven before I yield you to any man!'"

No, Gertrude Maisie Ellis did not blame the author. He wasn't there, anyway. She just blamed London. She blamed the decadent – I've used the word before, but it is a nice word – aristocracy; she blamed the servile and too-old-at-forty press; she blamed the manager – the English manager – and she attached no small amount of blame to the Court, which had inconveniently chosen that moment to be absent in India.

"You don't want real comedy," she said to the same unemotional reporter who had met her on arrival, "you don't want thoughtful interpretations – you want legs!"

"That's right," said the blushing reporter encouragingly. "Just tell me how you like London, and what is your impression of the House of Lords."

He also asked for a farewell message to the people of the metropolis, and she gave it him – good. The news editor, reading it over, reluctantly admired and as reluctantly turned it down.

"I don't think we can print this," he said – "not in the present state of public tension."

Gertrude Maisie Ellis expressed herself freely to the conductor on the boat train, to the chief steward of the *Kaiserin Catherin*, to such of her fellow-passengers who were not too sea-sick to be interested in the enormities of the British nation, to the neat little stewardess who tidied her cabin and brought her dried toast and weak tea in the morning, to the doctor – oh, to everybody.

She did not express her opinions about England so freely as did Felix Carfew, who was at that identical moment confiding his views on the American people to the skipper of the tramp steamer *Golden Dawn*, that was fighting its way through the broad Atlantic rollers, with a westerly gale on its quarter.

Carfew chose this moment of making his exit from the infernal apathy of New York – the great impresario had cabled that it was a pity the play had failed – because his broker, Parker, was the managing director of the company which owned the small steamer. The *Golden Dawn* was two thousand five hundred tons register, and, though no passenger-carrying boat, the accommodation was comfortable enough, and the company more agreeable than the company he had quitted, so he told himself. Carfew, as his best friends admit, was a talkative young man, and a good-looking young man if the truth be told. He was also a friend of the owners. Not only the captain, but the mate, the second officer, the engineer chief, and the second engineer, listened with polite interest to all that he had to say, though – let truth prevail – as uncomprehendingly as did the New York audience.

He orated at length on humour. He orated mostly to the captain because he seemed to have most time. Carfew discussed humour from many standpoints. He went back to the comic players of Aristophanes.

A gleam of interest shone in the eye of Captain Bigger when the passenger mentioned Aristophanes. "Oh, I know him," he said, with a sigh of relief, such as a man utters who feels the shelving beach beneath his feet after a long swim in deep water. "Keeps a little pub up at Hartlepool. Rare joker he is."

"The Aristophanes I refer to," said Carfew coldly, "was a Greek gentleman, and died thousands of years ago."

There was an embarrassing silence.

"Then it can't be my Harry," said Captain Bigger uncomfortably.

Carfew wrote the name on a piece of paper, and, leaning across the saloon table, the captain read it.

"Ah, to be sure," he said – "the *Arrystopeenus!* She is in the Black Sea trade. A regular tub of a boat. They took her into dock on the Tyne an' put a couple of rolling chocks on her! Comic? I should say she was comic! I've seen her crossin' the Bay with a twenty-five list on her – "

"You don't quite – " began Carfew wearily.

"All her starb'd boats awash," continued the enthusiastic skipper, "starb'd dead-lights fast all the voyage. Like livin' in a submarine havin' starb'd quarters. The only comfortable place in the saloon was to sit in the skylight, with your back restin' against the ceilin'."

Carfew gave him up. He tried the chief engineer on the subject of America's artistic soul, and spoke eloquently and without contradiction, at the end of which time the chief engineer protested that he had been awake all the time, and offered to repeat the last words that Carfew had said.

More than this, he took the American side of the controversy. "I don't agree with you, Mr Carfew," he said stoutly. "My opinion is that there is a sight more art in the United States than in any other part of the world. Look at their ads.! Get any newspaper you like and read the advertisements. Do you ever see anything like it in England? An' take

105

the Sunday papers. There was a bit I read about an ancient Babylonian temple havin' been dug up in Texas that was better illustrated than – "

Carfew groaned and gave up. He spent his time now on the unsteady deck of the *Golden Dawn*, revising the notes of his great work "America As I Saw It," which was to make eighty millions of people feel exceedingly small.

The sea was lumpy, though the wind had dropped; but five days out of New York, in somewhere about forty-five degrees west and forty degrees north, they made dead calm, with light mists, and in the middle watch the *Golden Dawn* struck a fog patch which was so thick that the man on the bridge could not see his mast-head light.

Captain Bigger slowed her down, though it seemed to Carfew that the boat could not go any slower without going backwards.

"How long will this last?" he asked the captain. Captain Bigger was drinking a strong cup of coffee in the chart-house, and made a rough calculation.

"We ought to get through in six hours," he said, "if we went full speed."

"What?" retorted Carfew incredulously. "Is it twenty miles thick?"

"It – " began the captain. Then the gross reflection upon his engines' capacity dawned upon him, and he relapsed into a silence which was at once a rebuke and an act of self-preservation. Every minute the siren of the *Golden Dawn* screeched fearful defiance at the elements, and every minute Carfew found himself listening tensely for the elements to answer back. He did not go to bed that night, having an absurd objection to being drowned in his pyjamas. This may be ascribed to the fact that Carfew was a Wesleyan till he found Art. Consequently, he was fully clothed when out of the fog, which had thinned somewhat, the *Kaiserin Catherin* leapt at the little *Golden Dawn*.

The captain and the chief officer had heard the siren of the oncoming German boat, and had worked out her position. By these calculations the *Kaiserin Catherin* lay four points off the port bow, and should pass two miles to port. Instead of which she didn't.

The skipper saw her coming – tiers of blurred lights looming out of the fog ahead – and, snatching the wheel from the quartermaster's hand, he put the head of the *Golden Dawn* hard a-starboard.

But a ship going dead slow is a lazy ship, and the *Golden Dawn* loafed to starboard hesitatingly, as though for two pins she'd have gone a-port.

Felix Carfew was sitting in the little officers' saloon, when the opposite wall of the saloon rushed across and hit him. He staggered up to the deck, and found the *Golden Dawn* settling down by the head, and far away, it seemed, a big steamer, blazing with lights, circling round in a big sweep, as though so proud of her accomplishment that she was loath to leave the scene of her exploit without another look.

"Muster all hands!"

He heard the captain's voice and the quick pattering of feet on iron.

"Lower all boats, Mr Carter. Where's that dude? Oh, there you are, sir! Get into that boat."

"I have some manuscripts below – " began Carfew.

"Get into that boat," said the obtuse chief officer. "There's plenty to eat, without troublin' your head about macaroons. Besides, this cow of a Dutchman will pick you up. Ready, below? Down you get!"

It was an awkward situation, and one which the young author had never contemplated. The ocean was beastly unsteady, and it was cold, and there were boat-loads of coarse men in his vicinity, who celebrated their rescue from an untimely end by violent language.

He came to the gangway of the *Kaiserin Catherin* with one cause for satisfaction – he was not in his pyjamas, though the decks were crowded with people, some of whom were not at all suitably dressed.

Carfew found himself in an ornamental smoke-room surrounded by a crowd of eager inquirers. People he had never met before offered him hot and pungent drinks, under the impression that they were rendering first aid. He learnt from them more than they had discovered from him – namely, that all the boats had been picked up, and the *Golden Dawn* had gone down, that the *Kaiserin Catherin* was undamaged, save for a buckled plate or two, and that everybody had been scared almost to death. There were a number of ladies in the throng about him, and one of these was indubitably pretty.

Moreover, she had offered him smelling-salts on his arrival in the smoke-room, and accordingly was entitled to also offer him consolation and comfort.

"Well, anyway," she smiled, after he had concluded an exciting narrative of his adventures – (" I heard the crash, and immediately sprang to the deck…" "I took charge of one of the boats…" "No, I assure you I wasn't a bit nervous…" "I lost a great many valuable manuscripts") – "well, anyway, you're going back to the only place for an artist!"

"I beg your pardon!" gasped Carfew.

"You're going back to America," said the girl, with animation.

"That," said the migrate deliberately, "is the greatest sorrow I have – the sorrow which transcends all others, the fly in the ointment. I am wondering," he said, "whether it wouldn't have been better to die!"

She was speechless with indignation. This was gratitude! She had saved his life – she and the ship and the sailors. She had assisted him aboard – at least, a Hamburg quartermaster had, and it was all charged for in the passage money.

"You – you – you Englishman!" she cried fiercely.

The next day they met again. She would have passed him in dignified silence if she had followed her line of thought to a logical conclusion. But she was not logical – she was a woman. (Wait a moment before you condemn the cheap sneer.)

He would have answered her salutation coldly, and resumed reading his book with significant earnestness if he had been consistent. But he was not consistent – he was a man. (Now you may criticise my conclusions, for I have shown that neither was perfect, except in the perfection of type.) Both obeyed the instincts of pugnacity.

ROUND I

"How are you feeling this morning, Mr Carfew?"

"Thank you, very well, though rather depressed."

"Ah, well, a little old New York will put you right."

Groan and a look of patience in suffering.

"You're the author of the play 'Dog-eared,' aren't you?"

"I am. They tell me you have had a London season?"

"London season!"

Oh, the contempt of it!

ROUND II

"Your play didn't seem to fit, Mr Carfew."

"The play was all right, Miss Ellis – the audience was wrong."

A sigh.

"Dear old New York! It *is* particular."

"Did you find the London playgoer – er – enthusiastic?"

A snort.

He glanced sideways at her. She was pretty, indeed. There was the dearest stray curl over the fine forehead, the lips were red with the red of health… Carfew unconsciously adjusted his tie.

ROUND III

"Did you see the National Gallery when you were in town?"

"Town?"

"London" – firmly. "There's only one town, Miss Ellis."

"Pouf! Yes, I think I did. It is that funny little shack on Waterloo Square."

"Trafalgar Square, Miss Ellis."

"Oh, I know it was named after one of your defeats."

Knock out.

The fighting progressed in spasms for the rest of the day.

The *Kaiserin Catherin's* damaged bow took a hundred miles a day off the usual run, and passengers who had carefully allocated their work or their play on the basis of a quick run, found themselves with time on their hands. Carfew was the candle which attracted

109

moth Gertrude Maisie. She simply could not leave the young man in peace.

In the first day she exhausted every possibility of the monarchy, the English aristocracy and their predilection for American heiresses, Bunker's Hill, the "Alabama incident," the Cockney accent, the funereal character of English humour, the Boer War, and the servility of the English servants.

He had retorted with the Panama Canal Bill, the vulgarity of Pittsburg millionaires, college football, the corruption of politics, the police scandal – a safe ground, for there is always a police scandal in New York; either the police are too strict or too lax – and the graft of corporation.

The conversation invariably swung round to audiences and their stupidity.

One morning – it was thirty-six hours distant from Sandy Hook – Gertrude Maisie came on deck in a pleasant frame of mind. The day was bright and sunny, the sea was smooth, she had eaten a good breakfast, and New York lay under the western horizon.

Carfew was reading "Dog-eared," a printed copy which was in his jacket pocket on the night of his rescue.

He would have thrust it out of sight, but the girl had already seen it; therefore he stuck to his guns valiantly, and was reading with evident enjoyment when the girl came upon the scene.

"Reading?" she asked.

She had the right motherly and domineering air due to the shipwrecked.

"I am."

"May I see it, please?"

She was very charming this morning, and really, beyond the ridiculous prejudice she had for New York, and the inflated value he placed upon the intelligence of Londoners, they were excellently disposed one to the other. He passed the book to her in silence. It was curious that he should know that, whatever might be her mental attitude toward the book, she would not hurt him.

She read the first act in silence. He, for his part, gazed abstractedly at the green waters rushing past in a simulation of disinterestedness in her perusal.

She turned to the second act – read it. Then the third act. He saw this out of the corner of his eye. She closed the little book and looked at him very seriously.

"And this was a failure?" she asked.

"In New York," he replied carelessly.

"Has it been produced in London?"

He shook his head. "Not yet," he said.

She turned the leaves of the play absent-mindedly.

"Your leading lady, was she English?"

Carfew nodded. Only a sense of loyalty prevented him from expressing his view that the leading lady had been responsible for much of its failure; for whilst the New York audience had no great appreciation of English humour, the leading woman in "Dog-eared" had no sense of humour at all.

She nodded. "I know where the play went wrong," she said, her eyes kindling – "I know just what's wrong in it, Mr Carfew." She rose from the deck-chair where she had been sitting and turned towards him with the frank friendliness of a sister-artist. "I'll revive this in New York – I've got pull enough – if you'll rewrite where I suggest."

He looked at her dubiously.

"My dear girl," he said, shaking his head, "you'd ruin your reputation. It's no use."

"I'll revive it. Will you allow me?"

He thought a moment. "On one condition," he said magnificently, "and that is that you play the lead when I produce it in London."

"Yes," said Gertrude Maisie Ellis to the representative of a London newspaper, "I love England. The sight of those cute little primroses just brings tears to my eyes. I can't tell you anything more about 'Dog-eared' than you already know. It played to big houses in New York, and it has won for me my European reputation."

111

"Yes," confirmed Carfew – he had come to see her off, and he was smoking a much bigger cigar than the great impresario had dared – "Miss Ellis made my play by her delightful representation of Mildred Banks. I'm vury sorry that business prevents me from accompanying her to Amurica, which is the vury forcing-house of genius and the home of art."

The reporter, who knew Carfew, looked at him wonderingly, for Carfew's drawl was distinctly American.

TOBBINS, LIMITED

Mr Carfew's broker called him up on the phone. Carfew was a man of many interests, and Parker was fortunate enough to catch him in one of his offices.

"Do you know Tobbins?" he asked,

Carfew, who knew everybody, said "Yes" nonchalantly.

"There's easy money there," said Parker's voice.

"Thank you for your good intentions," said Carfew, "but I never back horses."

Now, Carfew knew, or ought to have known, that Mr Parker was a good Churchman and a liberal subscriber to the Anti-Gambling League.

"It is not a horse," said Parker coldly; "it is a firm of bootmakers."

"Bookmakers?"

"*Boot*makers!" said the exasperated Parker. "B double o t – bootmakers! Come down and see me. What a chuckle-headed jackass Carfew can be sometimes!"

The last sentence was not intended for Carfew, and filled the interval between removing the receiver and hanging it up.

Carfew knew Tobbins, if the truth be told. Tobbins, Limited, had a "place" in Cannon Street. They had "places" elsewhere, but the Cannon Street Branch was "Tobbins." It was also "The Office" and "HQ." When, in other days, minor branches received complaints about the quality of goods retailed, they said, with an air in which awe with condescension was curiously blended, that they would report the matter to "The Office"; and the disgruntled customers, impressed by

113

the awe and abashed by the condescension, went away with the uncomfortable feeling that they had set machinery in motion which, before it could be stopped, would shake the boot world to its foundations.

Tobbins, Limited, sold boots and shoes, slippers and spats. It had sold boots and shoes in 1784. Soldiers who had marched across the peninsula of Spain had worn Tobbins' boots. The field of Torres Vedras, the trenches before Badajos, the sanguinary plain of Albuera, were strewn with Tobbins' boots attached to the feet of British soldiers. So the elder Tobbin would tell his guests at dinner, reserving the fact that the army had marched to Waterloo on Tobbins' boots, for a final impressive effort.

He gave you the impression that Tobbins had played no small part in the upbuilding of British prestige, and it was, indeed, a tradition of the family that Tobbins had been personally thanked by Pitt, or Fox, or somebody, for the patriotic endurance of Tobbins' soles and the extraordinary resilience of Tobbins' uppers.

Tobbins' greatness was of another day. Generations of partners had built country mansions at Kensington, Dulwich, and as far afield as Tonbridge, out of the enormous profits of the business. Generations of young gentlemen had had their tutors, their periods of study at Oxford University, their comings of age, their dog-carts and grand tours from the fat balances which accrued yearly.

When old Mr Charles passed from the control of the business, Tobbins affixed Limited after their name.

Some say the decay of Tobbins may be traced from that date and from that act; but there are minor Tobbins, who, possessing no interest in the business, were in the habit of receiving bonuses from profits every New Year's day. This pleasing custom was continued, but that did not affect the criticism, because, as everybody knows, there is no keener critic of municipal extravagance than the pauper, and the rich man's baker probably lived in terror of Lazarus and his judgment.

Certain it is that competition bit into the dividends of Tobbins, Limited. Business fell away, customers demanded new shapes and half sizes, and the firm, having no doubt in its official mind that Tobbins knew best, treated the requests with polite disdain.

For years Tobbins lived on its capital. Its members drew upon their private fortunes – none too large – for sustenance. The question of advertising had arisen.

A young and bouncing firm, the Exploitation Publicity Company, had bombarded Tobbins with letters, circulars, folders, diagrams, fat little hand-books and quotations, all going to demonstrate that the firm which did not advertise was half-way to ruin.

Tobbins acknowledged the first letter with the old-world courtesy which was part of its stock-in-trade, and ignored all subsequent communications. Tobbins did not advertise, because advertising was vulgar and new, and, so they fondly imagined, the hall-mark of mediocrity. Temptons advertised their "Wyde Welts" and survived – even thrived – on the disgraceful admission of their modernity; but what was good enough for Temptons was not good enough for Tobbins – except, of course, on the purely domestic side.

Which sounds cryptic. But I will explain later.

The crisis in the affairs of the house of Tobbins was reached when Mr Charles Tobbin called an informal meeting of his relations at his house in Sydenham, and, with some preliminary incoherence of speech, blurted out the fact that he was afraid – he hated to say it, but he had had losses on 'Change – he would be obliged to file his petition.

After which he broke down, and the assembled relatives remembered their own precarious condition, and, in some panic, what faith they had put in Uncle Charles. He had been their sheet-anchor. Considering the ragged rubble of their own defences, they had thought cheerfully and snugly of Uncle Charles in his turreted castle, his stout drawbridge ready for raising, his greased portcullis slick in its grooves, and his donjons stocked with broad pieces. And here was the first and last line of defence blubbering into a gaudy bandana! Here was the stronghold of Tobbinism in ruins, its portcullis rusted, its drawbridge, so to speak, overdrawn!

"Something has got to be done," said Mr Henry Tobbin. He was stout and ruddy and pompous, but neither weight, colour, nor a sense of his importance helped him in the crisis.

The remainder of Tobbins – the countable Tobbins – agreed that something must be done, but what that something was they did not know.

"The business, of course, is sound?" piped George Franklin Tobbin, a small man with side whiskers. Uncle Charles dabbed his eyes and said huskily that he didn't know, but he was afraid –

Somebody suggested a board meeting – a suggestion eagerly accepted, because it gave the party an excuse for dispersing.

"You see, Franklin," said Uncle Charles, who was a stoutish man with an unhealthy white skin, "I have had a lot of worries and expenses of which you boys know nothing. Maria was an invalid, poor soul! Thomas has cost me a fortune before he got his practice. Alice's husband – "

"Yes, yes, yes," said Franklin testily; "it can't be helped – it can't be helped. We must make the best of it. Something has got to be done."

He found his daughter, with other lady members of the Tobbin family, in the drawing-room. May Tobbin was tall and pretty and above the average in intelligence. A glance at Uncle Tobbin's red eyes told her the story of the calamity he had to tell. She kissed her tremulous girl cousins, and, collecting her father as a self-possessed girl might a parcel, she broke up the inquest, for an inquest on the dissolved meeting the after-talk promised to be. Their brougham was waiting in the road outside. Franklin Tobbin stood for a second on the pavement gazing at the equipage with a darkening eye, and was inclined to indulge in rhetoric.

"Let us make the most of our little remaining glory," he said bitterly. "The day is not far distant – "

"Please don't make a speech before the horses, father," she said. "Come into the brougham and tell me all that has happened."

He followed her meekly into the carriage, and, as they drove, he gave her a brief *résumé* of the meeting.

"Ruin, ruin," he said, "that is what it means! Over a hundred years' trading, and ruin at the end of it! I dare say I shall save enough from the wreck to buy a shop or something."

"Don't be silly, daddy," she smiled. "This has not come as a shock to you. You know very well that Tobbins has been going groggily."

"My dear," he protested, with a little shudder, "I do not like that word; it is not ladylike."

"It's the word," she said firmly. "Of course it has been going groggily. Tobbins!" she scoffed. "Why, there isn't a little general shop in Dulwich which isn't conducted on sounder lines! Tobbins' is a charitable institution run by slugs!"

"Newnham," he murmured, addressing the carriage roof, "expensive education – slugs!"

"There are too many men in Tobbins," she went on, unheeding his distress – "too many fat and lazy men puffed up with a sense of their suburban dignity. What are you going to do?"

"Perhaps, if we advertised – Something must be done," he said firmly.

"But what?"

He shifted uneasily in his seat, and was silent until the carriage was running through Dulwich village. "My broker, Parker," he said slowly and with evident distaste, "told me he could find a young man who'd put money into the business. It badly needs money, but Parker says this – er – young man would want complete control."

"Of course that would solve the difficulty," she said.

Mr Franklin nodded. "Yes, the money would."

"I don't want the money," she interrupted. "I don't think much money would be wanted. It is the control part of the scheme which offers a solution. What is the difficulty?"

Mr Franklin shook his head gloomily. He paid little attention to the irreverent attitude of his daughter towards Tobbins, Limited, for, as he was aware, women knew nothing of business.

"It is bringing a stranger into Tobbins," he said, lowering his voice. "It's worse than advertising."

"The Official Receiver isn't exactly a member of the family," responded May Tobbin brutally.

The carriage pulled up at Wildview Lodge, and May went into the house ahead of her father.

"Mr Tempton is waiting in the drawing-room, miss," said the maid, and the girl nodded.

She went to her room smiling. The family peril would at least serve her in this case. It would save her from the embarrassment of giving his *congé* to a young man who, if she knew him – and she thought she did – would now meet her more than halfway.

She and Arthur Tempton, a sleek young man, had been engaged for four years, and the engagement had been manoeuvred by the combined Tobbin family.

The general idea, as they say in military circles, was the eventual combination of Tobbins, Limited, with Tempton and Clark, or, as it is called, "Temptons."

Four years is a long time, however. In that four years Tobbins had retrogressed, in that four years Temptons had made extraordinary strides; Temptons' "Wyde Welts" had become almost famous, and the marriage which old Tempton had regarded with elation four years ago, he would now examine critically, for Tobbins' position was frankly discussed in the boot trade.

As for Arthur Tempton himself, his views were the views of the firm. He was a business-like young man who, for years, had secretly resented the mental superiority of his chosen partner.

He rose to meet her as she entered the drawing-room – a well-dressed young man with shiny black hair.

"How do, May?" he said briskly.

His attitude toward her during the past half-year might be summarised in the word "brisk."

He was a business man – he prided himself upon that fact. So he came to the point at once.

"I've called to see you, May," he said, "on a delicate matter; but I know that you're a practical, common-sense girl, and won't misunderstand me."

She nodded, absorbing him in an appraising gaze, which took him in from his lavender spats to his three-inch collar.

"There is a rumour in the City," he said, "about Tobbins, and, unfortunately, we know too well that the rumour is justified." He cleared his throat. "We know, you and I," he went on, "that our – engagement was not so much a – a love match; in fact, it was a sort of deal; in fact – "

"In fact," she said, with a serene smile, "you've come to break off our engagement because the deal hasn't turned out as profitable as you thought it would."

The young man went very red. "You're – you're doing me an injustice," he said. "I'm awfully fond of you, really, but I'm not worthy of you."

"I never thought you were," she said calmly; "and if it will be any relief to you to know it, I intend breaking off the engagement under any circumstances."

He did not seem as pleased as he might have been.

"Oh, indeed!" he said gruffly. "I'm sorry I didn't come up to your idea of what a man should be."

"You guess that, do you?" she smiled. She slowly unscrewed the ring from her finger and laid it on the table before him.

"I wanted you to keep that ring as a sort of souvenir," he said awkwardly.

"I need nothing to remind me of you, Arthur," she said with a little laugh, and, as he picked the ring up, "I think, and I have thought for some time past, that you are banking too heavily on Tobbins going under; but that doesn't alter matters between you and me."

"I don't know what you mean by 'banking' " – he had all the dislike for slang which a business man should have – "but I know – well, I know what I know about Tobbins."

He picked up his hat, stick, and gloves, and, having recovered something of his self-possession, endeavoured to take command of a situation which was not especially creditable to himself.

"For instance," he said, "we know all about Charles Tobbin – that's public property. I don't suppose you know – "

"I know all about Uncle Charles," she said with difficulty, "and it isn't pleasant to realise that all the enlarged shopkeepers in London are equally well-informed. You're not subtle, Arthur; there's a disagreeable 'Wyde-Weltiness' about you which is positively painful."

In a few seconds he was being shown out of the house by the prim maid, and it was an outraged and vengeful young man who caught the next train back to town.

When there is something to be known to the detriment of A or B, neither A nor B imagine for one moment that either C or D have the ghost of a suspicion, and it comes as a shock to them to learn that not only have C and D, but the rest of the alphabet, to say nothing of the cardinal numbers, been discussing the secret for months.

It was under the shadow of the knowledge that their infamy was known to the world that the board of Tobbins met. There were present: Charles Tobbin (chairman), Henry Tobbin, George Franklin Tobbin (directors), Augustus Albert Tobbin (secretary) – a young man who was never known to raise his eyes above the level of the third button of Mr Charles Tobbin's waistcoat – and Mr Harold Tobbin (auditor), a stout young man with a daring taste in neckwear. The solicitor Tobbin was not present, nor was the general manager Tobbin, because he was not a member of the board.

"Well, gentlemen," said Mr Charles, "I have advised you all – or, rather, Mr Augustus Albert has – of the object of this meeting. We have had an offer of twenty thousand pounds, subject to certain conditions, and you have to decide whether you will accept. If you do not, it may – um – it may" – Mr Charles blew his nose violently – "be necessary to call a meeting of Tobbins' creditors. We have – er – as you know, made a loss on trading for the past six years – er – a heavier loss than we realised."

He stood in silence, as though he had something more to say, then abruptly sat down.

"The question is," said the stout Mr Henry impressively, "is this Mr Carfew a sound man? Is he a practical man? Is he a man who could be admitted into the company with credit to the name of Tobbin? Is he a man who would be willing to be guided by the mature experience of those who, by their labours, their energies, their foresight, and their integrity, have built up and maintained a commercial undertaking – "

"That will do, Henry, please."

It was Mr Franklin's querulous voice.

"What we've got to face," he said, "is the evident fact that, if we do not get money, we go into liquidation. This young man, Carfew, was recommended by my friend Parker – an eminent broker in the City of London – and, if he is willing to come in, for heaven's sake do not let us put any obstacles in his way."

"I am satisfied," said Mr Henry, and lapsed into a dignified silence. There was a little pause.

"Mr Carfew is waiting," said Mr Franklin.

"I think we had better see this young man," said Mr Charles gravely.

Carfew came in, extremely cheerful, and, with a bow, accepted the chair which Mr Augustus Albert pushed toward him.

"You are very young, Mr Carfew," said Mr Charles benevolently, "and it may be some source of pleasure to you to know that you are the first stranger who has ever been admitted to a board meeting of Tobbins."

Carfew bowed and coughed expectantly.

"We have considered your offer," said Mr Charles, "and, subject to a rearrangement of shares which will be necessary, we are prepared to admit you into partnership. You may be sure" – his uplifted finger and his solemn tone was impressive – "you may be sure that the money you invest in Tobbins will be discreetly employed."

"I am perfectly sure of that," said Carfew heartily, "because I am going to employ it myself. In other words, it is on the condition that I secure absolute control of the business, and that your board grant to me irrevocably a free hand, that I come in at all."

"Young man," said Mr Henry, red in the face and glaring over his spectacles, "this is a business – "

"I think you are wrong," interrupted Carfew easily. "I have seen your figures, and it strikes me that, so far from being a business, it is the site on which a business once stood."

You can picture young Mr Carfew sitting easily in his chair, his knees crossed and one arm flung over the chair's back. On the long table, at one end of which he sat, was his glossy tall hat, by its side a pretentious bundle of documents. It would be slow work to follow the course of that meeting from there onwards. It lasted two hours, at the end of which Mr Charles Tobbin vacated his chair, and Mr Felix Carfew sat in the seat of High Tobbinism, undisputed tyrant of his little kingdom.

"If you will come to dinner tonight," said Mr Franklin, "there are one or two points I should like to talk over with you. I will pick you up anywhere you like and drive you down to Dulwich. You had some directors in your eye?"

Carfew had demanded and had received the resignation of the board of directors.

"I thought of asking my friend Lord Kullug," he said thoughtfully, "and I have some influence at Court – "

He did not, however, commit himself. He drove straight from his board meeting to Parker's, and that sardonic man kept him waiting for ten minutes, not because he was engaged, but for the good of Carfew's soul.

"My bright youth," said Parker, when his visitor had protested importantly, "sit down. I can give you exactly five minutes."

"From which I gather," said Carfew pointedly, "that the five minutes doesn't belong to you. I have just come from my board – "

"Your board! And only the other day it would have been your boarding-house," said Parker reminiscently.

"From my board," said Carfew, "and for a collection of Rip van Winkles they would be hard to beat."

"There's money in that business," said Parker, contemplating his elegant nails. "You chucked the board?"

"From Hades to Highbury," said Carfew extravagantly, "the road is encumbered with the mangled remains of Tobbins' late directors."

"You're an unpleasant devil," said Parker. "And now I suppose you want the balance of your money? You've got a controlling number of shares? Good! Now, Carfew" – he shook his head at the other – "we've got a big thing here, and, frankly, I shouldn't touch it if you weren't in it. But I've such a confidence in your nerve, your unfailing and colossal impudence, and, if occasion demands, your elastic notions of honesty – "

"I cannot stay," said Carfew, putting on his gloves, "much as I enjoy your naive confessions – by the way, why don't you write a book? – because I am dining with one of my junior partners."

"Poor fellow!" said Parker.

By arrangement, Carfew met Franklin Tobbin at the corner of Park Lane. There was no reason in the world why Carfew should not have met him in the City. In fact, Carfew made a special trip to the West End in order to keep his appointment, and narrowly missed the ignominy of being detected in the act of descending from a motorbus.

He drove with Mr Franklin to Dulwich, and all the way down his host sounded him cautiously.

"By the way," he said, as the car drew near to its destination, "I have a – er – daughter, Mr Carfew. Rather irresponsible, as young girls are apt to be. She may – er – be frank about Tobbins, and I should be glad – in fact, I should esteem it a great favour – if you checked any – er – disposition on her part to speak disrespectfully of the firm."

"You may trust me," said Carfew.

A tall, slim girl in white welcomed the new managing director warmly, for Carfew represented the fulfilment of an idea.

They chatted together on general topics whilst Mr Franklin was away from the room. It was not until dinner was halfway through that they touched upon Tobbins.

"What are you going to do with us?" she asked unexpectedly.

Carfew produced his most mysterious smile for the occasion. "My friend, Lord Kullug," he said, "has impressed upon me the necessity for preserving a discreet reticence as to future plans, and a becoming modesty regarding my past achievements."

"Is that why you have been talking about yourself all the evening?" she asked.

"May!" reproved her outraged parent.

"My friend, Lord Kullug – " began Carfew.

She was passing him the coffee and looking into his face with wide-eyed and unfeigned amusement.

"Swank!" she murmured.

Carfew grinned a little sheepishly.

"You can bet," he said, "that I'm going to make a fight to put Tobbins on top."

She beamed. "That is the kind of talk I like to hear," she said, "and I do hope you've turned out some of the Tobbins. Father's the best of 'em, but – " She shook her head sorrowfully at her indignant progenitor.

"I've asked them all to retire for a time," said Carfew.

"All!"

She leant back in her chair and laughed till the tears stood in her eyes.

"All!" she repeated. "You do not know the Tobbins. Why, if you got rid of all the Tobbins, you'd have no salaries to pay! Oh, I wish I were a man!" She thumped the table savagely and glared at Carfew. "I wish I were on that board with you. I'd make Tobbins' pay as it had never paid before!"

Mr Franklin's smile was at once forced, feeble, and apologetic. He looked toward Carfew for help and inspiration. The young man had no eyes for him; he was gazing intently at the girl.

"If I offer you a directorship, will you accept it?" he asked.

"But – you don't mean that?"

"I do," said Carfew.

"But can a girl – " she began, her eyes dancing with joy.

"She can," said Carfew. "Look here" – he leant across the table – "I want a Tobbin on the board, and I was wondering which of the gang – I mean, who of the family it should be. Will you take it?"

She was on her feet, shaking with the effort of controlling the desire for noisy demonstration.

Mr Franklin, a speechless spectator, could only look from one to the other, making protesting noises. She reached her hand across the table, and Carfew grasped it.

"I will," she said.

It was curiously like some Church ceremonial, of which Carfew had a hazy notion, and it gave him an extraordinary sensation – not at all unpleasant.

There is a legend in the City that when Mr Charles Tobbin heard of the appointment of his niece to the directorship of Tobbins, Limited, he took to his bed, and, having turned his face to the nearest wall – there wasn't much difference to choose between the walls, for his bed, as a matter of indisputable fact, is in the centre of the room – announced his desire for death. Be that as it may, there is no questioning the consternation which the appointment of a girl to the board of that ancient firm made.

In the meantime, Carfew had established himself in the comfortable office of the managing director. Beneath and around him the Tobbins hive was humming. Boots were being packed and unpacked. Crate loads and basket loads were coming in from the Tobbins manufactory at Northampton, to be repacked and distributed to the half hundred branches throughout England.

He was leaning back in his chair, his hands in his pockets, when May Tobbin came in. He jumped up and assisted her out of her long coat.

She wore a neat, tailor-made costume, and her hat was feathery. This she removed, jabbed it full of hatpins, and patted her hair.

They looked at one another solemnly.

"It's awful, isn't it?" she said.

"What is awful – getting up so early?"

"No, the bigness of it." She waved her hand round the room and indicated in her gesture the business of Tobbins, Limited. "How on earth did these relations of mine run it? Are they such simpletons, or are they much more clever than we think?"

"Child," said Carfew, "what motive power runs a ship when the engines are stopped? The ship doesn't come to a standstill, does it? It goes on and on and on, not because an engine is working, but because an engine has worked. I tell you, child – "

"Don't call me child," she said. "What are we going to do first?"

"We'll have a board meeting," said Carfew, and they adjourned to the big board-room. A young man with beetle brows was studying some papers at one end of the room.

"This is Mr Willetts, the secretary," said Carfew. "He is a friend of mine, and the trusted confidant of my broker, Parker. This is Miss Tobbin, Willetts, the new director."

"I've been looking through these salary lists," said Willetts, "and, really, these old guys – Oh, I beg your pardon!"

"Don't apologise to me," said the girl calmly; "they are my relatives, and you can say what you like about them."

Carfew took the sheet and sat down, the girl on one side, Willetts on the other.

"Thomas Andrew Tobbin, Director of the Machine Department, four hundred pounds," he read. "Who is he?"

"He's a cousin. He's supposed to be in Northampton."

"Is he any good?"

"He's worth about one hundred pounds a year," she conceded.

"Cut him down, Willetts," said Carfew. And the secretary struck out the four hundred and substituted one hundred.

"John Tobbin, Junior, Director of Travellers, five hundred pounds," read Carfew. "What is a director of travellers?"

"A Tobbin who wants a soft job," she said.

"Cut him off altogether, Mr Willetts."

"John Tobbin, Senior, Advisory Board, two hundred pounds," Carfew read, and glanced round inquiringly.

"The Advisory Board of the Tobbin family," explained the girl, "is a sort of old age pension scheme. When a Tobbin didn't know enough about boots to keep his teeth from chattering, he was put on the Advisory Board."

"Out him!" said Carfew coarsely. "Here's Arthur Tempton, AB, one hundred pounds – eh?"

The girl's face went red. "I didn't know he was on the list," she said.

She leant across him and, with a vicious slash of her pen, she wiped this unofficial member of the Tobbin family out of existence. One by one the list came down. The private prospects of the Tobbins grew bleaker and bleaker as the future of Tobbins, Limited, became more and more rosy.

"Notify all these people," said Carfew, "that in future they will have to work for a living."

He was leaving the board-room when the secretary called him back.

"Looking through the papers," he said, "I find a letter from a publicity agency – 'The Exploitation,' it calls itself – asking for business."

"I think we will give them some," said Carfew.

Willetts, a wise youth, looked dubious.

"A new agency?" He shook his head. "I like staid and sober firms best."

"You are unjust," said Carfew gently. "Let youth be served; hold out the helping hand to the struggling, and the generous hook of patronage to the novice. Six years ago, when I was young – were you ever eighteen, Willetts? You sometimes impress me with the idea that you were born at forty – I should have been glad of such a chance."

He left Willetts saying offensive things.

Tobbins, Limited, had always been a conservative firm, and the backbone of conservatism is an opposition to change, which means profit to somebody else at your expense. In knowledgeable quarters they say that the Tobbins of England came to London by the thousand.

May Tobbin, as the sole representative of the family on the board, was summoned to a council of kinsmen, and replied through the company's secretary that she regretted her inability to attend, "the affairs of the company being in such a condition that neither she nor her co-director felt it advisable to relax for one moment their efforts to undo the mischief which half a century of mismanagement had brought about." After which the minor Tobbins put their heads together and schemed a great scheme.

There were others who watched the progress of Tobbins with more than ordinary interest.

Mr William Tempton, a large and vulgar man, who, despite his affluence, wore side-whiskers and a cavalry moustache, discussed the situation with his sleek son.

"I give 'em a month," he said "then – compulsory liquidation. We've got too far ahead of 'em. We're alone in the market with 'Wyde Welts.' "

"It's rum, May taking on that job," said Arthur Tempton thoughtfully. "It's not ladylike, is it?"

"You're well out of that business," said his father.

A week later Arthur Tempton dashed into his father's office with a newspaper in his hand.

"Look!" he gasped.

The whole of the front page of a popular daily was dedicated to the use of Tobbins.

Mr Tempton, senior, looked and swore.

THE BOOTS THAT WON
WATERLOO.

First in 1815.   First in 1913.

TOBBINS' WYDE WELTS.

That was the beginning of it, but not all. Artistically arranged was every piece of information regarding shoeware that the average man would wish to know. There was the history of the firm in a neat "box." There was what Wellington said to Tobbin, and what Tobbin said to Wellington. There was a plan of the retreat of Corunna, and sketches of the boots that made it possible. There were descriptions of Tobbins' works in Northampton, and a portrait of the founder of the firm –

from an old print reputedly by Hogarth – and throughout the page ran the insistent claim that Tobbins' Wyde Welts were the only Wyde Welts in the world worth thinking about or wearing; that, before Tobbins, all other Wyde Welts hung out their tongues and looked sheepish.

It ended, this astounding announcement, with an appeal to the patriotism of every Englishman to reject with scorn all base imitation, and support the firm which made England what she was.

"This," said Mr Tempton, thumping the paper with a shaking hand, "settles Tobbins. I take them into court for an infringement of my idea."

But the case never went into court, because "Wyde Welts," as a name, had not been registered. Carfew had found that out. In fact, he had hardly troubled to make inquiries, so certain was he that a jealous Patent Office would refuse protection to the letter "y" in "wyde."

In pages, half-pages, double columns in newspapers and magazines, the story of Tobbins was told, the fame of the only genuine Wyde Welt – "the boot that beat Napoleon" – was extolled.

Arthur Tempton called at the office to protest.

The board was taking tea at the moment, and enlivening the interval with an exciting game of Halma. Carfew hastily concealed the board and pieces, put the tea-tray in the safe, and Arthur Tempton was met with becoming gravity.

"Now, look here," said the aggrieved young man, "we want to live in harmony – "

"Won't you take your hat off?" asked May.

"I'm sorry. We want to live in harmony – "

"Sit down, my son," said Carfew benevolently.

"We want," said Mr Tempton for the third time, "to live in harmony with everybody."

"Then your ambition won't be gratified till you get to heaven," said Carfew sadly.

"We don't want to have lawsuits. We've no grudge against Tobbins," continued the young man, "but we insist – we *insist* – on an understanding about this Wyde Welt ad. of yours. It's not business."

Carfew agreed. "It's not honest." Carfew agreed again. "It's not dignified."

"Quite right," said Carfew. "And now, what are you going to do about it?"

The young man was taken aback. "It isn't what we're going to do," he said irritably; "it is a question of what you're going to do."

"We're going to do nothing," said Carfew. "My fellow-director" – he indicated the self-possessed girl – "my fellow-director and I have decided that your firm is getting too much business, and we're out to take some of it away."

"You will be sorry," said the young Mr Tempton ominously. "There are developments pending of which you can have no idea. You will be sorry," he said again.

"I know I shall," said Carfew. "I've a tender heart, but I'll bear up."

"Temptons are not going to take this thing lying down," said the infuriated rival.

"I don't know," said Carfew carefully, "how you will do your lying, but I'll look out for your advertisements and find out."

"If there is a law in this land – " said the other passionately.

"There is," said Carfew, "quite a lot – enough to go round – and I warn you, Mr Tempton" – he was very solemn – "I warn you!"

At this outrageous innuendo, Tempton's face went red and white.

"Warn me!" he roared. "What the devil do you mean by warning me?"

"I warn you," repeated Carfew. "I have nothing to add."

Arthur Tempton staggered from the room dazed and bewildered.

"What did you warn him about?" asked the girl, with pardonable curiosity.

"I don't know," said Carfew. "I just warned him. He's bound to have some sin on his conscience. If we followed him, we'd probably find him taking out an extra dog's licence or writing an apologetic letter to the Income Tax Commissioners."

But Arthur Tempton was speeding back to his office, at once annoyed and exhilarated. He was annoyed for obvious reasons;

exhilarated because the Temptons had in hand a more powerful weapon against the new and unscrupulous tactics of their great rival.

Father and son were closeted together for two hours, at the end of which time a secretary was called in, and letters were addressed which began:

"We thank you for your offer of service, which we have pleasure in accepting." They were addressed to Thomas Bernard Tobbin, Albert Augustus Tobbin, to James Tobbin-Smith, to Richard Henry Tobbin – in fact, to all the disgruntled Tobbins in England, who, having lost their means of living without labour, had unanimously, and in a body, offered their services to a rival firm.

"It will cost money, but it will be worth it," said Tempton, Senior. "But we've got to get this fact into our advertisements. We've got to make it clear to all that all that was best and brainiest in the Tobbin firm is now with Temptons. It will ruin Tobbins' business. They depend on old customers."

"Who is going to do the ad.?" asked Arthur thoughtfully.

Mr Tempton, Senior, scratched his head.

"I'm going to try this fellow who's been writing to me so industriously," he said. "The firm is called the Exploitation Publicity Company."

A note to the enterprising firm brought a bright young man to Temptons.

"Here are the facts," said the elder man. "Against each of these gentlemen's names is the position he occupies in our business. You needn't say that they've deserted from Tobbins! that will speak for itself."

"I see," said the bright young man, and returned to his principals.

It made an interesting and attractive page when Mr Tempton saw the proof. It was headed:

TEMPTON'S EXPERTS.

Manager of Temptons' Works:
Thomas Andrew Tobbin.

Manager of Leeds Branch:
Frederic James Tobbin.

Manager of Cardiff Branch:
Richard Henry Tobbin.

And so on through an impressive list.

The advertisement was to appear on Wednesday, the first of a series of insertions.

On Monday the Press of England carried half pages on behalf of Tobbins, Limited. The wording was simple and to the point:

TOBBINS TEACHES THE WORLD.

Not only does Tobbins' produce the Best Boots
that ever shod humanity's Foot,
TOBBINS' WYDE WELTS
("The Boot That Won Waterloo"),
But Tobbins' is the Bootmakers' College of
Learning. You will find
Humble Members
of the Tobbin Family in every Branch of the
Trade, endeavouring to impart The Tobbin Touch.
But the real Tobbin Boot
("The Boot That Won Waterloo")
is Manufactured only by *The* Tobbin Company.

May Tobbin read the advertisement, and was puzzled. Then came Temptons', and she understood.

"How mean!" she stormed. "How Tobbinish! If you hadn't had the foresight – How did you know they were going to put that advertisement in the papers?

"There is very little," said Carfew modestly, "that I do not know. Yet, in this case, it was an accident. It illustrates," he said, directing his bland Sunday-school-superintendent smile at Willetts, "it illustrates the truth of the adage that a little kindness now and then brings profit to the best of men. I help the Exploitation Company; the Exploitation Company helped me."

"But," said the girl, with a troubled frown, "was that quite – "

"Honest?" said Carfew gravely. "I'm afraid it wasn't; in fact, I refused the information, but they insisted. I pointed out how reprehensible it was – how, if it was discovered, they would feel the draught."

The board-room door opened, and Parker came in. He smiled a greeting to the girl.

"They tell me you are making money," he said pleasantly. "I've just met young Tempton. He's going to give you best. As to this young man," he said, turning to Carfew, "he will be a millionaire."

Carfew was deferentially silent. He had a particular desire to hear himself praised before the girl.

"You've no idea how versatile our young friend is," said Parker. "Tobbins – he'll make a fortune here. There's his Exploitation Publicity Company. You make that pay, too, don't you, Carfew?"

"That's a very bad cough of yours, Mr Carfew," said the girl. "Did you feel the draught, too?"

CARFEW – IMPRESARIO

A thousand pounds is a lot of money, but a thousand times a thousand is an unthinkable sum, unless you are a financier, a Chancellor of the Exchequer, or an exceedingly dishonest person.

The easiest way to visualise a million pounds is to reduce it to hundredweights and pounds. Carfew had done that often, but he had never got any further than five figures. They were really four figures that were constantly climbing to the very lip of five, and as constantly slipping down again.

Carfew learnt a lesson which all successful men must learn, namely, that Fate fixes an iron grating across the path of fortune. It may be fixed at the thousand-pound stage, or at the ten thousand, or even the hundred-thousand-pound stage in the rock road. For many of us, alas! it is fixed away down in the foothills of the hundreds.

Try as a man may, with all the prestige and the influence and the good luck which is inseparable from success, he cannot turn that gate upon its hinges till the appointed time. Here he must sit amongst the ninety-nine, patiently, hopefully, uncomplainingly. Woe to him if he shakes the gate or seeks to climb it. Down, down, down he will slip and tumble, battered and bruised and torn. The gates lower down, which bar the progress of lesser men, will obligingly open and let him slip through, and it is well if he misses the altogether miserable, muddy pool on the edge of which all endeavours begin and in the cold depths of which every failure ends.

Let him sprawl into this, and hope of further exercise vanishes; he is expelled from Fortune's Alpine Club. No man climbs wholly by his own endeavour. He is hauled or pushed by fellow climbers, and honourable members of the excelsior brigade sniff at the malodorous figure of failure, and refuse the help of their dainty hands to the grimy and undesirable scarecrow who has taken a course of financial mud-baths.

Carfew was standing in exasperated calm in the 99's; but, stretching his arm through the bars, he could, so to speak, gather the flowers of the '00's, and it was an annoying situation. He was somewhat handicapped by the delusion that he was the only man in the world who had ever been in his trying situation. Anyway, he would not have taken advice, because Carfew never sought advice – he was not poor enough.

It was a distressing position, because, to continue the imagery, there, shining ahead of him, was the golden gate of the million, and Carfew was seized with an insane desire to reach that gate before the clock struck forty.

He went to his broker – not for advice, be it understood. He wanted somebody to approve of him.

"I am making no headway, Parker," he said.

"You're making a steady income," said Parker, "and a steady income is the most progressive movement in the City."

"A steady income is stagnation," said Carfew loudly. "A steady income means too fat at forty. A steady income – "

"We'll cut out the speech," said Parker, "and get to the bright, brisk business."

Carfew frowned at him suspiciously.

"That's very gay talk for a man who wears white spats," he said inconsequently. "Where did you pick it up?"

The middle-aged Parker blushed guiltily and looked out of the window.

"Oh, I don't know," he said vaguely; "one absorbs slang from the office-boy. You were saying, laddie – "

But Carfew was looking at him very hard.

"Laddie?" he repeated wonderingly.

"I'm busy," said Parker. With a look of preoccupation, he dipped his pen in the ink and looked round for something to write upon. "You stand here," he said irritably, "gagging – "

"Gagging?" repeated Carfew in awe. He drew a long breath. "You're on the stage," he said, in a hushed voice. "Oh, Parker, where are you appearing?"

"Rot!" snapped the other.

"You can't be one of the Parker Brothers," ruminated the other, "the thrilling Exponents of Aerial Flight. You can't be Billy Parker, the Brainy Boy, a Terpsichorean Performer on the Big Boot. You aren't Parky Parky, the World's Rare Rythmetic Ragtime Reveller. You're not Cissy Parker, the Pretty and Passable Principal Boy – "

"Oh, shush!" snarled the respectable broker. "If you want to know, I'm behind 'Calumney.' "

"That I will never believe. You don't mean the play?"

The broker nodded.

"Why, it has been running two hundred nights!" said Carfew.

"That's right," said Parker; "I financed it. I don't usually go in for that sort of thing, but I read the play – "

"Two hundred nights!" said Carfew, and there was admiration in his voice. "Why, you devil, you're making money!"

"A little," said Parker, in the complacent tone which meant "much."

"I'm not going out of this office," said Carfew, with determination, "until I find out how much you have made."

Parker raised his eyebrows offensively.

"You don't expect me to tell you my private business, do you?" he asked.

"Yes," said Carfew.

"Well! I'm jolly well not going to," said Parker. "And I'm a busy man. Get a wiggle on you!"

"Parker," cried the outraged Carfew, "restrain yourself! Tell me exactly how this sad affair came about."

Parker rang his bell ostentatiously, and his confidential stenographer came in with a notebook.

"I am going to dictate some private letters," he said pointedly.

"Don't mind me," said Carfew, settling himself in the easiest chair.

"Private letters," repeated Parker.

"I shan't tell anybody," said Carfew; "I'm awfully discreet."

"I'll ring for you in a moment, Miss Simmons," said Parker wearily. And, when the stenographer had gone: "Now, my friend, what do you want to know? There's little to tell. I happened to hear from a literary friend that the play was a good one. I knew that the usual syndicate had rejected it. I was interested, and am still interested, in that white elephant, the Minister Theatre, so I risked a couple of thousand and put it on. It was better than leaving the theatre closed. That's all."

"How much money have you made out of it?" demanded Carfew sternly.

"Oh, twenty thousand – or so," said the broker airily.

"Twenty thousand – or so!"

Carfew heaved a big and significant sigh.

"That's my business," he said, with tremendous emphasis.

"I must warn you" – Parker shook his forefinger of doom in the young man's face – "I must warn you that it was only by the greatest bit of luck that I made good – "

"Cut the scene," said the theatrical Carfew tersely; "it plays too long."

And he departed, his hat tilted on one side, his stick swinging, an impresario to the life.

There was nothing slow about Carfew. He moved like a hurricane. He hailed the first taxi-cab that came into view and ordered the driver to take him to Huggins. Everybody knew Huggins – even a cab-driver knew Huggins. Huggins has an estate agency – none of your "Flats-from-£5-to-£120" agents. He deals in real estates, thinks in shootings, and lets lakes. If you want a theatre or a park or a mountain, you go to Huggins. People who, in the innocence of their hearts, go to him for £80 Bayswater maisonettes are never seen again, or, if they are, are so broken in spirit and humbled in mien, that you may be excused if you overlook them.

Mr Huggins, the original Mr Huggins, is dead. The present Mr Huggins is the fashionable Huggins, the pomaded Mr Huggins. His trousers are creased, his hair is parted in the middle, and he lives in a boudoir into which dukes who want to sell or rent their estates are admitted one by one.

So he impressed one. There was a queue of dukes waiting when Carfew dashed up. "Excuse me, sir," said one of the dukes, as Carfew shamelessly demanded that he should be seen first, "I have been waiting half an hour."

"I've come on business," said Carfew.

The duke, who was an insurance duke, desirous of placing a policy, scowled horribly, and remarked audibly to an earl, who had come for a caretaker's job, that for two pins he'd kick the bounder down the stairs.

"Hello, Hug!" said Carfew, as he entered the room, circumnavigating the spindle-legged furniture. "I want to see you."

"Really, Carfew," murmured the languid Mr Huggins protestingly, "I'm afraid I can't see you without an appointment."

He sniffed a phial of perfume daintily.

"I want a theatre," said Carfew brusquely. "Take that look off your face and come down to life."

"A theatre?"

An unsuspected alertness came upon Mr Adolphus Huggins. He had a theatre; he wished he hadn't. It was a legacy from his father. It had been closed for twelve years. Once upon a time playgoers did not object to turning down side-streets, threading their way through costermongers' barrows, running the gauntlet of a fried fish shop on the right and a pork butcher's on the left, to reach their objective.

This was a long time ago – probably in the days of Shakespeare. In its day, Cander Street, Tottenham Court Road, was a fashionable neighbourhood, and the tide of alien immigration had not arisen, leaving on its doorsteps and beneath its corniced doorways a thin layer of all that may have been best in Poland, but which had undoubtedly deteriorated in transit.

The grimy doors of the New Time Theatre were ugly and discoloured. The iron gates which led to the entrance-court were rusted and broken, the boards affixed thereto, on which stars of the earth had been advertised, and such thrills proclaimed as "Shakespeare's Pathetic and Tragic Drama, 'Hamlet,' followed by that laughable farce, 'Did You Ever Take Your Wife to Peckham?' " which had appealed to the sensibility of the artistic, were now the happy hunting ground of the fly-poster.

"I have a theatre," said Mr Huggins, "a good theatre, and the only theatre available in London just now" – which was true – "and I am prepared to discuss terms with you. For how long will you lease it?"

"How long will it take me to make twenty thousand or so?" asked Carfew.

Mr Huggins looked at him long and compassionately. "About a year," he said softly.

"I'll have a look at it," said Carfew.

Mr Huggins hesitated. "I'd like to have time to brush it up a bit," he said.

Carfew went down to see the theatre next day.

It was slightly soiled, it was dingy, it was without an electric installation, but, to his surprise, the seating accommodation was in good condition. The stage mechanism, too, was workable, though here, again, the absence of electric lighting was a tremendous handicap. Carfew had a quick eye for possibilities. He saw them in the New Time Theatre. He struck a bargain with Huggins – a bargain that took away the other's breath when he came to realise how bad a bargain it was for the owner.

Carfew called in an electrical engineer. "Get some sort of an installation in for the stage," he said. "No fancy work – County Council requirements and nothing else – a good big splash of light in the roof of the auditorium, plugs for the projectors in every part of the house. I'm going to introduce a new art into the theatre. I'm the greatest reformer that ever happened."

Later Carfew sent an identically worded note to every paper in London. It ran:

"I have taken the New Time Theatre. I have taken it because I believe there is room in London for the stupendous art of Frac. Herr Wilhelm Emile Frac is a young Bavarian. His works are unknown; his artistry is the precious possession of the few. His extraordinary lighting schemes, unique and bizarre, have been perfected in the obscurity of his little village. Yet Herr W E Frac, shrinking modestly from publicity, has gained fame amongst those select connoisseurs who can best appreciate his art.

"My friends tell me I shall lose a fortune; I believe that I shall make one. I believe that the brilliancy of Frac's genius will astound, convince, and attract London."

"What is the name of the play?" asked a reporter, a little weary of the omnipotent Frac.

"The play?" said Carfew thoughtfully. "Oh, the play – well, that's rather a secret. In fact," he said, in a burst of confidence, "that is one of the secrets – the greatest secret."

"Who is the author?" demanded another inquisitive scribe.

"That I am not at liberty to say," replied Carfew solemnly; "in fact, he or she desires that the matter should be kept a dead secret. But" – he grew impressive – "if you knew the author's name, you would be in possession of one of the biggest sensations that has ever been published."

"Not – " asked the reporter eagerly.

"Hush!" said Carfew, finger to lips.

As a matter of fact, he had not thought of the play. He dined with Parker on the night of the interview.

"I suppose I ought to get a play?" he said dubiously, in a tone which implied that it was not

a matter which was really important one way or the other.

"You had better," said Parker gently; "the audience might be disappointed. Not even the sight of you in evening dress would be regarded as sufficiently humorous to compensate – "

"I'll write one myself!"

Carfew sprang up, fired with the splendour of the idea.

"Sit down!" begged Parker. "You are dining at my club, and I am responsible for the behaviour of my guests. Besides – oh, I am on the committee."

"I will, by George!" Carfew was bubbling over with inspiration. "Parker, I'll write a play that will set London talking!"

"You've started with my fellow-members," said Parker.

"Waiter!" He called a servant.

"Get Mr Carfew a piece of paper and a pencil. He wants to write a play."

The waiter, with an imperturbable face, bowed and went away.

"I'll put you into it," said Carfew, speaking rapidly. "You shall be a comic old man who marries the cook, who poisoned her master's dinner because she was hypnotised by a rajah whose sacred idol had been stolen by the master when he was in India. But you see through it – "

"Through India?"

"Don't be stupid – no."

"Ah, I see," said Parker, nodding, "through the idol – it's a crystal idol."

"That's an idea," said Carfew enthusiastically, "a crystal idol, stolen from a palace – "

"A crystal palace?"

But Carfew was scribbling furiously. One piece of paper was not enough for his needs; another sheet was sent for, another and another, then –

"Bring all the paper there is in the club, Robert, if there is as much," said Parker seriously; and Robert, who knew his Mr Parker, replied as gravely.

It may be said that never since the day when Lucullus dined with Lucullus had one man enjoyed his own company so much as Carfew enjoyed Carfew. As for Parker, he was a screen to reflect the brilliancy of his guest, a background to throw him into relief, a modern chorus to cry heartily, "Aye, aye, my lord!" or, in the sadder mood, "Oh, horror! Oh, horror!"

141

The play, the plot, and the cast underwent startling revolutions in the course of the dinner. In describing the evening to a confidant, Parker said: "The play began as a comic opera without music; by the time we got to the joint, it was a roaring farce… We had coffee in the smoking-room, and Carfew brought tears to my eyes as he described the death of little Rolando da Sforza, the natural son of the Duke of Milan, poisoned by Lucretia Borgia, who was jealous of the influence wielded by Beatrice D'Este over her husband, the Duke of Ferrara."

Parker preserved a scrap of the original dialogue.

Lucretia (entering drawing-room with a cup of poison): So at last I have you in my power.

Beatrice (looking up from her knitting): Hello, Lu! (With a weary gesture) You might ring for tea. I've got a thirst I would not sell for money. Hast thou seen Il Moro, my husband?

Lucretia (concealing poison behind piano): Nay. Did'st thou expect him? I suppose he's gallivanting about town with Lucretia Civilla, as usual. Ha! ha! ha! (sneers).

Beatrice: Dry up, Lu! You are always trying to make mischief.
[*Enter Mary with tray.*]
Put it down, Mary; don't fuss around. Get out, wench!

Mary: Yes, ma'am. The butcher called. Will you have chop or sausages?

Lucretia (aside): My chance! (Aloud) Methinks I would like to see those sausages, dear Beat, for are not the sausages of Milan famous all over the world? Prithee, girl, bring them.
[*Exit Mary.*]
Beatrice: You take an interest in my affairs, Lu?

Lucretia (carelessly): Oh, yes, I am considered quite a connoisseur of sausages.
[*Re-enter Mary with sausages on a golden tray.*]
Ah, yes! (She empties cup of poison over them surreptitiously.) At last! At last!
[CURTAIN.]

Carfew sat up that night to finish the play, then, thoroughly exhausted, he went to bed. He woke up at five o'clock in the afternoon, had a bath, and settled himself down to the enjoyment of reading his work. He read it through very carefully, then he read it again, then he laid the play, sheet by sheet, on the fire and watched it melt.

And somehow, with the burning of the play, a doubt as to his own wisdom arose. The papers which remarked upon his enterprise had damned it with praise so faint that one needed an ear trumpet to distinguish it.

All Carfew's friends who knew anything about theatrical matters – and it seemed he had not a friend who wasn't an expert – told him he was mad. They said this sadly or cheerfully or offensively, according to their several temperaments, but they were equally definite.

And time went on. He had not arranged for a play; he had engaged no company.

The theatre distressed him to tears. The unsavoury approaches, the neighbourhood, the impossibility of the whole thing oppressed him.

The New Time Theatre was flanked and faced by gloomy houses which at one time had accommodated snug *bourgeoisie*. Chairs had waited at these doorways to carry bewigged gentlemen to Lord Mayoral receptions; linkmen had diced away the weary hours of waiting before these portals. Now twenty families occupied each home. Broken windows were patched with paper, bare rooms echoed to the shrill and unintelligible voice of the alien child. Poverty, grim and uncleanly, lurked in the deep, unlighted basements, or strove vainly on top attics against the ravening wolf of hunger. Cander Street was a street of despair, a street of sin and sorrow, a stark, bleak street of hungry ugliness.

Carfew went down to the theatre one night to meet an unfortunate young scenic artist and to inspect the electric installation.

The artist was voluble and keen, in contrast to Carfew, who was gloomy and calculating. His calculations took the shape of working out the amount of money it would require to clear out of the business.

Usually he did not "clear out" of a business except with a profit to himself. He had cleared out of a certain Tobbins, Limited, a fairly rich man.

An idea struck him just as he was entering the theatre with the scene-painter. This Tobbins enterprise had brought him into touch with a singular girl. She had been his co-director in the great undertaking, and had acquitted herself well – for a girl. He went into the dusty box office and wrote a note. This he dispatched by taxi-cab to Dulwich, with instructions to wait for a reply.

His inspection of the lighting arrangements cheered him up. He switched on the footlights, darkened the gaunt stage, turned it blue and red and orange by the mere clicking of switches, and felt he was getting some of his money's worth.

He turned on all the lights of the auditorium and turned them off again; he manipulated the electric "limes" which he had had placed in the gallery, the dress circle, and the boxes. He experimented with every tint and colour he had at hand, and passed two pleasant and elevating hours in the amusement.

He came out into the vestibule, taking a tolerant view of the impetuosity which had landed him in a somewhat expensive position. He was in time to welcome a slim and pretty girl who came half running through the vestibule with outstretched hand. "It is good of you to come," he said.

"It is," she agreed, "remembering that you have so shockingly neglected me."

"Affairs," he said. He waved his hand wearily. He was weighted at once with the destinies of humanity. He was the busiest man in Europe, the sought and the pursued, the dictator to innumerable secretaries, the shaper of industrial policies. In that wave of the hand you saw, if you were willing, the crowded ante-room where sat the princes of commerce awaiting momentous interviews; you saw the presses of London working day and night on Carfew's prospectuses; you heard the buzzing of Wheatstone instruments transmitting cipher despatches from one foreign minister to another, and heard the dried-pea rustle of wireless words, waking the silence of oceans. You saw all this, if you were willing. May Tobbin was quite unwilling.

"You're a funny boy," she said. "You and your affairs! I've read about this." She nodded menacingly at the discoloured door of the dress circle. "Whatever made you do it?"

"Oh, this," said Carfew contemptuously – "this is just a – er – sideline – a little hobby."

She made no reply, but walked into the dress circle, Carfew following.

"Sit down by me," she invited, "and tell me the truth. You will be telling yourself something you haven't heard since the days of Tobbins, Limited."

Carfew began on the heroic note, continued flamboyantly, reached, under her calm and patient cross-examination, the level of cold fact.

"So you've got the worst theatre in London," she summarised the situation, "situated in the worst slum in the West End. You have no play, no players, no ideas worth tuppence" – Carfew winced – "nothing but some pretty lights and pieces of coloured glass."

"I haven't told you my great idea," protested Carfew.

"You haven't," she admitted, "and you needn't invent it on the spur of the moment."

They stood in silence, cogitating the position. In this silence, they became aware of the presence of a third party, the young scenic artist.

"Oh, yes," said Carfew awkwardly, for him, "I promised you that I would give a definite order – well – "

He glanced despairingly at the girl, but she was too absorbed to assist him.

"Now, suppose," said Carfew, still keeping his eye on May Tobbin, "suppose we have a castle scene, high mountains and things, and snow."

Still he received no encouragement from the slim figure that had seated itself in the one chair which the hall boasted. Her brow was knit in a frown, and she had clasped one knee in a very frenzy of thought.

"Suppose – " began Carfew.

She glanced round thoughtfully. Standing by the door was an old man, whose general dinginess and dilapidation was in keeping with the character of the building, which, for a miserable twenty-five shillings a week, it was his duty to cherish.

"What is his name?" she asked, in a low voice.

"He answers to the name of George," said Carfew; "but I am not certain if that is his name."

"George," she called, and the old man started violently and came towards her, the keys of the building in his hand.

"Closin' up now, miss?" he said hopefully.

"No. I want to speak to you. Do you know this neighbourhood?" she asked.

"Know it?" George smiled, as Lucifer might smile if anybody had asked him whether he used a sulphur bag for rheumatism. "Know it?"

"I gather you do," said the girl. "Tell me, do you ever have people here – nice people?"

George scratched his head. "I've lived in this neighbourhood," he began, "for nigh on forty-three years come October 28 – "

"We don't want the story of your life, George," said Carfew. "Do you know the neighbourhood, and do nice people come here?"

"Slummers," said George, "only slummers. We have had princesses down here – you've heard tell of the Blanket an' Coal League? – but, bless your heart, they don't come now; it's out of fashion, slummin' is."

"I thought so," said the girl, clapping her hands. "That is capital."

She swung round on the young painter.

"Paint a scene, a real good one, representing this street."

"Cander Street?"

She nodded vigorously.

"Cander Street," she said, "and an interior of Cander Street – the most wretched hovel you can find – and an attic of Cander Street – three strong scenes. You understand?"

She spoke rapidly, excitedly, and Carfew watched her in perplexity.

"Lock up, George," she said briskly. "Come along, Mr Carfew; we're going to write a play."

"The story of the play itself," wrote the dramatic critic of *The Daily Post Messenger*, "calls for little notice. Well acted as it is, with the extraordinary lighting effects by M. Frac, it brings home to the spectator something of the conditions of life in the foreign quarters of London – something of the conditions in which the underworld live.

"It was a bold attempt on the part of Mr Carfew to rename the theatre 'The Slum,' bolder still to portray the life of the very street in which the theatre is situated. It gave, and gives, fashionable London an opportunity of slumming without the discomforts and risks attendant upon that one-time fashionable practice. 'The Other Way,' despite its poor dramatic quality, will continue to draw crowded houses. The scene between Pepita and Lorenzo and the waif is the best thing in the play. But undoubtedly what appeals, and will appeal, to the playgoer is the novelty of the production – the programme girls in picturesque tatters, the pallid green lights over the entrance... Amongst those present were the Duke and Duchess of Wellfort – her Grace is the President of the Blanket and Coal League, which has done so much for this district – the Earl of Collborough, the Penservian Ambassador, and the Countess Czectiovic... The bookings are tremendous, and Her Serene Highness the Princess Pauline of Saxe-Gratz and suite will be present at tonight's performance."

CARFEW PRODUCES

There is an uninteresting part to every theatre – a part which is so isolated from the luxury of the auditorium and from the glamour and mystery of the stage as to be associated with neither. It is usually reached from a frowsy little side street through an ugly, narrow entrance. The stone stairs are steep, and the flagged landings are restricted to the accommodation of one portly tenor and a large soprano. As many as four juvenile "leads" have passed one another on these dismal gas-lit spaces; but then juvenile "leads " are notoriously thin and willowy and supple, and it is possible, by flexion and an adroit manipulation of bodies, for quite a number of juvenile "leads" of both sexes to pass and repass in the most confined spaces with no other misadventure than the catching of a loose hook in an astrakhan collar or the mysterious whitening of a politely-raised sleeve, due probably to the brushing against a damask cheek in passing.

No doors lead from stairway or landing. The walls are solid and unpromising. They are dull yellow, and have a make-believe dado of dull red, with an inch-deep black line to mark where wall and dado meet.

You climb and climb till you reach a door which ungraciously says "Manager, Private." Other information is occasionally displayed on a hanging card or on type-written notices recklessly pasted upon the panels of the door. These are to the effect that callers can only be seen by appointment, that silence is to be regarded as a polite form of refusal, that artistes will be kept to the strict terms of their contracts, and that gagging of a political character will be permitted.

The particular theatre which is dealt with here is in Wraybourn Street, London, West Central. It is the Gorgon, and the inevitable flight of stairs from the inevitable side-street leads to an office which, in addition to the announcements of which an assortment is given above, bore at the time covered by this narrative the magic words "Mr Felix Carfew."

His office was a small one. It conveyed the impression to anyone who had mounted the breathless stairs that it was hardly worthwhile. It had been papered daringly, by an earlier occupant, with a pattern which was unnecessarily busy. That this was the well-head of Art was indicated by the ceiling decorations, for a chromographic Cupid lounged on a couple of convenient clouds and amused himself, as boys will, by aiming a pink dart at Carfew's blue tobacco jar.

Carfew himself was an impresario.

He wore a tall, shiny hat on the back of his head, and lavender spats. The walls and the mantelshelf – on which reposed the tobacco jar aforesaid – were covered with unframed photographs.

Carfew had emerged from the chrysalis of management. A young man of sanguine temperament who finds a three hundred night success at the first time of asking may be excused the conviction that "failure" is a word which Fate has obligingly expunged from the lexicon of life.

Carfew had taken the Gorgon Theatre without one single doubt as to the wisdom of his proceedings. Parker, who was his broker, broke the habits of a lifetime and came westward in the forenoon, at Carfew's earnest request.

He climbed the interminable stairs, examined with great earnestness the notices pasted to Carfew's door, and found his client in his important occupation.

"Sit down, Parker," said the young man. "I'm frightfully busy, but I can give you ten minutes."

Parker, who knew his Carfew, ignored the impertinence.

"Well," he asked, "have you quarrelled with your leading lady yet?"

Carfew's smile exactly blended the qualities of pity and superiority which is calculated to reduce the person to whose subjugation it is directed to a condition of pulp.

"There's a lot of nonsense talked about the stage," he said. "The manager of the Oedipus told me today that he'd been two months casting a play. I cast mine in four hours."

"Perhaps he isn't as clever as you," reflected the unimpressed Parker, rubbing his chin with the gold head of his walking-stick.

Carfew eyed him severely. "There is no 'perhaps' about it," he said; "it's a question of instinct and intuition. I was born with the stage sense, Parker; it's a gift – you can't cultivate it. It grows with you."

"With you," corrected Parker, "not with me, I am happy to say."

"I cast the play in four hours," said Carfew complacently. "I took a trip from London to Margate by steamer, and did the whole thing between Old Swan Pier and the Pavilion."

"Who is your producer?" said Parker.

"I am producing 'Wastepaper' myself," said Carfew, with an assumption of carelessness. "After all, as I say, the stage sense is born with one; it is a divine gift."

Parker made a disrespectful noise.

"I've always thought you were a born something," he said crudely.

Carfew had chosen his play with some care. It was a problem play. It was the sort of play which, in book form, would have been barred at the libraries. "It dealt with life," explained Carfew enthusiastically – "real life that ordinarily is never touched upon save by daring Sunday newspapers with a large and decadent reading public."

The author was unknown.

"Theophilus Grudge," said Carfew impressively. "Have you ever heard of him?"

"No," confessed Parker. "Is it a man?"

"The name of Theo Grudge," said Carfew, in a voice shaken by emotion, "will ring through London. He has the original view. This play may not be popular. I do not aim at popularity. My object is to raise the theatrical art."

Parker yawned insolently.

The play, went on Carfew, was about two women and a man. One of the women loved the man, and the other was married to him. It was very sad. Then came another man who heard that the first man was a convict, and told his wife. The wife said "Ah!" and clutched her throat. Then the second man went to the lady who loved the first man, and told her, and she said "Ah!" too, but clutched his throat. Then the first man came in and said, "What does this mean?" to his wife, and she said, "I know all – all – all!"

"Ah!" said Parker thoughtfully. "Then it's not a musical comedy?"

Carfew choked. "It's a play," he said shortly, "which will pull all London."

Parker maintained his attitude of studied politeness.

"In the meantime," he said, "I am not sure whether you're pulling my leg or not. I think the best thing you can do is to get a little humour into it. Who is rehearsing it, by the way?"

"I am," said Carfew, with a cough.

"Ah, yes," said Parker offensively.

It is the easiest thing in the world to produce a play for a London audience, and "Wastepaper" was no exception. You simply assemble your company, hand the members their parts, and there you are. The responsibility thereafter lies very largely with Providence.

Carfew's view of life was that all the past had been ordered for his comfort.

Thus Edison had been born on a certain day in order that he might have his many electric appliances ready against Carfew reaching maturity. Stephenson had worked with no other object in view than that he should have railways shipshape by the time Carfew could afford to travel first class. Marconi – But why enumerate the folk who owed their existence and their fame to the fact that they were necessary to Carfew's well-being?

Carfew was a theatrical manager by accident. He had produced a play which had fluked a success. Carfew took credit for the joyful result, for the division of responsibility as between Carfew and Providence was so arranged that, if things turned out well, Carfew had succeeded in spite of Providence, and if they failed, they had failed in spite of Carfew.

He walked down the stone stairs after Parker had left, passed through a narrow passage, through innumerable iron-guarded doorways, and came to a large, open space of flooring which sloped gradually down to a congested border of electric bulbs. Beyond this was a dark and cheerless auditorium sheeted with holland.

The stage – for such it was, and it will serve no useful purpose to deceive you – was occupied by some dozen ladies and gentlemen. They wore ordinary clothing. The ladies wore furs and veils, and such as were on speaking terms with one another were discussing their former triumphs, each taking no notice whatever of anything the other said, but waiting for an opening which would allow them to continue their own stories which the other had so meanly interrupted.

"…I couldn't find my make-up anywhere, so I just dabbed a bit of powder on my nose and walked on. The play was going badly till then, but from the moment I stepped on to the stage it just woke up. There were three curtains after the first act…"

"Of course I had to gag. She was fluffing all over the shop – didn't know a line, my dear. If it hadn't been for me, the play would have been a dead failure. They called me in front six times, and naturally she was as wild – "

"I had to take on the part at ten minutes' notice, and learn my lines during the waits. I don't know how it is, but I seem to have the gift of acting… The papers were full of it the next morning."

Carfew heard the scraps with growing irritation. Nothing annoyed him more than egotism in people. His ideas of the stage had undergone an extraordinary revolution since his first association with the men and women who claimed it as their profession. They were so stupid; they listened to him with such evident boredom; they had so few interests, and knew so little about the world.

They had received his story of how he had saved Europe from war, by his dexterous handling of the German Ambassador, with polite "Oh, yeses!" and "How wonderfuls!" They had listened with patient weariness to his account of how he preserved the Spanish succession, and it was only when he spoke of the immense sums of money which he had made by the exercise of his qualities that they regarded him with the admiring interest which a small and select gathering of the Munchausen Lodge might have displayed toward Past Grand Master Ananias.

"Now, ladies and gentlemen," said Carfew briskly, "we will run through the first act. Clear the stage, please! Enter the Duke of Bulberry."

The Duke of Bulberry, a pale young man in a straw hat, took farewell of his friends in one comprehensive glance and retired to the wings. Here he rid himself of his inertia and came back briskly.

"Nine o'clock!" he said, addressing the melancholy stalls. "She promised to be 'ere by eight. Well, you can never trust a woman to keep an appointment."

Carfew raised his hand. "Where did you get that line from?" he demanded.

The Duke looked across at him with a pained expression. "I put that in, Mr Carfew," he said patiently. "It's a line that always gets a laugh."

Carfew breathed heavily. "You're not supposed to get a laugh," he said. "You are a tragic duke. You have lost money – you don't joke about such things. Please speak the lines that the gods – that the author has given you. And be careful about your h's."

The duke stiffened. "I 'ope," he said, with a touch of hauteur, "that I can speak the King's English, Mr Carfew. I 'aven't been told durin' my eight years' experience on the stage, both legitimate and the 'alls, that I've transgressed the bounds, so to speak. I've played the leading artistes of the day. I've been a top liner on the bill at the leadin' vaudeville – "

"Go on with the part, please," said Carfew.

The young man drew a long breath. "It is now nine o'clock," he said, "and she 'as not come! What can keep 'er? Ah, 'ere she is!"

"Come on, Miss Tilby," said Carfew. But Miss Tilby at that moment was explaining to an envious small-part lady the extraordinary fascination which she wielded over provincial audiences.

"Miss Tilby – Miss Tilby!"

In various tones, from the indignant one of Carfew to the gentler admonitory of her dearest friend, the presence of Miss Tilby was demanded.

She came on the stage a little flurried.

"Sorry," she said.

"Ah, 'ere she is!" said the Duke encouragingly.

"Why, duke," said Miss Tilby, coming forward on the stage and offering a gloved hand, "I have kept you waiting! But I've been to visit a poor woman, and it is better that dukes should wait than that the poor should suffer."

"In the name of heaven," said Carfew, pale but determined, "who told you to say that? It's not in the play, and it's nothing whatever to do with the play."

"I put it in, Mr Carfew," said the lady coldly. "It seems to me that this play wants strengthening up a bit, and it's a line that always gets the hand in the provinces."

"Cut it out," said Carfew.

Miss Tilby shrugged her beautiful shoulders.

"If I don't know what makes a play – " she began.

"You don't," said Carfew brutally.

"I know a great deal more than you," flamed the girl. "Mr Carfew, let me tell you that I am the idol of the provinces. I play to more money than any other lady in the business. When I was in Wolverhampton, they ran special trains to bring the people into the town to hear me. And I'm not going to be spoken to as if I was the dust beneath your feet!"

"I – " said Carfew.

"I am the idol of the provinces!" she went on, with an angry sob in her voice. "I've played in America, South Africa, and Australia. Merciful heavens, that I should have come to this!"

"You can say this," said Carfew to the representative of *The Dramatic News*, "that the idea of 'Wastepaper' being a problem play is quite erroneous. It is a forceful drama – in fact, by certain standards it is a melodrama. After all, is not melodrama the very essence of dramatic presentation? The scene where the duke throws the heroine into the Seine, and she is rescued by the hero disguised as a gendarme, is going to be the thrill of London."

The reporter went away, and Carfew returned thoughtfully to the stage. It wanted a fortnight to the opening, and his leading lady had thrown up her part, and, so far, no other leading lady had pleased him. Unless, of course –

A girl who was sitting on the angry waves which distinguished the second act, rose as he walked on to the stage. She showed her even white teeth in a smile.

"Hullo!" said Carfew, brightening up. "You're Miss Carrington, aren't you?"

"That's me," she said brightly. "I got your phone message. What do you want?"

He explained that Miss Tilby had left him. She was quite unsuitable for the part; she hadn't the voice or the presence or the manner. She couldn't "get it over the footlights." He did not say that Miss Tilby had thrown up the part. He was representing the managerial side of the business, and from that aspect a leading lady never throws up – she is just unsuitable and cannot "get it over."

The girl stared at him seriously as he outlined the plot, then shook her head regretfully.

"Drama isn't in my line," she said. "I'm straight comedy. Why don't you make it straight comedy? Cut out the murder in the second act and take them to Paris. I could do a solo dance that would bring the house down. Really, even straight comedy is a bit out of my line."

"My dear girl – " began Carfew, but she stopped him.

"Listen to me, Bright Eyes," she said kindly, laying her hand on his arm. "Your old play won't run two weeks. The public doesn't want murder – it wants amusement. Try it as a straight comedy – a foreign nobleman courting an American heiress, and all that sort of thing."

Carfew sent for his business manager.

"Have you put out the billing?" he asked. His business manager, who was known as Frank, and had apparently no other name, nodded familiarly.

"What have you called 'Wastepaper'?" asked Carfew.

Frank looked round the room for inspiration.

"We've called it 'Wastepaper,' " he said cautiously.

"Don't get funny with me!" roared Carfew. "Is it a tragedy, a drama, or a farce?"

Frank drew himself up. "It is called a 'play,' Mr Carfew," he said stiffly, "and I'd like to say that I'm not used to being addressed in this manner you employ. I've been managing houses now for twenty years, and I'm supposed to be the very best man in the profession. I've refused good offers to come to you. Every proprietor in London is after me."

"They've got you," said Carfew bitterly.

A pale and haggard Carfew sat in the stalls a week before the opening. His hands were pushed into his trousers pockets, his silk hat was on the back of his head.

A weary orchestra glared back at him with malice and resentment, but Carfew did not care.

The leading lady stood by the footlights, her hand on her hips, and scowled at him, and the remainder of the company stood around, looking at each other with significant smiles.

"Say," said the lady by the footlights, "you don't expect me to come on after the comedy scene?"

Carfew nodded.

"Well, you can have your part," said the lady. "I don't wonder Miss Carrington threw it up."

She spoke excitedly, and with an accent which told of a youth spent in an exclusive seminary in Portland, Maine.

"You understand, Mr Care-few, that I star in my country. I was the idol o' Broadway and the best-known actress in the Eastern States. An' if you think I'm going to stand for having my entrance killed – "

Carfew rose slowly to his feet.

"Miss van Ryan," he said, "to please you I've turned this play into a musical comedy, to please you I've engaged a ragtime chorus and dressed the play regardless of expense. If there is any other suggestion you care to make, just slip it across."

"Say," she cried, and leant across the footlights, "can't I make my entrance from the orchestra?"

Carfew laughed long and wildly.

"Make it from the roof, Amelia," he said.

The dress rehearsal of "The Wastepaper Girl" was not an immense success. Ever and anon the new American producer would say from the stage:

"How did it go?"

And as ever, Carfew would reply hollowly: "Rotten!"

The Duke of Bulberry was out of voice. His entrance song:

> "Though I am a duke,
> It is only a fluke
> That I managed the title to snaffle.
> My young cousin Fred
> Fell out of bed,
> And I won the rank in a raffle,"

did not "get over."

Then the new beauty chorus went all agley. Carfew distinctly saw three girls pointing their right toes when they should have been jiggling their left toes. And the leading comedian forgot his lines about Home Rule, and the second comedian said:

"Why, who is coming this way? By jove, it is Lydia Kinsella!" (Chord.)

The latest leading lady – she was English – was annoyed.

"You don't expect me to drift on to the stage like a piece o' paper, do you?" she asked wrathfully. "I want people to know who I am. I've played in the best theatres in England – "

"And you're the idol of Birmingham," said Carfew savagely, "and the police stop the traffic when you start singing. I know all about it. Give her a chord, Aleck."

This to the weary conductor, the only friend Carfew had by this time.

The first act proceeded, the second act was worse.

In the end Carfew made a little speech.

"Ladies and gentlemen," he said, "after this play has been produced, I hope you will all keep in touch with me, I am particularly anxious to mail you a verbatim account of my bankruptcy proceedings. In my evidence before the Official Receiver, I shall mention you all by name, and explain how much acting, singing, and dancing each one of you contributed to my failure. Good night!"

"The Wastepaper Girl" was obviously a success. Carfew knew that he was in for a long run before the curtain finally fell, before the frantic calls for "Author!" brought him to the footlights.

He supped with Parker that night.

"What I like about your play," said Parker, "is its uplifting quality. Never, in one play, have I seen anything so moving. Seriously, Carfew, you are rather a wonder. How do you do these things?"

"Parker," said Carfew solemnly, "I am the best producer in Europe. I've got Reinhardt lashed to the mast. I'm the idol of the profession, and the people will do anything for me. I just know what the public want, and I go for it. Do you get me, Steve?"

"I get you," said Parker, without exactly comprehending what he was getting.

WHY GELDEN MADE A MILLION

In the days when Carfew was living on the verge of poverty, he knew a man named Gelden.

Not a pleasant man, by any means, because he had habits which are not pleasant to nice men. He associated with people who did not move in the best of circles, and he drank more than was good for an ambitious junior reporter. For ambitious he was, this lantern-jawed, lank youth, with his crudities of speech and his scarcely hidden brutality.

Gelden lived with his invalid sister and his widowed mother in the days when he and Carfew had been reporters on *The Dallington Times and Herald*, and Carfew had boarded with them. Mrs Gelden had an income derived from an investment in Consolidated Funds, and it is probable that she accepted Carfew as a boarder at a ridiculous tariff because she stood in some fear of this wild scapegoat of a son. How far her fears were justified, Carfew learnt later.

Gelden lived in the faith that the future held a fortune for him, and he lived up to his expectations.

One day he came to Carfew – newly established in London – and borrowed twenty-five pounds. A month later Carfew learnt that his former landlady was taking the boarding-house business seriously, for with Carfew's twenty-five had disappeared almost all the unfortunate woman's capital. Gelden had had a scheme – one of many – for getting rich quick, and had cashed his mother's Consols and vanished with the money.

That was years before this story opened. At the period of which I write, things were not going as well with Carfew as he wished them to go. His investments had proved speculations, and his speculations were, of necessity, investments.

"Of necessity," because he found that the stocks he had bought at six to sell at seven, were quite unsaleable at four. There was nothing for it but to lock away these jumpers that would not jump until the great miracle day when all stocks reach for the sky, and the only thing which is flat and unprofitable is the "bear" who has sold short.

If there is one person in this bright and lovely world whom Carfew did not wish to meet at this moment of adversity, it was Gelden, and since Carfew's luck was freezing the mercury, you may not need telling that Gelden was the very man who came hideously on the skyline and refused to harmonise with the landscape.

Carfew was in his office one day, totting up his losses on 'Change. He had the arithmetic of the optimist, which is the science of counting nine as ten on the profit side, and omitting to count it at all when it lay under the "Dr" symbol. He was ever the apostle of the "round figure" system. A gain of nine thousand six hundred was in round figures ten thousand. A loss of nine thousand eight hundred was by simple adjustment a loss of nine thousand.

His banker, who was a born Jonah, had worked out Carfew's position into four places of decimals, and Carfew hated the bank manager for his cruelty.

The young financier threw his passbook into a drawer, banged the drawer into its place, and hunched back into his chair with a scowl which expressed his entire disapproval of existence as he found it.

It was at that solemn moment, when disaster was written so plainly, and when the only physical effort he seemed capable of making was the drawing of impossible old men upon his blotting pad, that the vision of Gelden obtruded itself.

There was a confident knock at the door.

"Come in!" said Carfew sternly.

A man stood in the doorway – a self-confident young man, who was, perhaps, twenty-eight, and who certainly looked forty. He was dressed a little extravagantly. The pearl pin in his cravat was just a shade too large. The spats which covered his glossy shoes should, by the strictest canons of fashion, have been of some other design than shepherd's plaid; and his entrance coincided with the arrival of a delicate and subtle odour of violets.

Carfew frowned up at him. This was not the Gelden he knew. The man's face was lined and seamed and sallow. There were little pouches under his tired eyes, his cheeks were hollow, and the hand that removed the amber and gold cigar-holder from his teeth shook a little.

His manner was buoyant enough as he stepped forward with a little grin and extended a lemon glove-covered hand.

"My dear boy!" he said. And Carfew, annoyed by the patronage in the tone, and impressed by the evident prosperity in the other's appearance, indicated a chair.

It was five years since Theodore Gelden had borrowed twenty-five pounds, at a moment when twenty-five pounds was a lot of money. Theodore was buying Siberian oil-fields with Carfew's good gold, and incidentally with his mother's pitiably small capital. I forget whether he was on the verge of clearing two millions profit or four. It was something fabulous, and all that was required to complete the impending negotiations were those twenty-five pounds. And Carfew lent them. And Carfew never saw Theodore again, or saw a prospectus, or smelt the faint, musty smell of oil, or heard one word in the Siberian language which might convey to him a sense of part proprietorship in that wonderful country. The oil-fields of Tomskovski faded away like a quivering mirage.

"Here we are," said Theodore, comfortably stretching his impressive feet.

"Here *you* are," retorted Carfew, in a noncommittal tone.

Suddenly Gelden straightened himself.

"By the way," he said.

He had a trick of employing inconsequent phrases, and his conversation was a very patchwork of speech. His gloved hand sought an inside pocket. From this he withdrew a large, flat pocket-book of green Russian leather, bordered and bound and initialled in gold. This he opened, and from a pocket therein extracted a flat pad of notes.

"Have you change for a hundred?" he asked, and peeled a thin, crinkly sheet from the mass.

Carfew took the note. There was no doubt as to its genuineness. That admirable institution, the Bank of England, through its chosen official, promised to pay on demand to the man who earned or stole this wonder-working slip of paper one hundred golden sovereigns.

"I owe you something," said Gelden carelessly. "Fifty?"

"Twenty-five," said Carfew. "I can give you a cheque for the balance."

Gelden replaced his pocket-book.

"Send it round to my hotel," he said, and relapsed into his attitude of ease.

Carfew was interested. He was always interested in people who had large sums of money.

Gelden watched him lazily.

"Things a-booming?" he asked. Carfew nodded gravely. "I've several things on hand," he said. "I'm interested in a new hotel, I've a concession in Bulgaria, timber, and that sort of thing."

Gelden chuckled. "Small," he said, and snapped his long, unshapely fingers. "Tiny – petty. Look at me!"

Carfew was looking.

"I've told you I'd be a millionaire," said Gelden. "A million or nothing, eh? How often have I said that?"

Carfew said nothing. He was thinking that the change from the hundred-pound note might with advantage go to the wronged mother, unless this son of hers indicated restitution.

Gelden had an uncanny knack of reading the thoughts of people.

"You're thinking of the mater," he said easily. "I suppose you know I ruined her? But, my boy, I've been cruel to be kind – she's a rich woman."

His smile of triumph, the sense of information suppressed which his attitude conveyed, were all imposing. Carfew was impressed.

"Getting along," said Gelden, and rose abruptly. He scanned the face of a gold chronometer which he extracted from his left-hand waistcoat pocket, pursed his lips as if dissatisfied with the inspection, and produced another gold chronometer from his right-hand pocket.

"One moment," said Carfew softly, when the other's hand was on the door-knob. "You haven't told me anything about yourself."

Gelden frowned a little. "I made a million out of tin," he said simply. "I am now making another million out of rubber."

Carfew was speechless. The man spoke with such conviction, was so evidently speaking the truth. Moreover, he referred to a million with such insolent familiarity that there was no wonder Carfew found himself a little breathless.

For he himself had secret ambitions concerning millions, vaporous nebulae of hopes and doubts which might, by the alchemy of time, solidify into a material something expressible in seven figures.

Gelden was watching him.

"I could make you a millionaire in a week," he said, and, returning to the chair he had vacated, he sat down and began to talk.

A taxi-cab carried Carfew to his broker, and Mr Parker forgot to be facetious as he entered. To a question Carfew put he replied readily.

"If one may judge by his style of living," he said, "there's no doubt about his having made a fortune, though I doubt very much if it is a million. Gelden has been bulling tin. He does a little business through Transome and Cole, but the bulk of his buying has been through some other firm."

"Am I to follow him in his oil speculations?"

Parker shook his head.

"I say 'No,' but I am aware that I may be advising you against your best interests. There is pretty sure to be an oil boom, but whether it is coming now or in ten years' time it is impossible to say."

Carfew bought a few oil shares cautiously, and that night dined with Gelden at the "Celvoy."

"It's dead easy," said Mr Gelden over coffee. "You've only to ask yourself sane questions. I ask myself questions. One: What will the traffic of the world be carried upon? Answer – Rubber. I bought rubber. Now I say: What is the motor power of the future? Answer – Oil. I buy oil. Everybody's nibbling at it. The big men who know most are hesitating because they're risking more; the little men wait for the big men. I know."

Gelden spoke with some reason. In a week from that evening London was in the delirium of an oil boom. On 'Change they call it the Gelden boom to this day. It was Gelden who amalgamated the Banker Fields with the Southern Odessa concern; Gelden who put Steam Oil up to six; Gelden who smashed the corner in West African Wells.

Carfew saw little of him. Now and again the young man would drop into his office, throw out disjointed comments on the condition of the market, and as abruptly as he had arrived he would go, without a word of farewell, save a slurred "S'long!" as he vanished through the swing doors of Carfew's suite.

Carfew was making money in little sums. He cleared three hundred pounds out of Bankers, and one thousand one hundred pounds from the phenomenal rise in Steam Oils.

What Gelden was making was conjectural. Parker shook his head when Carfew put the question.

"It isn't what he's making," he said gravely; "it is what he has behind him that is puzzling me. Do you realise that he should be in a position to produce two millions in liquid assets?"

"Can he?"

"His broker says he can find four," said Parker.

There was a long silence, the two men looking at one another across the table.

"He arrived in May from nowhere," said Parker, consulting a little table which he had compiled. "Beyond the fact that he seemed to have plenty of money, and made no secret of his having made a million in oil, I cannot discover anybody who had dealings with him before that date. And here is a curious circumstance: Gelden says he made a fortune in oil prior to May, but there has been no big market in oil before May."

Parker might have his doubts, and Carfew his misgivings, but the very apparent fact was that Gelden went from big to bigger things. His photograph was a daily occurrence in the papers. His house in Grosvenor Square was purchased on a Monday; on the Tuesday it was in the hands of three hundred decorators; on the Thursday it was furnished by eight of the greatest furnishing houses, each supplying the articles which the others had not in stock.

He bought seven motorcars in one week, and purchased at a cost of eighty-three thousand pounds, the steam yacht *Terra Incognita* from the Earl of Dambert.

London was oil mad. However important might be the news which monopolised the contents bill, be sure there was a subsidiary line: "Oil Boom – Latest," to supply the needs of the frenzied investors.

And Gelden had done this, Gelden the Magnificent, who had appeared over the horizon as violently as a tropic sun; Gelden the unknown, who had fallen into the City an unknown millionaire from nowhere, and, as he prospered, so prospered his friends.

Carfew was returning home late at night from the theatre, in an agreeable frame of mind. He was making money, he had discovered flaws in the play he had witnessed, he was smoking a rare and peculiarly fragrant cigar, and the people he had met at dinner had made a fuss of him. As to this last event, it may be said that his popularity was due less to his own qualities than to his known friendship with Gelden.

If there was an uneasy note in the harmony of his self-satisfaction, it lay in the fact that there was a something about Gelden which worried him. He had tried to trace this discomfort to its first cause, without any great success. References to the genius and wisdom and goodness of Gelden – he had today presented a new wing to a children's hospital – jarred him slightly.

It may have been, he told himself, because of his acquaintance with a Gelden that the public did not know – the earlier Gelden, a little vicious, a little unscrupulous, and something of a liar.

165

As he walked along the Strand, threading a way through the homeward-bound theatre-goers, the sense of distrust which was ever present, was for the moment overlaid by the material comforts which a pleasant evening had brought.

He turned into the covered courtyard of the "Celvoy" at peace with the world.

He hoped to find Gelden, but the inquiry clerk informed him that the millionaire had gone out a few minutes before. Gelden, in his splendour, maintained a suite at the hotel in addition to his new town house.

"Do you know where he has gone?"

The clerk shook his head. "He has been here all the evening," he said, "looking at his six new motorcars."

The man smiled proudly, as one accepting the reflection of Gelden's glory.

"Six?" gasped Carfew.

"Yes, sir; he bought 'em all today. You're Mr Carfew, aren't you, sir? Well, one of the cars is for you. Mr Gelden happened to be at the motor show this afternoon and bought 'em."

Carfew went out of the hotel a little dazed. He was living at Buckingham Gate Gardens in a flat which was neither modest nor magnificent. It was just expensive, and London is full of such unsatisfactory homes. His man-servant met him in the little hall.

"There is a lady to see you, sir," he said.

Carfew was not in the habit of receiving lady visitors in the neighbourhood of midnight, and the elderly woman who turned to him, when he entered his cramped drawing-room, was certainly not any friend that he recognised.

"Mr Carfew," she said, with a sad little smile, "you don't remember me?"

Only for a moment was he puzzled, then:

"Mrs Gelden, of course," he said heartily.

It was his sometime landlady, a faded woman whose richness of apparel went incongruously with the drawn, pale face and restless, nervous hands.

"I've come to see you about my son," she said.

His first inquiries satisfied Carfew that Gelden had made handsome amends for his earlier fault.

"But it is the money he has given me which worries me," she said. "Mr Carfew, a week before my son arrived in London I had to wire him money for his fare."

She said this quietly, and Carfew looked at her in amazement.

"But he came to London with a million," he said incredulously.

She shook her head. "A paper said that the other day, but all that I know is this: one week he was so poor he was obliged to telegraph to me for money, the next week he was in London spending money lavishly. I have seen the broker who transacted his earlier business."

"And – "

"He says that my son gave a hundred thousand pound order at a time when I knew Gregory could not have possessed a hundred pounds."

Carfew was troubled. He had accepted the meteoric rise of his friend without question. He accepted meteoric rises as part of the natural order of things.

"But he has plenty of money now," he said.

Mrs Gelden shook her head.

"I don't know – I can't understand," she said. "He has put two hundred thousand pounds to my credit in the bank; but though he is rich, I am worried, and I want you to see him tomorrow and find out the secret of his sudden wealth. I feel I cannot rest until I know."

Carfew looked dubious.

"I doubt whether he will tell me," he began.

"You are the only friend he ever mentions in his letters," said the woman, "and – and I was hoping, perhaps, that it had been you who gave him this start."

To any other person in the world Carfew would have admitted his responsibility, but here was one to whom he could not so much as boast.

He saw her to a cab and returned to review the situation. The next day he sought Gelden, and found him just as he was leaving his house.

Carfew thought the man was looking older. There were lines about his eyes, and the corners of his mouth drooped pathetically. None the less, he was cheerful, almost boisterously so.

"How's things?" he jerked. "Bought you a car – a fine car – sen'in' it along."

He would have passed out with that, but Carfew had a mission to perform. He induced the other, albeit reluctantly, to go with him to the library. Without any preliminary, and with the desperate sense of his own impertinence, Carfew dashed out the subject.

"Want to know where I got my money from – eh?"

There was an amused glint in Gelden's eye.

"Got it out of gold – Siberian gold-mine."

"But you told me tin!" protested Carfew.

"Gold – gold!" insisted the other. As he warmed to the subject, he spoke rapidly, dropping his lazy habit of clipping his short periods. "A whole mine given to me by – you'll never guess – a Grand Duke! No, I won't lie to you – given to me by the Czar!"

He leant back and looked at Carfew triumphantly.

"There is royal blood in my veins! Yes, yes, yes!" He laid his hand on Carfew's knee. "Carfew, I always had money – I can make you a rich man – I've twenty million pounds invested in Russia!"

He leant forward and dropped his voice.

"I've got enemies who hate me," he whispered. "They follow me wherever I go – but I am prepared for you!"

He glared at Carfew, and his face was horrible.

"You – you – you!" he yelled.

In a flash his hand went to his hip pocket. Carfew saw the revolver and realised his danger.

With one spring he leapt at the man as he fired.

Three days later Carfew interviewed Sir Algernon Sinsy, MD, and Sir Algernon is the most famous of alienists.

"My theory is that your friend was mad when he arrived in London, and that, like most madmen, he was most convincing. I think also that he came to London without a penny, and the enormous fortune which will now be administered on his behalf was made whilst under the influence of the mania."

"Will he never recover?"

Sir Algernon looked at him gravely

"He died this morning," he said.

CARFEW AND THE "MARY Q"

What kindness of heart was concealed behind the seemingly unsympathetic exterior of Mr Gustav Bahl nobody knows.

Carfew certainly does not.

I say "was concealed," having caught the habit from Carfew, who always speaks of Mr Bahl as if he were dead.

When Carfew talks of his whilom enemy, it is in that tone of good-natured contempt which one reserves for the foolish people who die in their prime as a result of matching their wits against yours.

Thus he would say that this or that was "enough to make poor old Bahl turn in his grave," or "when old Bahl was alive" – an attitude of mind offensive to Bahl, who very properly hates and loathes Carfew, and would, but for the disgusting restrictions which the law imposes, do him grievous bodily harm.

Gustav Bahl, as all the world knows, is an exceedingly wealthy man. He is a director of the Marine Mercantile Assurance, chairman of the Grey Funnel West Coast Line, and sole stockholder of the South Atlantic Steam Packet Company, Limited.

He is a short man, in stature and speech, and he is oppressed with the fretful fear that all the money in the world which is not circulated via Bahl is being misapplied.

Carfew met Mr Bahl at the dinner of the Mariners' Benevolent Fund. Our friend received an invitation in the form of a letter, written and signed by Mr Bahl himself, and the letter was accompanied by a ticket.

Too late – it was when he was sitting down to dinner – he discovered that the letter was a lithographed one, artfully circulated amongst the moneyed classes, and that so far from the ticket being gratuitously bestowed, some five guineas were extracted from the too-confident diner who had been lured to the function.

The suave secretary, who made the round of the diners during the meal, had a little difficulty in extracting a subscription from Carfew. Had the unwilling guest – for unwilling he was at the price – tumbled to the swindle a little earlier, he would have been seized with a timely illness which necessitated a hasty withdrawal; but the ghastly realisation of the plot only came to him when he had finished the second course, and had consequently incurred some thirty shillings' worth of liability.

"It is for a good cause," soothed the secretary.

"I already subscribe to a mariners' benevolent fund," protested Carfew, remembering the money he dropped into the collecting boxes on Lifeboat Saturday.

"It is for a good cause," said the secretary monotonously.

"I haven't a cheque with me," said Carfew hopefully.

The secretary, with diabolical ingenuity, produced an assortment of blank cheques.

"It is rather an act of brigandage," the unhappy donor said, as he signed the cheque with a savage flourish.

"It's for a good cause," said the secretary.

Mr Bahl himself gave nothing. On behalf of the companies he represented he presented a cheque for a hundred guineas, which had been collected from the various office staffs he controlled, and since the collection had been taken up on the principle that every name on the subscription list would be submitted to Mr Bahl when the summer holiday arrangements were under consideration, the sums donated had been amazingly and uniformly generous.

Carfew did not enjoy his dinner. He had never met Bahl in his life, but his instinct told him that the shipowner was a man who had too much money, and a complementary instinct informed him that he

(Carfew) was the one man in the world who might deal with this tight-fisted millionaire.

After dinner there was an interval, to enable the guests to express their views to one another on the socialistic tendencies of the Government, and Carfew, with the easy confidence of one who has nothing to lose, made his way to Mr Bahl.

That gentleman was the centre of a sycophantic circle, and through the ragged end of a cigar he was conveying his conviction that the country was going to the devil, when Carfew, bright and smiling, dawned upon him.

"Glad to meet you again, Mr Bahl," he said.

"Glad to meet you, Mr – er – "

"Carfew. Don't say that you've forgotten me," smiled Carfew.

"To be sure," said Mr Bahl, comprehending the other in one swift glance, which appraised the standing, the bank balance, and the habits of life of his guest.

"I wanted to see you," said Carfew easily, "if you could give me an hour any day next week, except on Thursday. On Thursday," he continued, with a hint of severity, "I am attending a meeting of my board, and, since we are expected to pass a dividend – "

His expressive hands told the remainder of the story.

Mr Bahl looked at him curiously. He had heard of Mr Carfew, and recollected that fact in a dim way. Whether Mr Carfew was a shipper or only a Life Governor of the Bank of England, he could not recall.

"Come and see me on Wednesday," he said, and Carfew nodded. It would have embarrassed him considerably had Mr Bahl displayed any curiosity as to the object of the forthcoming visit.

Carfew acted on his impulses, and his main impulse had been to get back a portion of the five guineas which, as he chose to think, had been stolen from him by a trick. Before he had left the awe-stricken circle which surrounded Mr Bahl, he had decided that the five guineas was too small game, and he walked back to his flat in Jermyn Street that night, weaving highly improbable dreams of "deals" from which he might derive future sustenance.

As for Mr Bahl, he promptly forgot all about the forward young man who had forced his conversation upon him, and turned to a more important question which was at that moment obsessing him.

Now, Mr Bahl was fabulously rich, and was therefore extremely mean, for it seems that the souls of the very rich are invariably in training for that eye-of-a-needle test which ensures their entrance to Paradise.

At the moment there was exercising Mr Bahl's mind the question of the tugboat *Mary Q*. He prided himself that he had never spent so much as a brass farthing more than was necessary, either domestically or commercially, and here he was saddled with a dead loss of three thousand golden clinking sovereigns, and, moreover, such were the unpleasant circumstances, was personally liable for this sum.

He had purchased the *Mary Q* from a syndicate because he had received an inquiry from a South American port of authority, which offered four thousand pounds for a sea-going craft of a certain capacity.

Unfortunately, the inquiry had been addressed to him personally, so that there was no necessity for passing the transaction through the books of his firm, and there was an immediate profit to be had for his own enrichment. He cabled to his buyer, only to discover that the need had been supplied, and thus it came about that he found himself with a tug on his hands for which he had no use whatever.

Worse than this, he had purchased the boat without a proper survey, and it would seem that the *Mary Q* suffered from certain engine infirmities, on the subject of which her previous owners had been discreetly silent.

The *Mary Q* from that day became a ghostly nightmare with Mr Bahl, and might indeed have brought him an early end, only that Carfew happened along.

Carfew came into the Bahl sanctum as the twenty-third possible purchaser of the *Mary Q* took his leave.

"You'll never have another chance," Mr Bahl was remarking, a little heatedly.

"We are willing to give two thousand, and put her into repair," said the agent, "and, of course – "

"Good morning," said Mr Bahl briefly. Then to Carfew, and in another tone: "Ah, good morning, good morning, Mr Carfew! Sit down and have a cigar," he said, pointing to a chair. "Fact is, Mr Carfew, I am annoyed. I was making an offer to Tangree, Smilson and Company – you saw that fellow going out? – a splendid offer. I have got a tug – "

And he unburdened himself of his trouble, yet in such a manner as to convey the idea that the main worry lay rather in the short-sightedness of people to whom he wished to act benevolently than in any desire on his part to carry through a profitable deal.

He spoke of the *Mary Q*, that splendid seagoing tug, built regardless of cost, fitted without parsimony – a tug capable of earning her owner a fortune, and now lying idle off Gravesend.

He was quick to seize an advantage, and when Carfew, with undisguised enthusiasm, questioned him on the point, he showed just how ownership of the *Mary Q* might lead an ambitious young man from comparative obscurity to a shining pinnacle of fame and affluence.

There was haulage – so much per ton burthen – salvage, tender work. One could get a Board of Trade certificate and use her in the summer months for a pleasure steamer – a yacht even. (This idea appealed immensely to Carfew.)

A tin of white enamel and a bit of polished brass, a few deck-chairs and a slip of carpet under the awning aft – awning aft and all accessories included in the sale price – and a man might go swaggering round to Cowes and take anchorage under the very nose of the Royal Yacht.

"I must say it seems an idea," said Carfew thoughtfully.

Then, pursued the tempter, suppose the owner wanted a holiday, he might work her down to Ushant, Bordeaux, Bilbao, Vigo, Lisbon, Cadiz, Gib, and by way of the Moorish ports to the coast. Think of the pickings for a man of spirit – and the adventure!

A sea-going boat, she could carry deck cargo out and home – Manchester goods to the coast, and copal, rubber, and bananas back to England. Likely as not, she would be saleable in one of those African ports, and the fortunate owner might return with a thousand or so profit. And he would sell this boat for three thousand, exactly the sum he had given for her. He produced a receipt as proof of his statements.

It happened that Carfew at that moment was weary of all the ordinary channels of speculation. There was in his bosom a sense of restlessness and oppression which comes to the man who eats too much and hails taxi-cabs automatically. He left the office of the Grey Funnel Line, his brain whirling with the splendid possibilities which lay ahead of him.

The very next day he went to Gravesend with Mr Bahl's confidential man, and inspected the boat from stem to stern. She seemed big and solid, the brass telegraph on the bridge was very substantial and imposing. Carfew had an insane desire to pull the steam siren – a desire he obeyed, to the embarrassment of another tug's skipper, for the signal he made was "Going to Port," when, as a matter of fact, he was crossing the up-river tug to starboard.

He went down the river to the open sea, and came back to Gravesend on the tiny bridge.

Altogether, Carfew spent a delightful day, and on the Saturday following his trial trip, the *Mary Q* changed hands, and Carfew added to the list of his vocations, which were inscribed on his office door, that of "Shipowner."

Parker, who was Carfew's best friend and most fluent critic, listened in silence to a recital of Carfew's grievances.

"Of course," he was saying – this was a month after the purchase – "I never realised that the hands on the *Mary Q* were all Bahl's men, and that they were alternately sitting on the cylinder head – or whatever they call the infernal thing – and praying, whilst we were doing the trip. I thought it curious that the skipper had a life-belt within reach, but I imagined that it was a Board of Trade regulation. It has cost me twelve hundred pounds to put her into working order."

Parker nodded.

"In fact," he said, "you've been had. What does Bahl say?"

"He says, if I call again, he'll send for the police," said the gloomy Carfew.

Mr Parker smiled sympathetically, but whether his sympathy was directed towards the disgruntled Carfew or the outraged Bahl, is a point for discussion.

"You've done the only wise thing," he said; "without the repairs she was worthless, according to your surveyor. What can you sell her for?"

Carfew shook his head. "Whatever happens, I lose a thousand," he said, with a catch in his throat, for he hated to lose a thousand.

"I've got a crew, and a man I know has given me a few haulage jobs; it will just about pay the coal and wages bill. I'm sick, Parker. What can I do?" he demanded.

"*Aequam memento rebus in arduis servare mentem,*" said Parker oracularly.

Carfew moaned.

"For heaven's sake, chuck Latin and talk English!" he pleaded. "What do you mean?"

"Keep your wool on," translated Parker, "and wait till you find a purchaser who is as big an ass as you are."

"Good afternoon," said Carfew.

For three weary months the *Mary Q* patrolled the river, a veritable child, a tramp amongst tugs. Other boats were regularly employed – had snug homes and regular hours, were even distinguished by a certain uniformity of funnel. They had slipways for their moments of disorder, quays where they might drowse in the shade of tall warehouses; but the *Mary Q* loafed away from Tilbury to Lambeth Bridge, doing odd jobs in her humble way, earning the scorn which is due to the unattached.

Carfew had offers for his floating white elephant, but they were ridiculous offers.

The *Mary Q* became as much a nuisance to him as she had been to her former owner, until there came to him an offer through an agent – an offer much nearer Carfew's conception of equity than any other. This was a tender made on behalf of the Monrovian Municipal Authorities, and, in the argot of the times, Carfew fell for it.

For the first time since the tug had been on his hands, a spark of the old enthusiasm glimmered, and he made his hasty preparations for departure in quite the holiday spirit which he had anticipated would accompany all his associations with his new profession.

"I have had a cabin rigged up pretty cosily," he explained to Parker. "I shall navigate her down to Vigo, and re-coal, then on to Gib. I shall put in a day or two at Tangier, then work her along the Moorish ports."

"I suppose you are taking somebody who understands navigation?" asked the sceptical Parker – "somebody who knows that the east is opposite to the west, and all that sort of thing?"

Carfew had engaged a captain, a mate, four hands, and a cook. The captain was a man of many attainments, for he combined his extensive knowledge of seamanship with a perfect execution of concertina solos. His cook had been recommended by the chef of the Witz Hotel, and two of the hands were lifelong abstainers.

"You should have an interesting voyage," said Parker. "I can picture your cook preparing *soles delice bonne femme*, with the captain encouraging him with a selection from Grieg, and at least two of your crew weeping into their lemonade."

But Carfew was in too cheery a mood to be annoyed. So elated was he, that he must needs call upon Mr Bahl. He might have been denied admission, but the clerk who took his card did not know him, and on the back of the card he had scribbled: "Sold the tug; want to tell you all about it."

"What did you get for her?" asked Bahl suspiciously.

"Five thousand," lied Carfew. "I am working her out to Monrovia tomorrow."

"To Monrovia?"

Bahl's eyebrows rose.

"To Monrovia," repeated Carfew.

Bahl looked thoughtful.

"Curiously enough," he said slowly, "I was selling the Monrovian people a boat. I've got a little two thousand tonner which isn't much use to us, and would be more useful than your tug. I suppose they know all about the engine troubles?" he demanded.

"There are no engine troubles," said Carfew wrathfully.

"Of course not."

"And look here," roared Carfew, thumping the desk with his fist, "if you spoil my deal, I'll – I'll break your infernal head!"

Mr Bahl smiled. He was a millionaire and felt safe, because people do not break the heads of millionaires. It isn't done.

"Curiously enough," he said, as though speaking to himself, "I am leaving for Monrovia the day after tomorrow; one of my boats, the *Shell King*, is leaving for the Coast. I shall probably be waiting for you in Monrovia, and we will talk this matter over."

Carfew did not trust himself to speak. He made his way to the nearest telegraph office and wired to Gravesend.

Fortunately, his belongings were aboard, and there was little to do in town, save to hand over the keys of his flat to a caretaker.

He left the river that night on a falling tide, and came out of his unsteady cabin in the grey of the morning to see the white cliffs of Dover appearing and disappearing with sickening monotony over the dipping starboard gunwale. The tug was a cramped, cheerless habitation, and long before the tiny boat had bumped and shuddered its way round Ushant, Carfew had lost all the good spirits that had been his when the voyage started.

"Why the deuce does she roll?" he demanded of the captain.

"Why does she roll?" Captain Walter Worth was a stout man, with a trying habit of eking out his conversation with whole sentences stolen from the previous speaker.

"Well, sir, all tugs roll; but they are very, very safe."

He pulled away at a short and foul pipe, and shifted his feet to give him purchase against the next heavy roll, which, with a master mariner's eye, he saw was due.

Carfew, whose eye was in no way nautical, clutched a stanchion, and gave himself up for lost as the blunt nose of the tug bashed itself into the heavy waters.

"You get used to tugs after a bit," said the captain philosophically. "They ain't like ships, where you've got twenty officers messin' about – engineer this and engineer that. A tug can go where a liner can't. They look down on tugs, but what do they send for when they've got a broken shaft? Tugs! Who goes out to a ship that can't live in a sea? Tugs! You can earn more money in a week with a tug than you can earn with a – with a – a Dreadnought!"

Carfew said nothing. He was thinking principally of land – happy motionless land; land that keeps still and doesn't fool about, throwing a chap off his feet and covering him from head to foot in dust.

"I haven't found a lot of money in tugs," he said at last, with some bitterness. "I wish I'd never seen this infernal craft."

Captain Worth pulled at his yellow-white moustache and eyed him severely.

"You've never found a lot of money in tugs, sir?" he said. "You wish you'd never seen this here tug? Come, come, sir! I don't like to hear a gentleman talk about tugs like that. Why, in my time, I've made thousands for owners and hundreds for myself out of tugs!"

He grasped the fore-rail of the bridge as a sea rose up and hit the little vessel a horrible nerve-racking buffet on the port bow.

Carfew, clinging on to the nearest support, saw the green waters pour smoothly over the tiny well deck, cream and swirl for a moment, then, as the stout *Mary Q* asserted herself and brought her bows to daylight, he gazed fascinated at the spectacle of the waters rushing back to the parent sea in two miniature waterfalls.

"Phew!" he said, and felt hot. "We're in the Bay now, I suppose?"

"You're in the Bay now, sir, as you suppose," agreed the skipper gravely.

Seven days out of Gravesend – seven years sliced clumsily from Carfew's life – the *Mary Q* struck a storm, which made all Carfew's previous experience on the tug comparable with punting on a Crystal Palace lake.

It seemed that the horizon was alternately a dozen yards and twenty miles distant. The *Mary Q* did every trick in her repertoire except turn somersault. She stood on her head, she reared up, she went to sleep on her right side, and appeared unwilling to change her position; then she went to sleep on her left side, and seemed to enjoy the change. She took seas whichever way the seas happened to be running, and as they appeared to be running in all directions, she obligingly accepted service to one and all at the moment. She lost her lifeboat; nobody thought it worthwhile to remark on the fact. Carfew's concern was centred on the problem: would she also lose him?

He had a horrible suspicion that, if she did, nobody would mention that fact, either. Perhaps, he thought, the mate might remark to the captain: "There goes Carfew – he floats very well for a landsman." And the captain might reply: "There goes Mr Carfew – he does float very well for a landsman."

The storm passed, and the wind dropped in six hours from its rising, leaving the *Mary Q* afloat on a sea which it would be erring on the side of moderation to describe as mountainous.

Carfew, weary of body and – amongst other things – of soul, went to his cabin, and was strapped into his bunk by a sympathetic cook.

From sheer exhaustion he fell asleep, and when he awoke eight hours later, the seas had subsided till there was little more than a gentle swell.

He might have slept twenty hours, but he was awakened by the captain's hand on his shoulder.

"Are we going down?" he asked, and struggled to free himself of the strap with which a too faithful chef had bound him.

"Are we going down?" repeated the captain. "No, we ain't going down; we're coming up."

With deliberation he unstrapped his owner, and helped him to the deck.

"We're comin' up smilin'," he went on. "Just get a cup of hot coffee for Mr Carfew an' bring it up on the bridge."

It was a cloudless night. Overhead the stars winked and sparkled cheerfully. "What is the time?" said Carfew. "What is the time?" replied Captain Worth. "It's three o'clock in the morning, or, as we say, six bells."

"And what the dickens do you mean," demanded an irritated and sleepy Carfew, "by calling me up at three o'clock in the morning, or, as you say, six bells?"

The captain, staggered no doubt by the plagiarism, made no reply. He led the way along the slippery deck and went clanking up the tiny ladder which led to the bridge, Carfew following.

"There," he said, and pointed westward.

Carfew looked, and saw somewhere on the horizon a faint glimmer of light. As he focussed his gaze, wondering exactly what it indicated, he saw a thread of fire rise slowly into the sky, describe a reluctant curve, and burst into a ball of blue stars.

He felt the captain's big hand on his arm, and it was trembling with excitement.

"Don't you go sellin' this tug to them niggers," said Captain Worth hoarsely. "You can make money out of tugs. Look at that signal!"

A Roman candle spluttered near the lights.

"Four blues, a green an' a red. That's the *Shell King*, one of old Bahl's ships, and if I know anything about signallin', she's lost her [unprintable] propeller."

Carfew gasped. In silence he watched as Captain Worth burnt an answering flare over one side of the bridge. The nose of the tug turned toward the distressed liner.

"Lost her propeller," said the captain, and his homely face was pleasantly fiendish in the blue light of the flare. "A passenger ship! She's worth ten thousand poun' to you, sir – we'll tow her into Bilbao. What a pity old Bahl ain't aboard!"

"He is!" said Carfew, and clasped the outraged captain in his arms.

A MATTER OF BUSINESS

Only Carfew knows whether he was ever truly abashed in his short but vivid life.

He himself has never given evidence of his abashment, nor, in his recitals of his career, which are not infrequent, has he ever admitted that he has been found wanting in self-possession in a moment of crisis.

A man owed Carfew a lot of money once, an amazing circumstance, only modified by the fact that the man stoutly denied that he owed anything at all. Carfew had not lent money, of course; that was an unthinkable possibility. What he had done was to force upon a reluctant speculator advice which he would have initiated of his own, even if Carfew had never been born into this world at all. Having tendered advice, Carfew had outlined a breathless scheme for the division of such profits as might accrue from the deal. He had – without waiting for the indignant repudiation of any agreement which trembled on the speculator's lips – hurried away, leaving a speechless jobber in the African market with a horrible sense of having committed himself to an arrangement of which he heartily disapproved.

Now it happened that the line of action Carfew suggested proved to be a very wise one, and the jobber cleared twenty thousand pounds profit. Carfew claimed two thousand pounds, which, as you may learn from the perusal of any popular educator, represents a ten per cent commission on the deal. The workings of Carfew's mind were peculiarly in the direction of Carfew's pocket.

He was an honourable young man; outrage that honour of his, and you invited trouble of a cyclonic and destructive character. He made it a point of honour never to forgo any monetary advantage that was due to him.

So he wrote to Zolomon, the fortunate speculator in question, congratulating him upon the success of the deal, wishing him every happiness in the future, inquiring tenderly after his family, and ending with a PS, which ran:

"Regarding commission due on the Sloefontein Goldfarm, will you send a cheque straight away to my bank, as I shall be out of town for a week or so?"

Mr Zolomon, taking upon himself the disguise of Zolomon and Davon, Limited, wrote back, expressing no solicitude for Carfew's family, offering no hope for Carfew's corporeal welfare, and congratulating him only upon the nerve which inspired a demand for a ten per cent commission, "of which," so the letter ran, "our Mr Zolomon has no knowledge and has certainly never contemplated."

So Carfew wrote again. On this occasion he was oblivious of Mr Zolomon's domestic affairs as though Mr Zolomon was no more than a name on a brass plate.

"I really cannot understand yours of the fourth," wrote Carfew, in stilted perplexity. "I am loath to believe that your Mr Zolomon would repudiate a solemn obligation entered into when in full possession of his faculties."

If Carfew was loath to believe any evil of Mr Zolomon, that gentleman himself had no such compunction. Indeed, he seemed prepared to flaunt his shame to the world, even going so far as to say he would mention the matter – doubtless in a spirit of boastfulness – to his solicitors, Messrs Dewit, Ambling and Browne. Whereupon Carfew mentioned his own solicitors, Messrs. Breyley, Fenning, Thompson, Cubitt and Sanderson – a triumphant rejoinder, since they outnumbered the others by five to three.

Here, then, began the great feud of Zolomon and Carfew. Carfew's solicitors were unimaginative people, and saw no reason in the world why Mr Zolomon should pay anything. Carfew changed his solicitors. He sought his broker, Mr Parker, and Mr Parker was equally unsympathetic.

"So far as I can see," said Parker carefully, "you are trying to bluff an unfortunate man out of two thousand pounds, and when you are arrested, as you will be – "

"Parker," said Carfew, with some emotion, "you are supposed to be a friend of mine."

"Am I?" said the alarmed Parker.

"You are supposed to be," persisted Carfew solemnly, "and you take the side of the people who have robbed me."

Parker nodded. "I should be glad," he said, "not only to take the side of people who were clever enough to rob you, but to take them into partnership."

A week later, Carfew, in the bitterness of his soul, openly dined in a Wardour Street café with a well-known anarchist, suspected of inciting an anti-Semitic programme.

He was in no wise reconciled to the Zolomon family by an encounter he had later with a cadet of that house – an American importation, and offensive.

By unhappy chance, or by the design of a young and indignant Zolomon, eager to come to grips with one who had dared to attempt to deplete the family surplus, Carfew found himself seated opposite young Zolomon on three occasions at lunch. Twice he had endeavoured to get into conversation with the enemy – young Zolomon's uncle – and twice he was repulsed. On the third occasion young Mr Zolomon broke the ice with a coke hammer.

"You British priddy wild about der Banama Treaty, I guess."

"Go on guessing," said Carfew, who was in no mood for high politics.

There was a pause.

"Ve don' stan' no nonsense, ve Americans."

Carfew preserved a stony silence.

"Ve licked you vonce," dared Zolomon.

"I am not aware that we were engaged in any war with you," said Carfew coldly.

"Vat!" said shocked Zolomon. "You never hear abote our var?"

"Never," replied Carfew. "I think you are mistaken. The British were not engaged in the affair."

Zolomon put down his napkin and fixed his gold-rimmed glasses more firmly on his thick nose.

"You have tell me," he said, "you neffer hear of der battle of der Bunker's 'ill?"

Carfew raised his eyebrows.

"Bunker's Hill?" he said in insolent wonder. "I beg your pardon; I thought you were talking about the siege of Jerusalem."

That was the beginning of an enmity which was pursued with bitter malignity on both sides. Carfew at this time had an office in the heart of the City. It was situated in a great block of buildings, and the office was only big enough to live in because the builder had made all the doors of the building one size, and no cubicle, in consequence, could be smaller than the door which gave admittance to it.

Carfew was in a condition of prosperity at the moment, being "in" concrete. In other words, with his usual acumen he had come in on the crest of the Ferro-Concrete boom, which created a mild sensation in the building trade a few years ago. He had bought out the Shamstone patents and was lord of a little factory at Erith which did a fairly good trade, and would have done more if Carfew could have found someone to put capital into the concern.

He could have put money into it himself, but Carfew had learnt that the important law of finance was: "Never put your hand into your own pocket."

When Gray's came on to the market, Carfew thought he saw a chance of amalgamation. Gray's was a big concern, with three high chimney stacks, and somehow this fact had always been a subject for Carfew's envy.

He might have cast an envious glance and let it go at that, for Gray's was an expensive proposition, and none the less expensive because it was in the hands of receivers appointed by unforgiving debenture-holders.

Unfortunately, Carfew was acquainted with a number of rich men, all of whom, upon convivial occasions, had pressed his arm and told him to "come to me if you ever want money for a legitimate speculation."

Carfew had discovered that a "legitimate speculation," in the eyes of most of them, meant something where the money was secured by a banker's guarantee of a twenty per cent return.

But it happened that Carfew had received a note on the very morning of the appointment of the receiver – a note which promised well, since it embodied an invitation to lunch with a man who was so rich that he could afford to be friendly to everybody.

Carfew was preparing for the momentous meal when there came into his office no less a person than the Right Hon. the Lord Tupping.

Tuppy, as everybody knows, was a bright young man of no particular financial stability, but with an unfortunate capacity for thinking out schemes upon which he could "draw."

Carfew, who judged humanity by uncomplimentary standards, was satisfied in his mind that Tuppy invented all his schemes between the front door of Langwood House and the fifth floor. Possibly Carfew was right, but certain it is that Tuppy was plausible. On this occasion Tuppy came on a most unselfish errand. It was to make Carfew's fortune. Midway between Middlekirk and Westende Bains, on the Belgian coast, there is an expanse of sand dune, a perfect beach, and a lot of sea, and Tuppy had an idea that if some person or persons built a casino, erected a magnificent kursaal, laid out a racecourse and put up a few thousand pounds for prizes, laid out a golf course and erected a swagger club-house, those persons would make a fortune.

"In fact, my dear old bird," said his lordship, with unwonted enthusiasm, "there's a million in it."

He was a small man, beautifully dressed. He wore the shiniest of silk hats on the back of the glossiest of heads, and the fact that he kept it on in Carfew's office – in Carfew's private office – revealed the measure of his friendship.

"I've just come back," he went on, stretching his snowy-spatted shoes to Carfew's waste-paper basket. "I've given the matter a most tremendous amount of thought – I get positively sick with thinking – I do, upon my word. Surveyed the ground most thoroughly – "

"What happened, Tuppy," interrupted Carfew, tapping the desk with an ivory ruler, "was something like this. You surveyed the ground from a motorcar travelling at sixty miles an hour along the road to Nieupoort, and your immense idea jumped at you whilst you were fastening your collar at the Belle Vue."

Tuppy eyed him with a look of injury.

"My charmin' lad!" he expostulated. "My cynical old dear! You didn't imagine I was going to get out amongst all those beastly dunes and things, gettin' my shoes filled with sand and muck of that sort, did you?"

"I didn't," admitted Carfew. He paused and frowned thoughtfully. "Your scheme is quite a good one," he said. "I should say that all we want is about five millions."

"Float a company," said Tuppy eagerly; "it's as easy as eatin' pie. Call the dem place Tuppyville-sur Mer – good name, eh? I thought it out comin' over on the boat. Make the company the Tuppy Development and Land Company. Capital, five million, divided into five thousand shares of one hundred pounds. You give me a few thousand in cash and a few thousand in shares for the idea, and make whatever you can out of the business."

"It seems simple," said Carfew. "The only objection I can see to the scheme is the absence of necessary capital."

"Float it, my dear feller!" said the exasperated Tuppy. "British public, my old bird – dear old silly BP, my lad. Get it out of 'em; issue a prospectus and all that sort of rot."

"Five millions is a lot of money," said Carfew, and he spoke in the tone of one who could lay his hand on the amount, but was disinclined to make the effort.

"It is nothing." Tuppy brushed aside the suggestion airily, as being too preposterous for consideration.

Carfew sat on the edge of his desk and thought, and Tuppy occupied the only other seat which the dimensions of the office allowed. Carfew was thinking of his lunch, and he was very anxious to get rid of his visitor; but Tuppy, scanning his face expectantly, thought he saw a great scheme taking shape. Which shows –

"Dear lad," Tuppy broke in upon the other's meditation excitedly, "you've a chance that another feller would jump at! There's a Johnny in the City, Kenneth Macnam – "

"Eh? Kenneth Macnam?" repeated Carfew.

"Kenneth Macnam," said Tuppy.

"Ugly devil, big nose, big glasses, coppery face?"

"That's the cove," said Tuppy. "Well, this Kenneth Macnam – "

"Zolomon!" said Carfew, with unpleasant brusqueness. "I know the blight – the gentleman."

Tuppy looked at him suspiciously, and in a weak moment became diplomatic, adopting a variety of diplomacy which has made his name as Machiavelli a byword in Fleet Street.

"Of course," he said carelessly, "if you don't want to take up my little affair I'll see Zolomon. I thought of seeing him. He bombards me – positively, old lad, bombards me – with letters askin' me to see him. I wonder if he's a relation of old Zolomon?" he asked.

"Of course he is. The young 'un's a moneylender," said Carfew impatiently, for he really had a most important engagement. "He writes to everybody, you silly ass! Why don't you go along and see him?" he questioned suddenly. "I'm going past his office, and I'll drop you there."

A good scheme from every point of view. Carfew was only five minutes late for lunch.

It was rather an unfortunate lunch, as it turned out, for Carfew engaged himself in the almost heartbreaking task of inducing a Northern ironmaster to take an uncommercial risk.

Yet Gray's made the finest artificial paving the world has seen, and there was no reason why, under vigorous management, the firm should not succeed. Gray's briquettes were fire-proof, they were dust-proof; they deteriorated neither to the action of the sun, moon, stars, nor any other solar manifestation; rain they laughed at; frost they ignored; "wear and tear" were words unknown in their vocabulary. Gray was dead; young Gray – whose name was Smith – was broke; the business could be bought from the receiver for a song. Would Carfew's *vis-à-vis* furnish the melody?

Mr Jasper Grittlewood, the gentleman under persuasion, was a typical Midland magnate. He was a young man of thirty, with an Oxford accent, a pretty taste in shirts, and a flat in Piccadilly. He shook his sleek head sorrowfully over Carfew's proposal.

"I'd awfully like to go into it with you," he said, "but my idea, when I heard of it, was that you, being in the same line, might like to take it up on your own. You're in Shamstone's, aren't you?"

Carfew nodded, and his host took a dainty little engagement-book from his waistcoat pocket. "I am going to Ascot for a week," he said, "and afterwards to my villa on Lake Como. Just let me know how matters develop. I might be able to assist you later."

Mr Grittlewood folded up his serviette carefully and neatly, after the manner of very rich men who have come by their money honestly, and shook his head again.

There is the mournful shake, the admonitory shake, the doubtful shake, the amused but mildly disapproving, the denying shake, and the puzzled shake, and Jasper included them all, with the exception of that which might indicate any amusement.

"It is a speculation," he said with some emphasis, "which a young man like yourself might take up with profit – that is why I wrote to you. I thought, perhaps – "

Carfew "thought, perhaps," too, but in a different direction.

Gray's did not strike him as a proposition to tackle alone. It had "gone down" the wrong way. There is a right and wrong way in these matters, and Gray's had deteriorated in a manner which was distinctly wrong.

It was probably true that young Mr Smith looked upon the wine when it was red, but it is certainly true that he looked upon the horse when it was last. To back bad horses is bad; to back bad bills is very bad. Combine the two pursuits and you reach Carey Street by the most rapid form of transit yet invented.

"I'll tell you what I'll do," said Mr Jasper, as he bit his cigar in the vestibule of the hotel. "If you can get anybody to get Gray's an order – a real big order, don't you know – I'll take up the option which you have, and you can make your profit."

"A real big order?" repeated Carfew. "And what do you call a real big order?"

The ironmaster looked at his cigar critically.

"Say a twenty thousand pound order," he said. "You can have commission on that, too. Anyway, you give a moribund business a certain vitality which at present it does not possess."

"If I could get a twenty thousand pound order," said Carfew, "it would pay me to buy the business myself."

Jasper nodded. "I think you would make a fortune," he said seriously.

Carfew returned to his office in the philosophical condition of mind which comes alike to those who have loved and lost, and to those who have hoped for the best and got an inferior brand.

He himself had no use either for Gray's cement bricks, or Gray's ferro-concrete drainpipes, nor for Gray's asbestos flooring. If he had, he would have taken it to Shamstone's.

His office was empty save for the scent of bad cigars, and he opened the window and unlocked his desk. Then it was that he saw, pushed into the space between the top of the desk and the desk itself, a folded note. It was written in pencil, and the fact that there were two "t's" in "waiting" showed him it had been written by a peer of the realm.

"Dear Carfew," it ran, "just seen – seen" – Tuppy had a trick of stammering in his epistles – "old Zolomon, young Zolomon's uncle, the chap you tried to swindle. Think Tuppyville idea will be taken up – up. Come over to Liverpool Street Hotel; waiting for you. TUPPY."

Carfew frowned, and his frown was justifiable. It was preposterous to suppose that anybody would take old Tuppy seriously. It was more than preposterous that the person to commit so insane an indiscretion should be the Zolomon of whom Tuppy wrote in terms offensive to his friend.

Carfew sat down to think the matter over. It was wrong, all wrong. Such things do not happen. People do not finance the wildcat schemes of impecunious peers – at least, people named Zolomon, who lived in the City of London, did not.

It was all Carfew's eye and maiden aunt. He had a wild hope that Tuppy, in his very innocence and child-like confidence, had beguiled the enemy to his undoing, but it was a spark of hope upon which Carfew immediately turned a cold and sparkling stream of reason. People like Zolomon were not convinced by the childlike, not the bland, since they themselves were dealers in similar quantities. Tuppy was lying.

Carfew rose and put on his hat. Liverpool Street Hotel was a stone's throw distant. He found Tuppy and his companions entirely surrounding an ashtray and three coffee cups in a smoke-room of the hotel.

Mr Zolomon smiled gravely as Carfew entered.

The eminent financier was stout and bald, and somewhat pallid by the dispensation of Providence rather than from any misgivings as to Carfew's possible attitude.

He offered his grave hand, and in his gravest tone expressed his desire that Carfew should find a seat somewhere.

"We meet under happier conditions, I trust," he said, and that was all the reference he made to the black past.

"You know my nephew?"

The two young gentlemen exchanged poisonous smiles.

"And you know Lord Tupping?"

"I should say he did," said Tuppy, with a chuckle. "Old Carfew and I are – " He interrupted himself full of good tidings. "Old Zolomon thinks Tuppyville is a cinch – the company is as good as formed. Carfew, my lad, we're on a million to nothing!"

Mr Zolomon, more coherent, was also more informative.

"You understand, Mr Carfew," he said. "Lord Tupping had only anticipated a desire I have often expressed to found a new Ostend to the west of the great *plage*. He has a concession – "

"You never told me that," said Carfew reproachfully.

"Didn't give me time, dear old bird," said Tuppy. "Got a concession from a Johnny named – forget his beastly name – owner of land, and all that sort of thing – gave me the option on an enormous lump of land."

"In fact," Mr Zolomon, senior, broke in, "the thing is virtually accomplished. Now" – he laid a large and plump hand on Carfew's sensitive knee – "I bear no malice, Mr Carfew, none whatever. You tried to get the better of me; I got away with it. I can't ask you to accept a commission on this transaction, because it is obvious you have had nothing to do with it; but what I will do" – he gripped Carfew impressively – "what I will do – I'll let you stand in in any way possible."

Carfew looked at him thoughtfully, and then turned his eyes swiftly in the direction of Zolomon, junior. In that brief second of time he caught a glint of excitement in the young man's eyes disproportionate to the matter at issue. Only for a second he saw it, and then the fire died down, and the eyes took on their usual dull and expressionless stare.

"We naturally want to create this new resort as cheaply as possible," old Mr Zolomon went on, "though we are not short of money." He smiled. "I am betraying no secret when I tell you that here, in this place, not more than an hour ago, I called up ten men, each of whom have guaranteed a hundred thousand pounds for construction purposes."

Carfew nodded. Such things had been done before, but – why should Tuppy have secured an option if it was worth anything? Was it possible for an ass like Tuppy to flounder into a fortune which patient schemers like Zolomon had worked steadily towards? The thought was revolting to a man of intelligence.

"Now," continued the older man – and his tone was friendly to a point of compassion – "if you have any line of business that can be helpful to us – why, I'll give you all the work you can do."

Gray's!

The thought leapt into Carfew's mind, and all his leisurely suspicions vanished in the contemplation of a new and magnificent opportunity.

What was it obsessed his mind at that moment?

Was it Gray's briquettes, unmoved and unworn by tread of foot or vagary of atmosphere? Gray's Ferro-Concrete Drain-pipes, designed to last for eternity, and to carry off surplus drainage from a new and promising *plage*! Gray's Asbestos Fireproof Flooring, such as no high-class modern hotel can afford to dispense with?

It was none of these. Still –

"I am interested in a patent concrete concern," he said, with an effort to appear unconcerned.

Mr Zolomon held up his large hand in delight.

"The very thing," he said. "You remember, Lord Tupping, I was saying – "

Tuppy nodded vigorously.

"By jove, old Carfew, you're made! Old Zolomon was remarking just before you came in – "

"I was saying," said Mr Zolomon, in his gravest manner, "concrete or nothing; ferro-concrete or nothing. If you can execute a fifty thousand pound order, Mr Carfew – why, you can have it!"

Carfew said nothing.

Again he had intercepted the eager gleam in young Zolomon's eyes.

Carfew looked at Tuppy. That happy man was beaming largely on the world, doubtless already spending the big and immediate profit which would be his.

"I'll tell you what I'll do." It was Zolomon, senior, again. "I'll get an architect friend of mine to submit me a rough idea of the quantities we shall want, and you can send me an estimate in the morning."

Carfew thought. He thought, and he thought, did Carfew. He had never thought so rapidly or so profoundly in his life.

"I want to telephone," he said, and went out. He was away for about ten minutes.

"I am going to be frank with you," he said when he returned. "I can arrange to carry out such a contract if I can borrow three thousand pounds. Will you lend me three thousand, taking the business as a security? I shall want the money for twelve months at six per cent."

Mr Zolomon was a quicker thinker than Carfew.

"You have the remainder of the money?" he asked. Carfew nodded.

"You understand," said Mr Zolomon, "I cannot absolutely guarantee you shall have any order from me in respect to this scheme of Lord Tupping's. I say this as a business man, desiring only to take every precaution for my own protection."

"I understand that," said Carfew.

"You can have the money now," said Mr Zolomon, and produced his chequebook. Carfew took the oblong slip and wrote a receipt in his vile hand.

It was an agreement, sufficiently binding, to repay the sum within twelve months, together with interest at the rate of six per cent per annum. It undertook, further, that the sum should constitute a first charge upon the assets of a business in which Carfew undertook the money should be invested.

"You would like the cheque open?" asked Mr Zolomon.

Carfew nodded. He had an eye to the clock. It wanted ten minutes to four. At four o'clock precisely he issued from the Merchant Jobbers' Bank with thirty notes, each of a hundred pounds' value.

Two days later Messrs. Zolomon, senior and junior, came to Carfew's office. They were both perturbed, or so Carfew imagined; but he greeted them with a seraphic smile.

"What is the meaning of this?" demanded Mr Zolomon, by no means grave.

"Of which?" asked the innocent Carfew.

"You have not purchased Gray's at all. You undertook to do so," stormed the other. "You shall return the three thousand pounds, unless you complete the purchase today."

Carfew shook his head.

"Pardon me," he said gently, "you have made a slight mistake. I never intended purchasing Gray's at all."

"What!"

"You see," explained Carfew, "when you and young Jasper Grittlewood – an admirable name – were appointed receivers for Gray's, and you looked round for what is known in the higher financial circles as a 'mug,' to whom you could sell the old iron which constituted your assets, you did not realise that there were other cement properties in the market of greater promise – the Shamstone Company, for example. And when you sent old Tuppy prowling along the Belgian coast looking for a site for Tuppyville, you did not appreciate my extreme suspicion of Tuppy and his business qualities."

"Do you suggest," asked Mr Zolomon, "that I have engaged in a conspiracy to rob myself of three thousand pounds?"

"I suggest," said Carfew carefully, "that you were engaged in a conspiracy with Jasper Grittlewood to rob me of thirty thousand pounds. If I paid for your poor old moth-eaten concrete works, you would have divided anything up to ten thousand pounds between you – you could afford to lend me three thousand pounds. You see," Carfew went on, "as soon as I tumbled to the business, I got on the phone to my broker to discover who the receivers were, and I found it was the Midland Commercial Trust. Then we discovered that the Midland Trust were Grittlewood and Zolomon. It was very clever."

"What have you done with my money?" roared Mr Zolomon, pink with anger.

"Invested it," said Carfew, "in a business, as per agreement."

"What business?" demanded the other, in a choking voice.

"That," said Carfew conventionally but with truth, "is my business."

ONE AND SEVENPENCE HA'PENNY

Carfew sat in his study in Jermyn Street, one bright June morning, in a happy frame of mind. It was a mental condition which, as a rule, he did not encourage, for happiness is one of the most unbusinesslike relaxations that man can allow himself

Happiness makes one receptive to impossible schemes and unbalances one's judgment. But Carfew had reason for happiness. He had spent a whole day working out his financial position with the aid of an accountant, and that marvellous man had discovered that Carfew was worth exactly thirty-four thousand nine hundred and ninety-nine pounds eighteen shillings and fourpence halfpenny. Those were the exact figures, though where the odd fourpence ha'penny came from, Carfew was at some loss to understand.

"If you lent me one and sevenpence ha'penny," he said, "I should have an even thirty-five thousand pounds."

The accountant smiled.

"If you wait until tomorrow," he suggested, "you will have more. All your money is in gilt-edged stock, producing forty pounds eight shillings per diem, and if I lent you one and sevenpence ha'penny, you would be no better off, because you would still owe me that sum."

Carfew pulled at his cigar, amused, but faintly irritated. The one and sevenpence ha'penny annoyed him unaccountably. It was the finest speck of sand in the smooth-running motor of his complacency.

Of course it was absurd, but then Carfew was absurd. He took absurd risks at times, and did absurd things at times. If he had not been absurd he would have been a poor man all his life. The eccentricities which unthinking people condemn in a mature and comfortable man are very often the forces which secure him that assured position.

"You have reckoned everything, I suppose?" he suggested hopefully.

"Everything – your furniture and household effects are put in at valuation," said the patient accountant.

Carfew rose and pushed the bell; he could be very determined in small as well as great matters. His man Villiers, a calm and gracious servitor, answered the call.

"Villiers," said Carfew, "have you anything in the pantry, such as syphons, baskets, or cases, for which money has been deposited?"

"No, sir," said Villiers promptly. "I have ordered some new syphons."

Carfew thought.

"Go through the pockets of all my clothes," he said gravely, "and see if you can find one and sevenpence ha'penny, or something worth that amount."

"One and sevenpence ha'penny," repeated Villiers in a tone which disguised, as far as a well-bred servant could disguise so apparent an emotion, his contempt for odd coppers. "Have you lost that sum, sir?"

"I haven't exactly lost it," said Carfew sharply, "but I want to find it."

Villiers bowed and withdrew.

"I don't like his face," said Carfew, shaking his head at the laughing accountant. "I never did like black-eyebrowed people." He frowned thoughtfully. "Perhaps he's robbed me at one period of his service, and his conscience will get busy to the extent of one and sevenpence ha'penny."

But if the superior Mr Villiers had ever succeeded in robbing Carfew, his conscience, so far from getting busy, was exceedingly lethargic, and in ten minutes he returned from his search with no more tangible evidence of unexpected prosperity than a crushed and discoloured rosebud.

"This was the only article, sir," he said, handling the withered flower gingerly. "I found it in the breast pocket of your dress-coat."

Carfew wriggled and went painfully red. "Thank you," he said loudly, and took the flower with all the unconcern which accompanies the process of feeling a fool.

"Perhaps," suggested the accountant, when Villiers had departed, "we might regard that as worth the money."

Carfew deliberately placed the rosebud in his pocket-book, and as deliberately slipped the book into his inside pocket.

"I regard that," he said a little stiffly, "as beyond the value of anything in the world."

Whereby he succeeded in establishing a painful silence, broken only by the murmured apologies of the man of figures.

It was this embarrassing situation which brought about one of the most remarkable and momentous days in Carfew's life. From being a whim, the pursuit of the one and sevenpence ha'penny became a serious purpose in life.

He started up from his chair and examined his watch. It was eleven o'clock. He snapped the case viciously.

"You may think I'm mad," he said, "but I'm going out to earn that one and sevenpence ha'penny, and I'm going to earn it in solid cash."

He went out into the world and hired a taxi, and was halfway to his broker's before he realised that by the time he reached his destination, his deficiency would be three and a ha'penny, for taxis cost money. To be exact, the fare and the tip brought him three and tuppence ha'penny on the wrong side. He might have given away the odd ha'penny, but it wielded a certain fascination over him.

Parker was busy, but saw him after a minimum wait.

"Well, my bright boy," he greeted him, nodding towards a chair, "and what have we to thank for this visitation?"

"Parker," said Carfew earnestly, "I want to earn three and tuppence ha'penny."

"I didn't quite get you," said the puzzled Parker. "You want – "

"I want to earn three and tuppence ha'penny," repeated Carfew.

Parker leant back in his chair and surveyed him approvingly.

"At last," he said, "you have decided to earn your living – to get a little money by honest toil."

Carfew kept very calm.

"I desire that you refrain from being funny," he said, with admirable self-restraint. "I have a particular reason for wishing to earn one and sevenpence ha'penny – I mean three and tuppence ha 'penny – four and eightpence ha 'penny," he corrected himself, for he remembered that he had to get back to his flat.

"Make up your mind," said the patient Parker; "but how do you want to earn it?"

"I don't care how I earn it, but I just want to get it – that's all."

Parker settled himself comfortably in his chair, resigned, but polite.

"What's the joke?" he demanded. "If there's a catch in it, I'll be the victim. Let me hear it, and perhaps I'll be able to pass it off on one of those clever Alecs in the Kaffir Market."

Carfew rose slowly and reached for his hat.

"I want to earn four and eightpence ha'penny," he said, "and if you can't give me a job keeping books or sweeping out the office, or something for that amount, I'll go somewhere else."

Parker smiled politely.

"The joke's a little elaborate," he said; "but I'm quite willing to laugh – ha, ha!"

Carfew closed the door quietly behind him as he went out.

His blood was up. It was absurd that a man of his attainments should have the slightest difficulty in raising one and – in raising four shillings and eightpence ha'penny.

He bought a paper in the street, giving the boy a penny. He hastily scanned the market intelligence. Of all the days in the year this would appear to be the most deadly. The earliest report showed that all markets were stagnant. There were no one market or group of stocks which looked as though they would move in any direction.

He walked along Moorgate Street, turned into Liverpool Street, and stood irresolutely before the gateways to the station. He walked over to where a newspaper seller stood.

"George," he said, hazarding the name which is common to all newspaper sellers and to the hansom cabmen of old – alas! that the taxi and the motor-bus have introduced the Horaces and the Percies to public life – "George, suppose you wanted to make four and ninepence ha'penny, how would you do it?"

George looked his questioner up and down. "I should back Razel for the Stayers' Handicap," he said. "Back it both ways, an' double it up with Brotherstone for the Nursery. That's what I'd do, and that's what I've done."

"You would back Razel and double it up." Carfew repeated as much as he could remember.

Razel was evidently one of those unwieldy horses that had to be folded in two before he could be carried in comfort.

"That's what I'd do," repeated George; "an' if you want a real cast-iron racin' certainty for tomorrer, you have a little bit each way on Lord Rosebery's horse in the Royal Hunt Cup."

"Is he running each way?" asked Carfew, interested for the first time in the sport of kings.

"That's what I'd do," said George gloomily.

It was obvious to Carfew that four and ninepence ha'penny was not an easy sum to earn. He felt that racing – even if he had known the slightest thing about it – was too hazardous a means. After all, the horses might not win, and he had a suspicion that George might not be right in his prediction.

Strolling up Broad Street he ran against Wilner, a man in the shipping trade. Wilner was a hard-headed Lancashire man, with whom Carfew had done business on several occasions. At least, he was a Lancashire man, and people have got the habit of applying the prefix to anybody who counts his change and bites dubious-looking half-crowns. In all probability – the theory is offered for what it is worth – North-countrymen aren't any harder-headed than people who live in Balham.

Wilner would have passed on with a nod, but Carfew had an inspiration and stopped him.

"Give me five shillings," he demanded.

Wilner drew back a pace, then he grinned, and his hand wandered to his trousers pocket.

"Come out without money?" he said. "Shall I lend you a sovereign?"

"I don't want you to lend me anything," said Carfew firmly. "I want you to give me five shillings."

Mr Wilner looked hard. "Give you five shillings – for a charity or something?"

"I want five shillings for myself," said Carfew doggedly.

"I'll lend you a fiver – " began Mr Wilner.

"I don't want you to lend me anything," snarled Carfew, hot and angry. "I want you to give me five shillings."

Mr Wilner was pardonably alarmed. "Of course I'll give you five shillings," he said soothingly. "Look here, Carfew, my boy, you wouldn't like to get in a taxi with me and come along and see my doctor?"

Carfew groaned. "Merciful heavens!" he appealed to the patch of sunlit sky above Broad Street, "I ask a man to give me five shillings and he offers me a medical examination!"

"But why?" demanded the exasperated Mr Wilner. "Why the devil do you want five shillings? Haven't you got plenty of money?"

"Of course I have, you ass!" bellowed Carfew, to the scandal of the neighbourhood; "but I want thirty-five thousand pounds, and I must have five shillings. I really only wanted one and sevenpence ha'penny, but I took a taxi and bought a paper, and I am going to take a taxi back. As a matter of fact, I want three and threepence ha'penny if I walk."

Mr Wilner drew himself away significantly. His attitude was that of a man who did not wish to be mixed up in an unpleasant and painful situation.

"Well," he said hastily, "let's hope for the best." And with a sympathetic pressure of Carfew's hand he hurried away.

From the Bank to Dulwich village the fare works out at approximately three and tenpence. Carfew gave the driver five shillings, so that he arrived at the home of May Tobbin exactly eight and threepence ha'penny on the wrong side of thirty-five thousand pounds.

May was at home, and it seemed to Carfew's prejudiced eyes that she had never looked so beautiful as she did in the domestic garb she wore that morning. Her sleeves were not rolled up, nor did she wipe the flour from her hands as she offered him a grip which betrayed her athletic propensities. Nor was her print gown open at the neck, or her face flushed with the healthy exercise of making up a kitchen fire. Such things do not happen in the suburbs except in good books.

She was wearing a simple morning frock, a modified Poiret model, and nothing short of a tin-opener would have rolled her sleeves up. But she was beautiful enough, with the clear eye and the firm line of confident youth.

"I am glad to see you," she said, with a smile that went straight to Carfew's heart. "I suppose you've come to lunch?"

"I never thought of that," confessed Carfew, brightening up. "That's half a crown saved, anyway."

He could say as much to May, because she knew him; because, a year or so before, they had worked together, he and she, to put a tottering business upon its feet.

She had worked with him in his high-principled effort to revive interest in the modern drama, and had taken her share of the profits. Moreover, though Carfew would never guess this, she had settled down, at the advanced age of twenty-three, to the calm contemplation of lifelong spinsterhood for no other reason than because – well, just because. She surveyed him now with a little anxiety in her grey eyes.

"You look a little under the weather. Would you like to lie down?" she asked.

Carfew braced himself. "Would you give me eight and threepence ha'penny?" he asked with great resolution, "or shall we say ten and threepence ha'penny – I think I can get home for two shillings."

She was bewildered. He saw the distress in her eyes, and felt a brute.

"The fact is," he said, laying his hand upon her arm, for she appeared to be on the point of taking flight, "the fact is, I discovered this morning that I was one and sevenpence ha'penny short of thirty-five thousand pounds, and, half for a joke, I went out to get one and sevenpence ha'penny. But now it is eight and threepence ha'penny – that is to say, I have thirty-four thousand nine hundred and ninety-nine pounds eleven shillings and eightpence ha'penny. Unless I raise eight and threepence ha'penny – I only wanted one and sevenpence ha'penny, but it has been awfully expensive – "

May rose. "I'll call father," she said gently. "Perhaps if you sat in the garden under the awning for a little while you'd feel better."

"You misunderstand me!" expostulated Carfew. "I want eight and threepence ha'penny – "

"I'll lend you anything you like, you poor boy," she said, and there were tears in her eyes.

"I don't want to borrow anything!" moaned Carfew. "I – " But she was gone.

Mr Tobbin appeared after a while, a tactful Mr Tobbin, a coaxing, humouring, infernally irritating Mr Tobbin.

"Hot weather, my boy," he said, and patted Carfew's shoulder cautiously, not being quite sure in his mind whether his guest would bite, or whether he was merely the King of Siam.

"Come along and smoke," he said. "You young fellows overdo it – just a wee bit overdo it. There's no repose in business as there was when I was a youngster. It's this infernal American method of hustle, hustle, hustle." He led his captive to the big garden at the back of the house. "You stay and have a little lunch," he said, when he had Carfew seated in a position where he could be patted without risk to the patter.

"One moment, Mr Tobbin," said Carfew, warding off the marks of his host's friendship. "I want to ask you this: Will you give me some work to do – something I can earn ten and threepence ha'penny before to-night? I don't ask you to give me the money – I prefer to earn it. This thing started as a joke, you understand. If I hadn't been an ass I should not have gone fooling round for one and sevenpence ha'penny."

"Naturally – naturally," murmured Mr Tobbin sympathetically.

"Now" – Carfew spoke rapidly – "you and May – Miss Tobbin – think I'm off my head. Well, I'm not."

"I'm sure you're not," said the other, in simulated indignation. "If anybody said such a thing I should be extremely vexed."

"There is no sense in borrowing one and sevenpence ha'penny," pursued Carfew confidentially. "I should be no better off than I am. What I want to do is to find somebody to give me a job to earn the one and sevenpence ha'penny, or eight and threepence ha'penny, as it is now – that is to say, ten and threepence ha'penny – "

"Calm yourself," my dear boy, urged Mr Tobbin. "Here is May."

Unless Carfew's eyes were at fault, and May Tobbin's eyes were being particularly disloyal, she had been crying. Mr Tobbin retired with every evidence of relief, announcing – from a safe distance – that he was taking lunch in his study, and May sat herself by Carfew's side.

"You've got to be very quiet," she said softly. "We'll have lunch together – "

"May," said Carfew desperately, "will you please listen to me whilst I recite you a perfectly coherent and consecutive narrative of what has happened since this morning?"

"I think you had better – " she began. Then, as Carfew jumped up in genuine annoyance, she pulled him down again. "Tell me," she commanded.

Carfew began his story – the story of the audit, the story of his happy breakfast, gloating over his balance, the story of the accountant's arrival with the true total of his fortune, and as he went on, the anxiety died away from the girl's eyes and her lips twitched. Then, as he described his meeting with Wilner, her sense of humour was too strong for repression, and she leant back in an ecstasy of laughter.

"You poor creature!" she said, wiping the tears from her eyes. "And you want – "

"Ten and threepence ha'penny," said Carfew mournfully. "But I can't take it from you now, after I have told you. Isn't there any work I could do – genuine work that you'd have to pay somebody else ten and threepence ha'penny for, if they did it?"

She thought, her chin on her palm, her lips pursed. Then she went into the house. Carfew judged she was interviewing her father, and his calculation was correct. She came back in ten minutes, and her return synchronised with the booming of the luncheon gong.

"Come along," she invited, with a smile. "Come to lunch, and I will explain just how father wants the coal-cellar whitewashed."

It was a happy lunch. Mr Tobbin, by no means convinced that Carfew was not a dreadful example of how the evil, hustling tendencies of the age may affect a man, lunched in his study and listened apprehensively to the bursts of insane laughter which floated up from the dining-room.

"And so poor Villiers found nothing?"asked May.

Carfew blushed. "Nothing," he said.

She looked up at him quickly:

"What did he find?" she asked.

Carfew hesitated, then he took out his pocketbook and from the pocketbook an ill-used rosebud. She took it in the palm of her hand, and the colour came and went in her face.

"Who is the fortunate lady?" she asked quietly.

"As a matter of fact," stammered Carfew, " it was from a – a sort of a bouquet. Don't you remember? One night – a sort of dance that Tobbins, Limited, gave their employees when I was managing director, and – and you were managing me? You had some flowers – "

He was pardonably disturbed. The girl looked at the rosebud in her hand and did not raise her eyes.

"Was it really mine?" she asked, in so low a tone that he thought she was speaking to herself.

He nodded.

She put out her hand across the table and he clasped it.

I forget who whitewashed Mr Tobbin's cellar.

EDGAR WALLACE

BIG FOOT

Footprints and a dead woman bring together Superintendent Minton and the amateur sleuth Mr Cardew. Who is the man in the shrubbery? Who is the singer of the haunting Moorish tune? Why is Hannah Shaw so determined to go to Pawsy, 'a dog lonely place' she had previously detested? Death lurks in the dark and someone must solve the mystery before BIG FOOT strikes again, in a yet more fiendish manner.

BONES IN LONDON

The new Managing Director of Schemes Ltd has an elegant London office and a theatrically dressed assistant – however Bones, as he is better known, is bored. Luckily there is a slump in the shipping market and it is not long before Joe and Fred Pole pay Bones a visit. They are totally unprepared for Bones' unnerving style of doing business, unprepared for his unique style of innocent and endearing mischief.

EDGAR WALLACE

BONES OF THE RIVER

'Taking the little paper from the pigeon's leg, Hamilton saw it was from Sanders and marked URGENT. *Send Bones instantly to Lujamalababa... Arrest and bring to head-quarters the witch doctor.'*

It is a time when the world's most powerful nations are vying for colonial honour, a time of trading steamers and tribal chiefs. In the mysterious African territories administered by Commissioner Sanders, Bones persistently manages to create his own unique style of innocent and endearing mischief.

THE DAFFODIL MYSTERY

When Mr Thomas Lyne, poet, poseur and owner of Lyne's Emporium insults a cashier, Odette Rider, she resigns. Having summoned detective Jack Tarling to investigate another employee, Mr Milburgh, Lyne now changes his plans. Tarling and his Chinese companion refuse to become involved. They pay a visit to Odette's flat. In the hall Tarling meets Sam, convicted felon and protégé of Lyne. Next morning Tarling discovers a body. The hands are crossed on the breast, adorned with a handful of daffodils.

EDGAR WALLACE

THE JOKER

While the millionaire Stratford Harlow is in Princetown, not only does he meet with his lawyer Mr Ellenbury but he gets his first glimpse of the beautiful Aileen Rivers, niece of the actor and convicted felon Arthur Ingle. When Aileen is involved in a car accident on the Thames Embankment, the driver is James Carlton of Scotland Yard. Later that evening Carlton gets a call. It is Aileen. She needs help.

THE SQUARE EMERALD

'Suicide on the left,' says Chief Inspector Coldwell pleasantly, as he and Leslie Maughan stride along the Thames Embankment during a brutally cold night. A gaunt figure is sprawled across the parapet. But Coldwell soon discovers that Peter Dawlish, fresh out of prison for forgery, is not considering suicide but murder. Coldwell suspects Druze as the intended victim. Maughan disagrees. If Druze dies, she says, 'It will be because he does not love children!'

OTHER TITLES BY EDGAR WALLACE AVAILABLE DIRECT FROM HOUSE OF STRATUS

Quantity		£	$(US)	$(CAN)	€
	THE ANGEL OF TERROR	6.99	11.50	15.99	11.50
	THE AVENGER	6.99	11.50	15.99	11.50
	BARBARA ON HER OWN	6.99	11.50	15.99	11.50
	BIG FOOT	6.99	11.50	15.99	11.50
	THE BLACK ABBOT	6.99	11.50	15.99	11.50
	BONES	6.99	11.50	15.99	11.50
	BONES IN LONDON	6.99	11.50	15.99	11.50
	BONES OF THE RIVER	6.99	11.50	15.99	11.50
	THE CLUE OF THE NEW PIN	6.99	11.50	15.99	11.50
	THE CLUE OF THE SILVER KEY	6.99	11.50	15.99	11.50
	THE CLUE OF THE TWISTED CANDLE	6.99	11.50	15.99	11.50
	THE COAT OF ARMS	6.99	11.50	15.99	11.50
	THE COUNCIL OF JUSTICE	6.99	11.50	15.99	11.50
	THE CRIMSON CIRCLE	6.99	11.50	15.99	11.50
	THE DAFFODIL MYSTERY	6.99	11.50	15.99	11.50
	THE DARK EYES OF LONDON	6.99	11.50	15.99	11.50
	THE DAUGHTERS OF THE NIGHT	6.99	11.50	15.99	11.50
	A DEBT DISCHARGED	6.99	11.50	15.99	11.50
	THE DEVIL MAN	6.99	11.50	15.99	11.50
	THE DOOR WITH SEVEN LOCKS	6.99	11.50	15.99	11.50
	THE DUKE IN THE SUBURBS	6.99	11.50	15.99	11.50
	THE FACE IN THE NIGHT	6.99	11.50	15.99	11.50
	THE FEATHERED SERPENT	6.99	11.50	15.99	11.50
	THE FLYING SQUAD	6.99	11.50	15.99	11.50
	THE FORGER	6.99	11.50	15.99	11.50
	THE FOUR JUST MEN	6.99	11.50	15.99	11.50
	FOUR SQUARE JANE	6.99	11.50	15.99	11.50
	THE FOURTH PLAGUE	6.99	11.50	15.99	11.50

ALL HOUSE OF STRATUS BOOKS ARE AVAILABLE FROM GOOD BOOKSHOPS
OR DIRECT FROM THE PUBLISHER:

Internet: www.houseofstratus.com including author interviews, reviews, features.

Email: sales@houseofstratus.com please quote author, title and credit card details.

Please allow for postage costs charged per order plus an amount per book as set out in the tables below:

	£(Sterling)	$(US)	$(CAN)	€(Euros)
Cost per order				
UK	2.00	3.00	4.50	3.30
Europe	3.00	4.50	6.75	5.00
North America	3.00	4.50	6.75	5.00
Rest of World	3.00	4.50	6.75	5.00
Additional cost per book				
UK	0.50	0.75	1.15	0.85
Europe	1.00	1.50	2.30	1.70
North America	2.00	3.00	4.60	3.40
Rest of World	2.50	3.75	5.75	4.25

PLEASE SEND CHEQUE, POSTAL ORDER (STERLING ONLY), EUROCHEQUE, OR INTERNATIONAL MONEY ORDER (PLEASE CIRCLE METHOD OF PAYMENT YOU WISH TO USE)
MAKE PAYABLE TO: STRATUS HOLDINGS plc

Cost of book(s): —————————— Example: 3 x books at £6.99 each: £20.97

Cost of order: —————————— Example: £2.00 (Delivery to UK address)

Additional cost per book: —————— Example: 3 x £0.50: £1.50

Order total including postage: ——— Example: £24.47

Please tick currency you wish to use and add total amount of order:

☐ £ (Sterling)   ☐ $ (US)   ☐ $ (CAN)   ☐ € (EUROS)

VISA, MASTERCARD, SWITCH, AMEX, SOLO, JCB:

☐☐☐☐☐☐☐☐☐☐☐☐☐☐☐☐☐☐☐☐

Issue number (Switch only):

☐☐☐

Start Date: **Expiry Date:**

☐☐ / ☐☐   ☐☐ / ☐☐

Signature: _____

NAME: _____

ADDRESS: _____

_____

POSTCODE: _____

Please allow 28 days for delivery.

Prices subject to change without notice.
Please tick box if you do not wish to receive any additional information. ☐

House of Stratus publishes many other titles in this genre; please check our website (**www.houseofstratus.com**) for more details.

OTHER TITLES BY EDGAR WALLACE AVAILABLE DIRECT
FROM HOUSE OF STRATUS

Quantity		£	$(US)	$(CAN)	€
	THE FRIGHTENED LADY	6.99	11.50	15.99	11.50
	GOOD EVANS	6.99	11.50	15.99	11.50
	THE HAND OF POWER	6.99	11.50	15.99	11.50
	THE IRON GRIP	6.99	11.50	15.99	11.50
	THE JOKER	6.99	11.50	15.99	11.50
	THE JUST MEN OF CORDOVA	6.99	11.50	15.99	11.50
	THE KEEPERS OF THE KING'S PEACE	6.99	11.50	15.99	11.50
	THE LAW OF THE FOUR JUST MEN	6.99	11.50	15.99	11.50
	THE LONE HOUSE MYSTERY	6.99	11.50	15.99	11.50
	THE MAN WHO BOUGHT LONDON	6.99	11.50	15.99	11.50
	THE MAN WHO KNEW	6.99	11.50	15.99	11.50
	THE MAN WHO WAS NOBODY	6.99	11.50	15.99	11.50
	THE MIND OF MR J G REEDER	6.99	11.50	15.99	11.50
	MORE EDUCATED EVANS	6.99	11.50	15.99	11.50
	MR J G REEDER RETURNS	6.99	11.50	15.99	11.50
	MR JUSTICE MAXELL	6.99	11.50	15.99	11.50
	RED ACES	6.99	11.50	15.99	11.50
	ROOM 13	6.99	11.50	15.99	11.50
	SANDERS	6.99	11.50	15.99	11.50
	SANDERS OF THE RIVER	6.99	11.50	15.99	11.50
	THE SINISTER MAN	6.99	11.50	15.99	11.50
	THE SQUARE EMERALD	6.99	11.50	15.99	11.50
	THE THREE JUST MEN	6.99	11.50	15.99	11.50
	THE THREE OAK MYSTERY	6.99	11.50	15.99	11.50
	THE TRAITOR'S GATE	6.99	11.50	15.99	11.50
	WHEN THE GANGS CAME TO LONDON	6.99	11.50	15.99	11.50
	WHEN THE WORLD STOPPED	6.99	11.50	15.99	11.50

Hotline: UK ONLY: 0800 169 1780, please quote author, title and credit card details.
INTERNATIONAL: +44 (0) 20 7494 6400, please quote author, title and credit card details.

Send to: House of Stratus Sales Department
24c Old Burlington Street
London
W1X 1RL
UK